What readers are saying about *If I Should Die*

'[A] brilliant read . . . You will not be disappointed'
5* Amazon Review

'Twisty and full of suspense . . . I was on the
edge of my seat'
5* Netgalley Review

'Anna at her wonderful best . . . Full of
tension throughout'
5* Amazon Review

'This is truly amazing. And I can't wait for
the next one'
5* Goodreads Review

'This is an exceptionally gripping thriller with tense
nail-biting action, suspense, drama and twists
and turns, [and] so many fantastic characters'
5* Amazon Review

'Amazing storyline and captivating characters'
5* Netgalley Review

'Anna Smith is yet to write a bad book! Stunning
writing, gritty plot, this has it all'
5* Amazon Review

If I Should Die

Anna Smith has been a journalist for over twenty years and is a former chief reporter for the *Daily Record* in Glasgow. She has covered wars across the world as well as major investigations and news stories from Dunblane to Kosovo to 9/11. Anna spends her time between Lanarkshire and Dingle in the west of Ireland, as well as in Spain to escape the British weather.

Also by Anna Smith

THE ROSIE GILMOUR SERIES

The Dead Won't Sleep
To Tell the Truth
Screams in the Dark
Betrayed
A Cold Killing
Rough Cut
Kill Me Twice
Death Trap
The Hit

THE KERRY CASEY SERIES

Blood Feud
Fight Back
End Game
Trapped

THE BILLIE CARLSON SERIES

Until I Find You

If I Should Die

ANNA SMITH

A BILLIE CARLSON THRILLER

QUERCUS

First published in Great Britain in 2023
This paperback edition published in Great Britain in 2023 by

QUERCUS

Quercus Editions Ltd
Carmelite House
50 Victoria Embankment
London EC4Y 0DZ

An Hachette UK company

A CIP catalogue record for this book is available
from the British Library

PB ISBN 978 1 52941 586 5
EB ISBN 978 1 52941 585 8

10 9 8 7 6 5 4 3 2 1

Typeset by Jouve (UK), Milton Keynes

Printed and bound in Great Britain by Clays Ltd, Elcograf S.p.A.

Papers used by Quercus are from well-managed forests and other
responsible sources.

For Jude. Dream on. Be brave. Stay gold.

PROLOGUE

Astrid is beyond freezing now. She's starting to feel tired and her eyes dart around looking for a place to lie down and sleep. It's all she wants to do. Just sleep and forget, make it all stop, find some peace. She's clutching the half-empty vodka bottle in her freezing fingers, and in her jacket pocket is the foil packet of co-codamol she's been swallowing, hoping to make all the pain go away. She feels sick from downing so much vodka. She thought it would make things easier. She's wandered off the main road out of the town and into the forest, yet she can't even remember doing that. It's dark here. Eerie and silent. She staggers, her feet sinking into the melting snow, and she nearly loses her balance as she turns her face up to gaze at the tall trees that seem to stretch all the way to the pale grey sky. It reminds her of Sweden, and suddenly the picture is blurry as tears spring to her eyes and she remembers herself back home playing games with her family, swimming in the lakes and running through the forests. She stumbles on a branch, which snaps, and she falls. On all fours she looks up and around her, but now she has no idea how to get out of here. In her stupor, she doesn't really know if she wants to anyway. Maybe if she can sleep for a while she will feel better. She pushes herself against the broad bark of a tree and sits, drawing her knees up to her chin. Then she swigs from the bottle, retching as the raw alcohol burns the back of her throat. She rests her head back.

But when she closes her eyes all she can see is the video, the hazy images and masked faces, the sounds of laughter, the groans of the men in raw, brutal pleasure on top of her. Then when he finishes, as she lies there, he steps back and the one who was filming hands the friend the phone and unzips his trousers. She can see this happening, but she is powerless to stop it. Her body and arms feel heavy. She tries to push herself back with her feet but the man who has just been inside her puts his knee on her chest. She can smell him. Then it's so quick. Thrusts, groans, and she tries to speak but can't. How can she be this drunk, she now remembers asking herself. She wasn't that drunk in the bar with her friends. When it was over, they stepped back, laughing, replaying the video, showing it to her. They even sent it to her mobile.

When she woke up in the flat this morning, at first she had no idea how she got there. Her jeans and pants were in a heap on the floor, but she had no recollection of taking them off. She'd been woken by her friend Jenny banging on the door of her flat. She'd come to check if she was all right because she said she had disappeared from the bar the night before. It was only then that it began to come back to her in little torturous flashes, how after the attack she'd run all the way home, and showered and scrubbed and then collapsed into bed. She'd shown Jenny the video, and Jenny had asked her to WhatsApp it to her so that there would be more than one copy. Her friend told her they had to go to the police. As they'd watched it again, Jenny begged her to call the police, told her she would go with her. But how would they believe her? Astrid had wept. People must have seen her leaving the bar with those guys. Asking for it, they'd say. She could phone her brother Lars in Sweden. He would understand. Her parents, stiff and reserved, had pleaded with her not to go to Scotland but to stay studying in her own country. This would destroy them. Distraught, Astrid had told Jenny she would be okay, that she just wanted to be left alone. She'd paced the flat all day, images coming back to her. As the afternoon wore on she began to drink vodka, hoping it would calm her down, make her sleep. She forced it down because she very rarely drank. Then she found some painkillers in the flat and took a few of them. It seemed to help, take the edge off things, so she drank more vodka, followed by more pills. It was dark when she'd left her flat, drunk and unsteady, dressed only in a T-shirt, jeans and rain jacket. Somewhere in her head she knew if she kept walking away from town she would be in danger. Yet it didn't seem to matter.

She sits, her eyes getting heavier. She's not so cold now and feels warm under her neck and chest, and she opens her jacket. She looks up again at the darkening sky. She knows she should get up. But she's so very tired. Just five minutes' sleep and then she will get up, and she will find the courage to call Lars. Her eyes are closing, her breathing slow and steady as she sleeps.

CHAPTER ONE

You think you've left much of your early life behind you, or at least filed the painful parts away in a box marked 'do not open'. I've managed to accomplish it so that a lot of the dark places are buried and I seldom let my head wander into them. Not all of them, obviously, because there's stuff that shapes who you are, walks beside you every step. Like my Lucas, my boy, my heart. But long before Lucas, long before I was who I am today, I was in a different world, with a landscape and life so far removed from this one. I hadn't completely left it behind though – you never do. There was so much to love about it and so much to cherish because it was in my blood. But I had moved on. Until the day the telephone call came in and clawed me right back.

I was in my office, three floors up, slap bang in the centre of Glasgow, where the sign on the half-frosted glass, half-wooden door, says Billie Carlson, Private Investigator. It's not just a job, it's my story, and it's where people come as a last resort when every conventional way of getting to the truth has failed them. But the truth doesn't always result in a happy ending for them, and I tell them that from the get-go. So we proceed with the betrayed spouses trying to trap their partner, the insurance jobs, the missing. This morning was my first day back after a harrowing three weeks on the other side of the world wading through my own personal hell. I was feeling jet-lagged, exhausted, wasted, and planning to take an early cut, when Millie, who you might call my front-of-house lady who fields my calls and helps me operate, stuck her head around the door.

'There's a guy called Lars Eriksson on for you. He says he's an old friend from Sweden. It's about his sister.'

I looked up at Millie, somewhat bewildered. Lars Eriksson. Jesus! There was a name from my past life. Millie slipped into my office and lowered her voice to a whisper.

'Listen, this guy was on the phone yesterday, but you were travelling from the US. It's about his sister. You won't know, but while you were away, there was this Swedish student found dead up in Caithness. Her name was Astrid.'

'What?' I muttered as the words hit me. 'Astrid? Dead?'

An image flashed up of the little sister with the mop of platinum-blonde hair, who used to follow Lars around like a puppy when he and I were teenagers in Sweden. I remember the day she was born and she was only a toddler by the time I left Sweden.

'My God!' I stood up, walked from behind my desk. 'I can't believe it. Where? How?'

'It's been in the papers,' Millie said. 'And on the television last week. Suspected suicide, they were saying. Or froze to death in the woods near Thurso.'

I looked at Millie, then at the handset on her desk where Lars Eriksson, my oldest childhood friend, the boy who was always there for me, the boy I lost touch with, was waiting to talk to me.

I took a long breath and let it out slowly.

'Put him through, Millie,' I said, and went back to my desk.

A second later I had the phone to my ear and I could hear his breathing.

'Lars?' I whispered. 'Oh Lars! I . . . I'm so sorry.'

The long silence sent a shiver through me. Then he spoke.

'Billie. Oh, Billie! I am so, so sad. My little Astrid.' His gentle voice was as I remembered it, the way he'd always said my name – laced with clipped Scandinavian tones.

My desktop screen pinged and I could see it was a message from Millie which I clicked on to see a brief newspaper story. It said police had been investigating the death of a young Swedish student who was found in a snow-covered wood outside the Highland town of Thurso. She may have frozen to death. A post-mortem was being carried out.

'Lars,' I said, 'I don't know what to say. I'm so shocked and so sorry. I've been abroad and only got back yesterday, so I knew nothing of this. Millie just told me. I'm stunned. I didn't even know Astrid was here in Scotland.'

I stopped, afraid I was beginning to babble, the way we do sometimes when we are lost for words after being given terrible news. I felt a pang of guilt for losing touch all those years ago.

'It's okay,' Lars said, in the way he always did, exonerating people because he was bigger than anger, always beyond rage or resentment, always thinking of how other people felt. 'We lost touch. I'm sorry about that too.'

A long, awkward silence followed as we both acknowledged that contact goes both ways. We were both guilty of abandoning each other, something that would have been unthinkable when we were twelve years old and inseparable. But life does that to you. Moves you on. Bombards you with new experiences, friends, relationships, life. You forget. And now we are two people on either end of the phone, faced with unimaginable sorrow.

'Billie, I want to talk to you. Do you have time?'

'Of course I have time. Of course,' I said quickly.

'I wanted to come to Scotland. To see what happened. But I can't. You see I teach in the secondary school and I cannot get away because my parents are quite frail now and I cannot leave them alone as they are completely broken. I have to be here. But, they say that Astrid seems to have taken her own life.' His voice trailed off, and there was silence, then a sniff. 'Not Astrid, Billie. She would never do anything like that. She loved her life.'

I didn't know what to say to that. Suicide was the thief that stole into the tormented soul, suffocating all hope. It snatched people away without explanation, and left those behind not just bereft, but broken, because for the rest of their lives they would wonder if they could have stopped it, whether they could have done more, and how they didn't see it coming. I know this, because my father committed suicide when I was just twelve, and there had been no sign, no inkling that he was so unhappy with my mother and me that he had to leave us the way he did. It has scarred my whole life because there was always a time as a child when I wondered if it was my fault that he went away.

Lars's voice brought me back. 'I found out you were a private investigator, a detective.'

'I am. I was a police officer before. Long story.'

'I want to ask if you will investigate Astrid's death for me. Will you do that? I mean as a case?'

'Of course,' I said, because I knew that's what he wanted to hear. But I've done these kinds of investigations before and nobody wants to know the truth – that it was in fact suicide after all – and it's never anything but painful when they have to face it.

'I'll pay you, obviously. Whatever your rates are.'

'Please, Lars. Let's not talk like that. It's not important.' I said and meant it. 'Where is Astrid now? Are you talking to the police? What is the plan? Is there to be a funeral? Is she coming home?'

Too many questions, I knew. But I found myself shifting into private-eye mode very quickly because it was easier than the long, heavy silences of grief and I didn't know what to say to him that would go anywhere close to helping him.

'Her bo—'

He stopped and I knew it was because he couldn't bear to say 'body' or to accept that that was all Astrid was now – a body, cold and alone on a hospital slab so far from home. Then he went on.

'She is being held in a mortuary. She was identified by a student friend, and there was a post-mortem. The police called me this morning with the results.' I heard him swallow and take a breath.

I waited in the silence for him to continue. I know from experience how distressing post-mortem results can be for loved ones. Often there are details they don't want to hear, details that may shock them. After a few beats Lars continued.

'It appears she died from hypothermia. Her heart stopped. She had been dead for at least four hours by the time the dog walker found her in the woods.' He stopped, choked on his words. 'My Astrid. So alone like that, Billie. I cannot bear it.'

'I know, Lars,' was all I could say.

'And, also,' he continued, 'there was alcohol and drugs in her system. Recent, they said, and the level of alcohol may have contributed to her going into the woods alone in the night, dressed the way she was, with no proper winter clothing on. They are more or less saying she took her own life by her actions, her recklessness.'

I was seeing Astrid suddenly having become some depressed teenager far from her family, alone, desperate, drinking and taking pills. How could it have come to that? Why had she not reached out?

'And,' Lars went on, 'there was . . . Well. There was evidence that she'd had sex. There were traces of semen inside her.' His voice trailed off.

That put my mind into overdrive. That Astrid had had sex some time before she died alone in a freezing wood was something that would make me want to look twice if I was a police detective. They should be testing the semen, not that they could automatically find out whose it was, but it occurred to me she may have been raped. Was there bruising on her body that would indicate rough or unwanted sex? It wasn't something I even wanted to broach with Lars right now. What if this wasn't suicide, or if it was, what if something unthinkable had happened to Astrid before she died?

'Billie,' Lars said when he composed himself, 'I don't think Astrid even had a boyfriend. We spoke every week or so and she never mentioned a boy. She was studying hard – for a degree in Equine Studies at the university in Thurso. She loved horses and planned a career working with them in Europe. She could have studied here in Sweden, but she wanted to go to Scotland, to the Highlands. You see she was always interested in the history of the Scandinavians – the Vikings – who sailed to that part of the country. She was a little introverted and bookish. I know she didn't have a lot of friends. But I think she would have mentioned if there was a special boy in her life, don't you? She wasn't secretive like that. Not with me.'

'Yes, I agree,' I said, more to comfort him, because I had no idea what kind of teenager she'd become. 'Have the police interviewed all of her friends and asked where she was in the night leading up to her death? I presume they have investigated.'

'Yes. They say they have. She was in a bar in the town. She'd been drinking. Normal, student things. They said that she had some drinks. But everyone said they were drinking heavily on the night and they didn't see her leaving. I've never known Astrid to take a lot of alcohol. She wasn't like us in our crazy times back in the day, Billie. She was sensible. I can't understand why she would be very drunk. Then the sex?' He took a breath. 'But the night she left the bar is not the night she died. It was the next night that she went into the woods alone. I just don't get why she would do that.'

Part of the story was not unfamiliar to me as a detective having to relay to heartbroken parents the double life their teenage son or daughter was living when the post-mortem results threw up some unsavoury facts. But I was intrigued to know more. Mostly because this was Astrid, the sister of my friend, but also because it didn't ring true. Had she left the bar alone, drunk? Who does that? Could she have been so drunk that she didn't know where she was? How could that happen, and that she ended up alone? What kind of friends allowed their mate to stagger alone into the night? What happened after she left? And why did she disappear the next evening into the woods alone? So many unanswered questions.

'I agree, Lars. There's a lot to find out. Look, I just got back and I need to get my head around what has happened to Astrid, but I'll investigate for you and I promise I will do everything I can to find out what happened.' I paused. 'But are you sure you want me to do this? Because sometimes, no matter the circumstances, the result of the post-mortem and the cause of death is the same, in that if she froze to death as a result of too much alcohol it might be deemed as inconclusive. Some would take that to mean she contributed to her own death by her recklessness. And we may never get all the answers. But I want to find out if she went out of that bar alone, and why the next night she went out again dressed like that and headed to a wood on a freezing snowy night. I will try my damnedest, Lars. You know I will.'

In the long silence I could hear him sniff and I knew he was struggling to talk. I waited. Eventually he spoke.

'The police are releasing Astrid in the next two days and she will be flown home to Sweden. I can't be there with her—'

'I'll be with her, Lars,' I heard myself interrupting. 'I'll bring her home to you.'

CHAPTER TWO

I stayed in the office longer than I had intended, but by the time I left in the mid-afternoon I had read and reread every newspaper story about Astrid's death. It had happened only twelve days ago, but I got the impression that the case was being wound down and suicide or death by misadventure would be the judgement. In the absence of any injuries or witnesses to the contrary, that wouldn't be so surprising. When a young person dies suddenly in mysterious circumstances there is always a flurry of stories in the press as reporters try to build up a picture of the person and what could have happened prior to their death. And social media – where grieving often becomes public to the point of obsessive – becomes awash with the chatter of friends paying tribute. Then, unless there is a case for the police to investigate, the story fades, and the families are left to live with their heartbreak. I checked out Facebook and Instagram, but Astrid didn't seem to have a profile, which surprised me. But if she was quiet and bookish, as Lars had said, perhaps she hadn't felt compelled to post her private life all over social media, the way so many young people do these days, craving constant affirmation for every little thing they do. But for me, trying to get a handle on her friends, it was disappointing, as there was nobody to reach out to for information. I wouldn't have been emailing them anyway, and would definitely attempt to see them when I headed north, but it would have been a good start to see how Astrid had interacted on social media.

I got to my house on Blythswood Square just as the darkness was beginning to fall and the rush-hour traffic was starting to build up on the motorway. When I got out of the car, I stood for a moment, just taking in the place, glad to be home. The elegant buildings that looked onto the gated, leafy gardens gave this side of the city a calmness that belied what went on after dark, when skinny, drug-addled prostitutes stood in doorways waiting for cruising punters who would give them the means for their next fix. I decided to take a stroll around the square because although I was beyond shattered, I wasn't quite ready to go into my flat. Although it's my home, it sometimes feels sad and empty, and I knew that tonight I would feel it more acutely. Also, I was still a little shocked by the news about Astrid. And suddenly being plunged into this huge tragedy was hard to get my head around, having just arrived back from the USA after a surreal three weeks that at times felt as though I was watching someone else's life unfold before me. I walked around the square a couple of times, vaguely conscious by the second lap that a couple of cars were slowing down as they passed me and the drivers had that look about them that you just knew they were on the prowl. I'm pretty sure that in my walking boots, denim jeans and heavy padded jacket I didn't look much like a hooker, but there's a grim desperation about men who go on the hunt for women for sex that maybe they see anyone walking in this red light area as fair game. Eventually, I climbed the four stairs to my apartment building and turned the key in the huge oak front door. My flat is on the ground floor to the left, and from the big windows in my living room on any given evening I can see a myriad of life laid out in front of me like a cold buffet. I've seen enough tragic figures from this window to make me want to move to the country, or at least away from here. But this was the home I grew up in, where I lived with my parents until I was twelve, where every room was filled with the memories of our life, the cooking, the chatter, the music. I inherited it after they died, but I was only a child and was shipped off to Sweden when I became an orphan, so it had been kept in trust for me until I finally came back to Glasgow to study at university.

In the flat, I ate some pasta in the kitchen with the television on and the evening news in the background for company. If I was going to take on Astrid's case for Lars I was going to need some help from my old friends in the police. People who knew my name and reputation might say that I left the force under a cloud after I shot dead a murdering paedophile. But that isn't actually true. I was cleared by an extensive, exhaustive internal enquiry that accepted my plea of self-defence. But there was always the whiff that would hang over me and it eventually drove me out. By that time, my life was in meltdown, because the unthinkable had happened. My toddler son, my reason for living, was taken away, stolen from me by my American husband. He was just over two years old at the time. He will be turning four very soon. I look for him every day, I wait for news every hour, but it never comes. And each night I put my head on the pillow and pray for the morning light so that I can keep myself busy until I finally find him and bring him home to me.

My first call for help would have to be Danny Scanlon, my best friend who I trained with at police college and worked alongside during my time as a rookie uniformed cop, then as a detective. He has picked me up so many times from the depths of despair, and he was there for me every single time. I love him as much as I think I can love anybody, and while he is attractive and handsome, we've never pursued any thoughts we might have in that direction – though we did have one brief kiss recently after dinner, which keeps resurfacing in my mind. Probably would spoil a beautiful friendship, I've told myself, and that's fine by me, because the last thing I'm looking for at the moment is a relationship. But I knew Danny would help me if he could. I took my mug of tea into the living room, sat on the sofa with my feet on the coffee table and punched in his number on my mobile.

'Carlson! You're back?'

Just hearing his voice immediately made me feel less lonely.

'I am. Last night. Shattered. But I was in at the office today.'

Two beats passed before he spoke, and I knew he would be choosing his words carefully.

'So,' he said. 'I'm almost afraid to ask. How did it go?'

I took a breath and puffed out. 'Long story, Scanlon. Too long for the phone. We should meet and talk.'

'Are you okay, though? I mean, with whatever happened?'

'I'm okay. Thanks. I'll keep going.' I paused, not wanting to go into anything on the phone. 'Listen, did you see in the press that story about the Swedish student girl who died up north, in Thurso?'

I could almost hear his brain tick over.

'Ye-es. It rings a bell. It was nearly two weeks ago though.' He paused. 'It's not someone you know, is it?'

'Yeah. It is. Astrid Eriksson. I knew her brother really well. We grew up together and for a while he was my best friend. He called me today. Obviously I knew nothing about her death. They're saying it's a possible suicide, but he's asked me to take her case.'

'Jeez, Carlson! You know what these things are like. Suicides. People never want to accept it.'

'I know. But there's some stuff, some things I'm intrigued about.'

'Okay. How about I'll see what I can dig up tonight and meet you for a coffee tomorrow?'

I hesitated for a moment.

'Well, actually I want to make an early start tomorrow and drive up to Thurso so I can get a full day chasing things.'

Scanlon didn't answer straight away, and I knew he would want to tell me I should rest up for a day after my trip before I started digging. But he knew me too well.

'Okay. If that's what you want to do. I'll see what I can find and email you or give you a call.'

'Perfect. Thanks, Danny.'

I was about to hang up, but didn't, because it was just good to know he was there at the other end of the phone for me.

'I missed you, Carlson,' he said.

It kind of took me by surprise, but I was touched by his words, and probably should have called him while I was away, because he really does care about me.

'I would have called. But what can I tell you? Frantic doesn't even cut it.'

'Really?'

'I've got a lot to tell you when I see you. Hopefully before I go to Sweden.'

'Sweden?'

'Yes. I promised Lars I would accompany Astrid's body home.'

There was a silence and I sensed that Scanlon would

be concerned that I was going from one heartache to another.

'You sure that's good for you to be doing that?'

I sighed. 'I just think it's something I have to do. Lars was my first and best friend when I was only twelve. He's hurting. I want to do this for him. The police are not releasing the body for a couple of days, so I'll be going up to Caithness briefly to make a start on my investigation and to touch base.'

'Okay. We can talk tomorrow. Get some sleep and drive carefully.'

By the time I'd had a long, hot bath and gone to bed I was overtired. My eyes were stinging but I couldn't shut my mind off. I knew sleep would eventually come, but for a while I would have to let my head roam wherever it wanted. And as I closed my eyes I drifted back to where I knew my heart would be until I found him . . .

When I'd arrived in the city of Cleveland, Ohio, three weeks ago, I was as mentally prepared as I could be to stay for as long as it took. I knew deep down I wouldn't be able to sustain that financially, but somehow I'd convinced myself that this time I would be able to track down Lucas. The shock phone call that had made me jump on the first available plane had come from Dan Harris, the US private eye who had taken my case over a year ago, when all official avenues had come up with nothing. Over the past eighteen months he'd become something of a friend and we spoke in lengthy transatlantic phone calls or FaceTime chats where he'd inform me of every agency he'd involved, every line he'd chased. His last call had taken the feet from me. The day before, he'd phoned to say he had tracked who he believed to be my runaway husband Bob and my son to a trailer park somewhere in the south-west of Ohio state. But the next afternoon was the bombshell. By the time he'd flown down there from his office in Baltimore, there had been a fire in the trailer and Bob's remains had been taken out by firefighters. I'd listened, shell-shocked, but never anywhere in my heart had I felt upset or sad that Bob was dead, because this man had stolen my child from me. It didn't matter that he was his father. When Harris had got on the scene in the trailer park, there had been no sign of Lucas, and the police and fire service had said there were no traces of a boy. Whether he'd been there the night before I'll probably never know. But all I knew was that he had been there at some stage in the days before, and now he was out there, somewhere, perhaps with someone, perhaps with no one.

I'd taken a flight out of Glasgow to Pittsburgh and a connecting flight to Cleveland, where Harris picked me up at the airport. On the way to a small hotel in the city he talked about what he'd found so far. I listened with a kind of strange, unreal sensation that this was someone else's life he was talking about, not mine. He told me that the police and forensics were still at the scene and that the local television station had been interested as he'd spoken to a female reporter at the scene and given her the background. He asked if I was up for an interview, and I agreed. It was all happening so fast. Dan got us booked into the hotel – a tired-looking, dated building in the centre of the city, next to a line of cut-price stores and a sauna. We are used to the idea of American life mostly from watching television or reading books. And if we visit as tourists, it is usually the bigger cities like New York, or Las Vegas. But when you get to places like Cleveland you feel you've not come very far from Glasgow or Manchester, or any big city that's fallen on hard times. I noticed that downtown and towards the outskirts there were shuttered, abandoned storefronts, much the same as you see in any city across the UK. Dan took me for dinner in a little Italian restaurant around the corner from the hotel that looked like it had seen better days. I was glad of his company because my gut felt edgy and cold, and I was so far out of my comfort zone that I wanted to run back to the airport, find a place to sit and just cry all the way home. I had to keep telling myself I was going to have to man up big time, because anything could happen on this trip.

In the restaurant we ate pasta and I tried hard to shake off the exhaustion and sense of hopelessness that threatened to overwhelm me. Dan attempted to coax me into a second glass of red wine, telling me it would help me sleep, but I stuck to one. I told him nothing helps me sleep. As the waiter took our plates away, I looked at Dan's worn-out face, the wrinkled forehead and deep-set tired eyes, and waited for him to start.

'Okay, Billie, here's the situation.' He pushed back the cuffs of his shirt and leaned forward, swallowing a glug of wine. 'I'm going to level with you as I have done all the way.' He studied my face. 'I spent all day yesterday and most of last night chasing up people who might have an inkling into what happened with your husband.'

I nodded, said nothing, picked up my glass but put it back down again without drinking any.

'The way it looks is that Bob had got himself into a whole heap of trouble.' He raised his thick black eyebrows. 'Big trouble. With the kind of people that can burn down your trailer while you're still in it. You get my drift?'

I shook my head. I got his drift all right, and it terrified the hell out of me. How could Bob do that, take those kind of risks, when he had our son with him? If he was getting into trouble, all he needed to do was pick up the phone and tell me to come and get Lucas. Why would he not do that? I would never have asked questions or judged him. I would have done anything he'd asked to get my son back.

CHAPTER THREE

It was still dark when I got on the road north by seven in the morning, and it was going to be a long day. You can't go much further in Scotland than the coastal town of Thurso in Caithness at the very tip of the country, and there is no quick way to drive there. I strapped myself in for the long haul up the A9, a never-ending, monotonous road, and the further I went the more I felt I was leaving behind the Scotland I am used to. When you live in the city you are attuned to the sounds and the traffic and buzz of the people coming and going. The north, especially this far north, is like a different world of vast sweeping landscapes, sparsely populated, the wind whipping and rattling the car the further I went. And the rain coming in sheets across the fields. I had been up in this direction a few times, but just once as a private eye – one of the first cases on my books – trying to track down a lawyer who had embezzled elderly clients out of their fortune. I was told he had fled to the Highlands, and as the police seemed to have lost the trail, the family of two of the old souls he'd swindled hired me to track him down. What I found everywhere I looked were closed doors, especially in the smaller towns where he was rumoured to be holed up. People seemed to clam up when outsiders came into their patch, even when I explained to them what he had done. I eventually tracked him to a farm miles outside Inverness, and he buckled when I told him who I was. He pleaded with me not to go to the police, and I told him if he transferred the money back to his two clients I might consider it. To my astonishment he agreed. While I was in the farmhouse, I called the families and relayed this news and they gave me the bank details. I stood in the room while he tapped at his laptop and, just as he promised, I saw the money, eight thousand and nine thousand pounds, being transferred to the clients' accounts. I wondered how many more people he'd fleeced who had just given up. By the time he was finished transferring the money he broke down in tears telling me he had a drink problem and promising me it was only these two clients. He looked a wasted wreck of a man, with a blotched face and smelling of days-old unwashed clothes. I'll never know if he was telling the truth, but the bleeding heart in me gave him a break. He was sobbing at the table when I left, and I wasn't quite sure if he was crying because I'd given him a break, or because he'd lost the money he'd stolen.

I needed to stretch my legs after the five-hour drive, so I parked up in a side street at the edge of Thurso and went for a stroll to the town centre in search of somewhere I could sit and decompress. My mobile had been chiming with emails all the way up the road, as I had asked Millie to get me details of the course Astrid was on at the university here, and who her lecturers were. It would be a good place to start. I found a quiet café in the town precinct, went inside and took a table at the back. At the counter a couple of female staff stood chatting, staring in my direction, and I guessed it was because they would know I wasn't local, and they would be curious as to what I was doing there. Locals could be clannish in small towns and suspicious of incomers, and they probably had every right to be. The waitress was an older woman with short greying hair. I ordered a tuna toastie and a mug of tea.

'You here on business?' she asked, barely moving her thin lips.

I looked up at her, meeting her pale grey eyes.

'Yes, kind of,' I said, hoping that would be the end of it.

'Staying long?'

I tried to keep my face straight.

'No,' I said.

She lingered.

'Aye, we don't get a lot of people in the winter. Not like the summer when the place is heaving with tourists.'

I nodded, not really sure what to say and hoping she would just go so I could get on with reading my emails. I took my laptop out of my bag and opened it up, and it seemed to be a sign.

'Oh, I'll let you get on with things,' she said brightly. 'By the way, is that brown bread or white for the toastie?'

'Brown, please.'

She marked it on her pad and smiled again as she turned and headed towards the counter where the woman behind looked as though she was waiting for her to come back with any news.

When the food arrived I ate it as I read through Millie's emails and took the phone number of the department at the University of Highlands and Islands and the address, along with the name of the head of the Equine Studies course, a man named Jack Reilly. Then I had a quick look through the university website at the various courses and photos showing eager young faces on the threshold of life. I thought of Astrid and wondered who her friends were, how she'd lived her life until whatever drove her to the woods that night. There was also an email from Lars telling me the address of the small flat she rented in the town and that it was paid up until the end of the month. He told me I could pick the keys up from the shop downstairs to have a look inside. He also gave me details about which bank she used, and the names of a couple of friends she had mentioned, but he didn't have phone numbers for them. I immediately fed their names into Facebook and profiles came up that matched the names and students at the university. I scrolled down one girl's timeline and it was all the usual photos of nights and other random posts. Then I scrolled back to the date after Astrid died, and there was a single candle burning in a window, and some poem about loss and love and pain – and at the bottom, 'RIP Astrid'. A few friends had posted hearts and little emojis with tears, but no words. I sat back staring at the screen, trying to imagine Astrid's life, her final days. I would send her friend a message, but not right now, because I wanted to go to the university first. I finished my food and packed away my laptop. As I did, the waitress approached with the bill.

'You staying local?' she asked as I was getting the cash out of my pocket.

'Yeah, nearby,' I said.

'You staying long?'

I could barely keep my face straight. I was bursting to say why don't I just sit back down, have a coffee and tell you my life story, but I had to remind myself the north was indeed another planet. People took the time to ask you how you were doing, expected you to share your story with them. In a city, especially in Glasgow, people were open and friendly to strangers, but they wouldn't probe too deep. But once you got into the countryside people always wanted to know more about you. I wasn't threatened by it, but I really wanted to play things close to my chest until I found out a thing or two about what had happened to Astrid.

'No,' I finally said. 'Couple of days.' I pulled on my jacket. 'I'll see you again. Food was lovely.'

I left some pound coins on the table for a tip.

*

The University of the Highlands and Islands (UHI) was only a few minutes' drive from the town centre, out past the local secondary school on the quiet road where big, staunch sandstone houses had been home to generations of families. A biting wind came in gusts and was sweeping across the fields as I got out of the car and headed to the reception. I'd decided not to phone the university first as it would give them the opportunity to say no. At the reception I merely enquired where the equestrian centre was. When I was asked if I had an appointment, I didn't say yes, but told her I was seeing Jack Reilly.

'What's it about?' she asked.

'It's about a former student, Astrid Eriksson.'

She gave me directions.

The big indoor equestrian centre was impressive, and I stood for a few moments taking in the atmosphere of the place and watching students working with horses in one open arena, and others inside stables. I could see a few of what looked like lecturers chatting together. One of them turned around, then the others. I raised my hand, not quite in a wave, but in acknowledgement as one of the men came towards me and I realised the receptionist must have called the stables. But I was relieved to see that he didn't look like he was going to throw me out.

'Jack Reilly,' he said, his eyebrows raised. 'What can I do for you?'

'Billie Carlson,' I replied, reaching out a hand. 'I'm a private investigator.'

I was glad that he shook my hand warmly.

'Come over this way and I'll make a cup of coffee. Have you just arrived?'

So far so good. He seemed chipper enough. He was wearing black Hunter wellies, the kind you don't see much in Glasgow unless it's posh people in four-by-fours dropping their kids off on the school run, or out for a walk in the woods. These were proper, used, working wellies with horse shit on the heels. He wore a navy-blue fleece zipped up to his neck and had the rosy cheeks of someone who spends a lot of time outdoors. I followed him to an alcove that looked like a small kitchen.

'Take a seat.' He pulled up a white plastic chair.

I sat down and he looked at me as though he was waiting for me to start.

'Astrid Eriksson,' I said. 'I've been asked by her family in Sweden to see what I can find out about her death. As you can imagine, they are distraught.'

He nodded, looking beyond me to the arena.

'Yes, tragic. Do you know much about it?'

'Only what I've read in the newspaper reports. I haven't talked to the police yet. I'm kind of trying to tread lightly at the moment, see if I can build up a picture of who she was, you know, and what led this to happen.'

He shook his head and seemed genuinely perplexed.

'Nobody was more shocked than the team here. Astrid was a lovely girl, very hard-working, studious, and she loved her course. She was a very promising student. None of us saw this coming. If we'd even thought for a moment she was in any kind of trouble emotionally or otherwise we would have been there for her. It's just inexplicable.'

'Do you know any details of the post-mortem, or what the police are saying?'

He looked at me, a bit furtively.

'Nobody is telling us anything. We aren't family so they won't tell us any of that, and the newspapers haven't had any details apart from saying that she had alcohol and drugs in her system. That was the biggest shock of all for us. That just wasn't Astrid. Not the girl we knew.'

'Did she have many friends here? On the course, or in other courses at the university?'

'She did have a couple of friends, but from what I gather, she wasn't one for socialising too much. She had a flat in the town somewhere. But as far as I can see she didn't go out a whole lot, unlike a lot of the students. This area, to be honest, it might surprise you to know, is a bit of a hotbed of drugs and young people and it can be a problem. But Astrid was not that kind of girl.'

He seemed honest enough and cared about her and I got the impression he was telling me the truth.

'She seems to have been with someone the night before she was found. Would you be able to throw any light on that?'

He glanced at me. 'How do you know that?'

'Her family told me. Her brother. Forensics from the post-mortem.'

He said nothing then shook his head. Then looked at me.

'It all seems a bit out of character for Astrid. There's something not right.'

'Why do you say that?'

He took a breath and pushed out a sigh.

'Look, Billie, I can't really tell you any more, and you probably know more than me. But one thing is, I have a friend of mine, an ex-cop, who lives near here, and he still gets some info from time to time. I think he might be someone you would want to talk to.'

'Really? You think he would talk to me?'

'I can ask him. He's a good guy.' He leaned forward. 'But they're not all good guys, if you get my drift.'

I waited for him to elaborate, but he didn't.

'I'd be very grateful if you could call him for me, Jack, and ask if he'd meet me. Total discretion all the way, please tell him.'

I took out my business card and handed it to him and he put it in his pocket. We both stood up.

'Thanks for seeing me,' I said, shaking his hand. 'You've been really helpful.'

'We're all just so sad here at what's happened. It shook us all to the foundations. A lot of students who come here, if they're not from the area, can find it a bit bleak, especially in winter if they've not been away from their families before. So some stay for a short period then go back home and do the course remotely, which we're all set up to do. But Astrid came a long way and chose this area apparently because she had a friend who told her it was a fantastic place to study and enjoy life. What a terrible way it has turned out.'

I nodded. 'For sure. Tragic. Her family are heartbroken.'

He walked me to the door of the centre and we stood for a moment looking out across the landscape.

'Good luck with your investigation, Billie. I really hope you get to the truth.'

I held his gaze for a long moment and wondered if there was more he knew but wasn't saying, or if, like Lars, he was looking for a reason, or some explanation, or someone to tell him that it wasn't true, and that Astrid didn't take her own life.

CHAPTER FOUR

The sight of the sea and a blast of salty air would stave off the exhaustion that was beginning to overwhelm me. Millie had booked me a hotel a few minutes' walk from the beach, and once I'd checked in and thrown my overnight bag in the room I could easily have lain on the bed, closed my eyes for a few minutes and rested. But the hotel was dreary and deserted, and although my body was screaming to rest, I needed to be outside. I zipped up my puffer jacket and bulked up the scarf around my neck, pulled on my sheepskin gloves and headed for the shore. I had already sent a Facebook message to Jenny Barclay, the girl who'd posted the candle and the poem in memory of Astrid, but I wasn't holding my breath in hope.

By the time I got to the seafront the low sun was trying to break through and there were patches of bright blue sky, but a vicious wind was almost blowing me off my feet the closer I got to the beach. I watched, hypnotised by the huge, menacing waves that, if you stood close enough to the edge, would swallow you up and drag you out to sea. They crashed onto the rocks, and every now and again a massive swell lashed onto the road, soaking cars and anything in its path. I could feel the salt spray on my cheeks, numb from the freezing wind. I wondered if Astrid had sometimes walked this shore road on a day like this and if it lifted her spirits or if it depressed her. Places like this, coastal towns and villages with their faces set to the sea, can be mesmerising and beautiful, but they can also be bleak and brooding and lonely if you're a troubled soul. Looking out to the rampaging water, a stab of desolation washed over me. I felt far from home, and much further now from Lucas, who was somewhere across this ocean, beyond where the North Sea meets the Atlantic in what might as well have been another world. I sniffed in a sharp breath to stem the lump in my throat, but I couldn't hold back the tears that spilled warm on my freezing cheeks. I brushed them away and put it down to tiredness. My mobile pinged and I pulled it out of my pocket and saw a message from Jenny. She was agreeing to meet me but she would only be in Thurso for the next hour. I turned and walked briskly back to the hotel, trying to shrug off the shadows.

I waited outside my hotel for Jenny. When I'd messaged her back, she'd said she didn't want to go anywhere in the town where she might bump into any friends or other students. I told her we could drive somewhere quiet, and my car was parked outside waiting for her to arrive. Bang on time, a tall, willowy girl came around the corner and looked in my direction. She was dressed in black leggings and trainers, T-shirt and a cropped leather jacket, which made me freezing just looking at her.

'Jenny?' I said as she approached.

'Yeah. Billie?'

I nodded. 'Thanks for coming. You want to go for a drive?'

'Yes, that would be good. There's a car park facing the sea up the road. We could sit there for a bit.'

We got into the car and I drove the few minutes with her directing me. I parked the car, and handed her a cup of coffee I'd bought from a café near the hotel.

'I wasn't sure what kind of coffee you like, but this is just white. Is that okay?'

'Yes. Thanks. I'm kind of cold.' She glanced at me. 'And to be honest a bit nervous, you know, about talking to you.'

I raised my hand in acknowledgement.

'I understand. But don't worry. I promise you nobody will know we spoke.'

I kept the engine running and the heater on as we looked out to the sea and for a long moment there was just the sound of the waves.

'So what I'm trying to do here, as I told you,' I began, 'is build up a picture of Astrid, her life here, and what could have happened in the lead-up to her death. How well did you know her?'

She sipped her coffee from the steaming cup, then put the lid back on.

'She was a quiet girl. We didn't go out together much. I mean, I did. I go out a lot, but Astrid didn't really go anywhere at the weekends. That's why I suggested she start coming along to the bar with us on Friday nights. There's a few of the girls from uni, and some of the lads, and there's a live band in the pub.' She half smiled. 'Basically, we get a bit wasted and sometimes go back to someone's flat. You know. Student stuff. It's all good fun. Most of the students are away from home and they don't have the money to travel to Inverness to go clubbing, so we just make the best of it here. But there are a few arseholes around too.'

'What do you mean?'

'Guys that come in from other areas. Because of the students, the girls and stuff, they come around a lot and try to muscle in. Some of them are all right, but some are not. They try to push drugs on us. Weed mostly, and a few of the guys take it sometimes, but not me. And definitely not Astrid. There's cocaine too, but as far as I know, none of us has ever taken it.'

'Did you see Astrid in the days before she died? I mean, were you out together or anything? Police reports have said she left the bar the night before she was found, and that she was a bit drunk. Were you there that night with her?'

Silence. She nodded slowly but said nothing and stared out of the windscreen. I waited. She was either processing how to tell what she knew or was deciding whether to tell anything. I wondered if she was being completely honest with me. Her lips tightened.

'I . . . I'm worried,' she finally said.

I let it hang to see if she'd expand on that but she didn't.

'Were you interviewed by the police? The press reports said they spoke to everyone who was in the bar.'

She nodded, swallowing. 'Yes. But I didn't tell them everything.'

'What do you mean? About that night?'

She didn't reply and we sat again for a bit, until I spoke.

'Jenny, Astrid's brother, Lars, called me because we were old friends from years ago in Sweden when I lived there as a kid, and I knew Astrid. I remember her as this lovely little girl.' I paused. 'That's why I'm here. Her brother doesn't believe that Astrid took her own life, or was careless and drunk. And I promised him I would try my best to get to the truth. This is a small town, so somebody must know something. Can you talk to me about that night or the days before she died?'

I hoped my line about knowing Astrid as a little girl and my friendship with the family would open her up a little, and I watched patiently as she took a sip of her coffee.

'We were out together in the bar. It wasn't the first time. Astrid had been there with us three or four times recently and she really enjoyed it. It was good for her to get out, as most of the time she's cooped up in that flat she lives—' she glanced at me, 'lived in. So she was good that night. It was a birthday night for one of the guys and we were all a bit drunk.'

'What about Astrid?'

'Yes. She had a few drinks too. She'd have been tipsy. We were drinking beer and shots, but we didn't have a lot of shots. The pub was noisy and got busy. Then ... Then the guys came in. These locals. They're like chancers, hard men, and they seem to run the show around here. They're always hanging around us. And they liked Astrid. I mean, she's, was, gorgeous. Different-looking from the rest of us, her being Swedish, the long blonde hair and tall. She was like a model.'

She glanced at me, my hair.

'Are you a bit Swedish? Is that why you lived there?'

'Yes. My father was Swedish, hence the blonde hair.'

'It's nice.'

'Thanks.' I waited for her to go on.

'So there was a live band playing, and when the guys came in people were up dancing and it was all a bit mad. Just a Friday night but more of a party atmosphere.'

'What about Astrid? Was she dancing and enjoying herself?'

'Yes. She was. For a bit. Then later, two of those guys I was telling you about, they were hanging around her at the bar and she was chatting to them. And ... And ...'

She stopped, put her hand to her mouth and shook her head.

'And what, Jenny?'

'That's the bit I feel bad about. I don't know what happened. I was on the dance floor with a few of the other students and we were having a carry-on and dancing in a circle and stuff and just messing around, and then when we came back to the bar, Astrid wasn't there.'

'What do you mean?'

'She was gone. I went to the toilet to see if she was there after a few minutes, but there was no sign of her, and by this time the bar was in full swing.'

'What about the guys who were talking to her?'

'They were gone too. The three of them.'

There was a picture building up here and it wasn't looking good.

'I went outside and along the road a bit but there was no sign of her. I asked the bouncers and they just said they didn't see anything. But they must have seen something, because she didn't just walk out of the bar and disappear. Somebody must have seen her.'

'Did you try her mobile?'

'Of course. I rang it loads of times and texted it. I mean she could just have gone home, but she wouldn't have done that without telling us. Her flat isn't that far away, but I was meant to be staying with her that night, as I live with my parents in Scrabster which is a few miles away, but there's more freedom staying with a friend than being at home. But I couldn't get hold of her.'

'So what did you do?'

'I told the rest of the guys that Astrid was nowhere to be seen. But to be honest, people were all drunk and I think they just assumed she'd gone off with a boy.' She paused.

'I'll be honest. I was a bit drunk myself, and, and . . . that's what I feel so guilty about.'

'So where did you stay that night? Did you go to her flat? Knock on her door?'

'Yeah, I did. I banged on the door a few times but it was after midnight and the neighbours were raging, so I gave up. I thought maybe that she'd come home and crashed out. But that's why I feel bad, because there was this niggle with me the whole night and the following morning that something wasn't right.'

'So what did you do?'

'Well I got a taxi home. Then in the morning I tried her mobile again, but it was ringing out and she didn't answer any texts. So that was when I got my dad to drop me off in Thurso to try her house again.'

'Have you told police all this?'

She looked at me then dropped her gaze.

'No.'

'Can you tell me why not?'

'Because I'm scared.'

'Scared of what?'

She leaned forward, her head in her hands.

'Scared because of what Astrid told me the next day.'

'What? You saw her the next day?'

She nodded. 'When I went to her flat and hammered on the door, she eventually answered, and she was in a real state. Sobbing, hysterically. But she was staggering around as though she was on drugs or drink and I was trying to calm her down and asked her what had happened. She just kept sobbing and saying she didn't know. She said one minute she was in the bar and the next minute she was walking somewhere down the road with a guy and didn't know where she was. Then a car stopped and this other guy told her to get in and that they would take her home. But when she was talking, she kept saying that's what she thinks happened, but she didn't know for sure. She was really confused.'

'Jesus,' I said. 'Someone spiked her drink?'

She nodded again, sniffing. 'I think so. But I don't know. I'm sure it was them.'

'Does she know who picked her up in the car?'

'She didn't know for certain, but she said it was the guys she was talking to at the bar. She doesn't know them, but everyone does. They're arseholes. I think they must have drugged her.'

I sat in stunned silence, trying to imagine the confusion and the fear of Astrid, whatever happened to her.

'Why are you scared to tell the police this, Jenny? Have you been threatened?

She didn't answer. She looked like she was about to crumble.

'Look,' she said, 'that morning when I went to Astrid's place, she showed me a video. It was horrible. She was lying on this table or bench thing and two guys were having sex with her.'

My mouth dropped open.

'You saw this?'

'Yes. It made me sick. I pleaded with her to go to the police there and then, but she wouldn't. She said they wouldn't believe her, because in the video she is not fighting back. She's just lying there looking helpless. Like she's drunk or drugged.'

'Did you see who was in the video?'

She bowed her head. 'There were two of them. But they were wearing masks.'

I waited for a moment, watched as she looked at me then out of the windscreen and down at the back of her hands.

'Jenny,' I said. 'Do you have a copy of the video? Did Astrid send it to your phone that morning?'

It took her so long to answer that I knew in my gut she would not tell the truth.

Finally, she shook her head.

'No. I was so upset and could see that Astrid was too, and I didn't want to ask her to share it with me.'

I looked at her, but she didn't meet my eyes.

'Jenny, are you telling me the truth? I know you're scared. But if you do have the video then it's really important evidence.'

She swallowed and shook her head.

'Astrid wasn't fighting back. She couldn't. But who is going to believe that?'

'If I could get that video, I will make sure someone believes it and we can find these guys.'

CHAPTER FIVE

How could I ever tell Lars that his sister's last hours were
filled with such terror? I shivered as I stepped into Astrid's
flat above a baker's shop in the centre of town. It was icy
cold, and the landlady who took me there seemed huffy
when I asked her to turn on the heating and if I could
spend some time there.

'Why?' she asked.

The question and her manner irritated me, and I glared
at her.

'Because as I told you when I called, I am here on behalf
of Astrid's family. And they have assured me that the rent
on the flat has been paid until the end of the month.' I
stood, arms folded, ready to take her on.

From her po-faced expression, she wanted to tell me that
the tenant was no longer with us therefore the contract
was obsolete, but she backed away and shrugged.

'Well. The police told me they were finished with their

investigation. They were here, you know, looked around, but said there was nothing to see.'

'That's fine,' I said. 'Astrid's family have asked me to bring some personal items back, so if you don't mind, I'd like to be left alone.'

Her face hardened.

'Fine. You can come down to the shop with the keys when you are finished. I'll be there till six.'

When she left, I walked around the room taking in the pictures on the wall, the leather jacket still on the back of the chair, papers and study books on the table. An unwashed mug. It was as though life had stood still, as though the room was just waiting for her to come back. I opened the bedroom door and saw rumpled bedclothes, clothes on the floor – a teenager's bedroom, but this teenager would never come home. I stood looking out of the window onto the quiet main street and imagined Astrid, all day in this flat, traumatised, drugged, bewildered, and ultimately unable to make any rational decision. I wondered at what moment she decided to go out of the house with the alcohol and drugs and head to the woods. If only she'd called someone – Jenny, her brother, her lecturer. Just one phone call and she might still be here. I picked up the duvet and pulled it back, then saw her jeans and underwear on the floor as though she'd stepped out of them. Had the police not even thought about taking anything out of here? Why were they so quick to dismiss this as some kind of routine story of a teenager getting drunk and staggering into the woods? There was no mobile phone lying around that I could see. Was it on her when she left the flat that night? Why had they not looked further? I sat on the sofa, rested my head back and closed my eyes for a moment.

Standing once more, I paced the floor, then went back into the bedroom. I looked down at her jeans and pants and wondered if that was what she'd been wearing the night it happened. I took out a pair of surgical gloves from my bag and slipped them on, then very carefully picked up the jeans, rolled them up, and did the same with the pants. Then I went into the kitchen and found a couple of white bin liners and gingerly placed the jeans and pants inside. It was twelve days since the attack, but if there were traces of sperm on the clothes then it belonged to someone. I knew the lab would be able to get DNA from it and it was then a question of finding a match. I'd have to ask Scanlon to pull some strings for me. But what I couldn't understand was why the police hadn't taken anything away from her flat for investigation, especially after the preliminary post-mortem found that there was sperm in Astrid's body. They either assumed she just happened to have had sex a day or so before she died, or they were hiding something. I could imagine the cops' defence – they questioned several people who had seen her in the bar chatting to some boys, but they were all so drunk nobody seemed to know their names. Case closed. But why? I went into Astrid's wardrobe and pulled out her hard-shell suitcase, a brightly coloured job with the Scottish and Swedish flags fixed onto it. I pictured her packing to leave Sweden, the excitement and trepidation she must have felt taking the first faltering steps away from her family. She'd be packing the things that would remind her of home, photos, jackets, jumpers, boots. I wasn't sure if Lars would want these things brought back, but I decided to pack most of them anyway, thinking it would be part of his grieving process to have her possessions at home. I went into the living room where there were photos of her family on a bookshelf. One picture on the wall was of the harbour at Västervik, and a pang of something like homesickness tugged at my chest as I saw myself there so many years ago, growing up, making the best of it, finding new friends. I thought of Lars and the other teenage troops, and the warm summer nights swimming and trips out to the lagoons. And now this, the remnants of a life cut short. I swallowed the lump in my throat as I took the picture down and packed it into the case. Then I took the unwashed mug and a hairbrush, anything I could find that might help establish that they belonged to Astrid and would match the DNA from her post-mortem. I did this in the event that there was any question that the DNA they found on her body was different from items in her home that she had used. I was conscious that I had now crossed over from private investigator into police mode, but I was driven by finding the truth not just for Lars but for Astrid. Before I left the flat, I called Jenny.

'Billie?'

'Yes. Jenny, I want to ask you a couple of things. I'm at the flat, taking some things of Astrid's home to her family.'

'I understand.'

'Can you remember what Astrid was wearing that night in the pub when you were all out?'

'Yes. She had her jeans on, ankle boots and a black blouse. She looked lovely. She always did.'

'Thanks.' I paused for a moment as she sounded choked. 'And the day you went to the flat to see her, can you remember did the video she was showing you have any name or anything attached to it?'

'We were both crying as she showed it to me and I was really upset. Astrid said she didn't know the name and that she never gave the boys her mobile number so she was confused how she'd even been sent it. Maybe they were able to get into her phone settings that night and find her number. Or maybe with bluetooth or something. The video message she got was from someone called Rab, but there was no phone number.'

'Do you know anyone called Rab?'

'I know of a couple of guys – one from Thurso, and another, who is the son of this guy, Donny Mason, who owns one of the hotels here and a string of others in the area and in Inverness. But that might not even have been the real name on the phone. If they were trying to torment her they could just have used a name.'

'Yes. I see. What do you know of this Rab Mason?'

'I don't really know him, but I know of him. From what I hear he's a right bastard. But this. I mean raping a girl. That's just sick.'

'And one last thing, Jenny. When the cops talked to you the day after Astrid had been found, were you not tempted just to tell them everything? About the video?'

There was silence and then I could hear her sniffing.

'Yes, but I didn't. I was scared. I was terrified to be pulled into something because the guys who did this are evil, and I'm scared of them.' She paused, crying. 'But I'm ashamed of myself. I let Astrid down. I should never have left the flat that day and should have forced her to come to the police. But she was absolutely never going to do that, and she said she just wanted some sleep and pleaded with me to do nothing and just to leave her alone.' I heard her swallowing. 'I did, and I will never forgive myself.'

'What about now, Jenny? Would you come to the police now? With me?'

Silence. I waited. This was a no-brainer question for me.

'Jenny?' I eventually asked.

Again with the tears.

'I can't, Billie. I . . . I just can't. I'm too scared. You have no idea how powerful these people are.'

'What people?'

'It's not just these boys, it's who they are, what they do,

how connected they are. They run everything up here. I can't stick them in. They'd kill me.'

There was no answer to that, and by the silence at the other end of the phone I knew that she had only told me some of the truth. The rest I would have to find out myself.

'But Jenny—'

'I have to go,' she said, and hung up.

I stood staring at my mobile, bewildered. Darkness had fallen and the house was gloomy, the shadows in every corner where scraps of Astrid's life lay. I walked across to the window and looked down at the street. A couple of cars passed and I watched them until they were out of sight. As I stood there, one of them came around again, slowed down opposite the flat and two male occupants looked up at the window, and they stayed that way, just staring up. A chill ran through me and I stepped back behind the curtain. Then I went back into the bedroom and hurriedly packed as much as I could get into Astrid's suitcase and a smaller holdall, with a gut feeling that this might be the only chance I would have to get her possessions out of the flat. But I'd made my mind up that I wasn't going return the keys to the landlady, as I wanted to come back again and check if anyone had come in after I left. I opened a couple of drawers a fraction, taking a snap on my mobile so I would remember how I'd left them, and also moved a couple of things around the flat into positions that I'd be able to see if someone moved them. Call it paranoia, or instinct, or whatever, but there was something beginning to creep me out about this whole affair and who was involved in it, and I sensed I would have to watch my back. I took the luggage downstairs, threw it into the boot of my car, and drove quickly to my hotel, all the time with the feeling that I was being watched.

As I got into the car park at the rear of the hotel, my mobile rang but no number came up on the screen. I pushed the answer key but didn't speak.

'Billie Carlson?' A male voice, soft spoken.

'Who's this?'

No answer for a moment.

'Jack Reilly passed me your number. You might want a chat?'

The penny dropped and I was relieved. Reilly had said he would pass my number to an ex-cop who might be able to help. I didn't even have his name, but this was good.

'Yes, sorry,' I said. 'I didn't have your name.'

'Dave Fowler. Ex-cop. Detective.' He spoke in staccato, like he was reading a description of a suspect to a police briefing room. 'I'm told you're investigating the death of the Swedish student.'

'Yes. Astrid,' I said. I wanted to say she was a real person, not just a Swedish student, which was how everyone would remember her up here, but I knew her a whole lot better.

'Astrid. Awful tragedy.'

'It was,' I said. 'Dave, I'm not going to be in the area long, would you be able to meet me any time soon?'

'When?' he asked. 'I'm in the town just now, but I live near Scrabster so I'll be going back in a couple of hours.'

'Now would be perfect. I'm staying at the Manor Hotel. There's a bar in there. Do you want to meet me there, or would you prefer one of the pubs?'

'The hotel is fine. I can be there in fifteen minutes.'

CHAPTER SIX

The hotel bar was like a morgue, and just as cold. In the dead of winter in a town like this I wouldn't have been expecting many people propping up the bar at five in the evening, but the barman looked crestfallen when I walked in, as though he was giving it five more minutes without a customer and he would pull down the shutters.

'What can I get you?' he said grimly.

'A heater would be good.' I did my best to smile as I rubbed my hands together. 'It's freezing in here.'

He looked back, flint-faced, my attempt at banter barely registering.

'Aye, well, we don't get many folk in here at this time of the day.'

I glanced away from him at the fireplace across the room, coal and kindling fixed up ready to be lit.

'Are you wanting the fire lit?'

'Well, that might be an idea,' I said. 'Heat the place up a bit.'

He put down the cloth he was using to clean a tumbler.

'Are you resident?'

'Yes.'

If I hadn't been resident, I was clearly going to have to freeze. It crossed my mind to ask for a sandwich just for the sheer hell of it to see what kind of face he would throw.

'Okay. I'll light the fire. Can I get you a drink?'

'Some tea would be good.'

He nodded, stepped to the other end of the bar and switched on a kettle. Then he came out from behind the bar and crossed the room, bent down and struck a match on the fire. I watched as the flames caught the kindling and within seconds began to burn brightly, suddenly making the room feel welcoming. I thanked him as I went over and sat on an armchair by the hearth. By the time the tea arrived, the fire was well ablaze and I was hypnotised by the flames. I was beginning to feel the heat on my face and the tiredness of the day and the travel starting to catch up with me, when the door of the bar opened bringing in a chill blast of air, and a tall, chunky figure that I thought might be Dave Fowler. He glanced around the empty bar, where the barman was standing his face deadpan, then at me, and walked over to my table.

'Dave?' I looked up at him. 'Thanks for coming.'

He didn't stretch out a hand, and he stood for a moment, his eyes scanning my face as though there was some vague recognition, then he nodded.

'Billie Carlson,' he said. 'You're a long way from home, are you not?' His leathery face was ruddy, and the bags under his eyes looked like he had seen the wrong end of too many boozy nights. But his smile was the friendliest I'd seen since I left Glasgow.

'Yep,' I said. 'It certainly feels that way.' I stood up, motioned him to sit opposite me. 'Let me get you a drink.'

'Thanks. Pint of lager, please.'

The barman already had the glass under the font as I approached, and I made a mental note that my chat with Dave would have to be sotto voce, because this guy would no doubt be hanging on every word. I brought the pint back to the table and sat down. Dave raised his glass to his lips and took a small sip, then set it down.

'So how long you been out of the force, Dave?' I asked, thinking it best to start with a bit of small talk.

'Five years now. Soon as the clock struck forty-five I was out. I'd had enough by then.' He looked at me, then at the fire for a long moment, and I wondered if it was my cue to ask what he meant. But then he turned to me and put me on the spot.

'You're an ex-cop yourself, aren't you, Billie?'

He'd been checking me out. I'd have done the same with him if I'd had more time. He half smiled and lifted his pint, taking a good swig.

'I've got a couple of mates down in Glasgow still in the force,' he said. 'It's not a problem that I checked you out, is it?'

'Course not.' I shrugged. 'I wouldn't have expected anything less from a detective.'

He looked at me. 'Actually, your name was familiar and I couldn't place why, then when my mate mentioned your background, I remembered the story that was everywhere at the time.'

I nodded, didn't reply, but hoped I wasn't going to have to rake over my past.

'Any regrets?' he asked, his eyes narrowed.

'What do you mean?'

'Leaving the force, I mean. Not shooting the murdering perv.' He paused. 'No loss to the world, that.'

I really didn't want to get into that, so I just nodded and said nothing. He looked like he was waiting for an answer and when it didn't come, he spoke.

'Anyway, not trying to dig up your past, but good that you've moved on. I thought about the private investigator scene myself. But way up here, I don't think there's a seam for it, if you know what I mean.'

'Yes,' I said. 'Unless some poor girl turns up dead in the woods and nobody wants to talk about it.'

He ran a hand across his chin and sat forward, lowering his voice.

'What do you know?' he asked, leaning a little closer.

I waited a few seconds then I looked straight at him.

'I'm hoping you might tell me what you know,' I said. 'I mean about the police investigation. There's something not right about it.'

'It feels like the police just want the case closed.'

I was surprised at his frankness, and it fuelled my own suspicions.

'There are unanswered questions,' I said.

I didn't want to give anything away, but I got the feeling there was more to come from him.

'For example,' I glanced at the barman who had his back to us fixing one of the optics, 'where is Astrid's mobile phone? It's not in her flat. I have keys as the family in Sweden asked me to come up here and see what I can find out. But I've searched the flat and it's not there. I know the police were in there after she died. So maybe they took it. Or maybe she lost it when she walked into the woods.' I paused. 'I have to take some of her possessions back to Sweden with the body; that's what I agreed with the family.'

He gave me a long look and was silent for a moment, then he leaned over and spoke.

'I still have close connections in the force. The cops took her mobile phone from the flat, so I'm told, after she was found in the woods. But don't expect them to hand it over to you.'

It wasn't easy to read his face and what he was trying to tell me, but I thought he might be fishing to see how much I knew.

'Why would that be?'

He sat back giving me a wry look and I wasn't sure if he suspected I already knew the answer.

'Think about it.'

I paused long enough, but I could see he wanted me to say something.

'Evidence? Text messages?' I said. 'Something on the phone that would mean Astrid didn't just get drunk and walk into the woods for no reason?'

He didn't answer. Took a long breath and exhaled slowly, then looked me in the eye.

'Tell me, Billie,' he said. 'How far do you want to look in your investigation here?'

I looked right back at him.

'All the way.'

For a while he said nothing as he gazed at the fire. Then he said, 'It would be a lot easier for you to go back home, take that poor girl back to her family, and tell them it was all just a tragedy. Poor, lonely girl so far away from home she couldn't cope.'

'But that's not the truth,' I said. 'I want the truth. Astrid deserves better.'

'She does. But digging up the truth is not safe.'

'For who?'

'For you, Billie. For anyone who starts raking over the coals in this town.'

'What do you mean?'

'Okay, I may have quit the force, but I still have information about what goes on there. One of my best mates who worked with me in the CID in Inverness has sources very close to the investigation of this case. He gets inside information, and he has passed stuff onto me.'

'About Astrid's case?' I raised my eyebrows.

'Yes. But over and above all that, there's some corrupt shit that goes down here and everything is just brushed under the carpet. People look the other way. It's always been like that in certain matters. That's one of the reasons I left the force.'

'What do you mean, "corrupt"?' I asked. 'Who? The police?'

'Yep. And the connections. They're all tied up.' He paused. 'And I don't mean all of the police, because most of them are good guys. But some of them aren't.'

I sat for a moment. This was away from what I wanted to do. I wanted to get to the truth of what happened to Astrid and I was clear something wasn't right, but uncovering corruption in high places wasn't why I was here. And I also knew that some cops when they leave the force become bitter and look for conspiracy theories everywhere. If Fowler was one of them, he was no use to me. I had to stick to the case I was here for.

'That aside,' I said, 'do you know what happened to Astrid? I know the police were asking everyone in the bar that night before she was found, asking the friends she was with. And also the bouncers in the bar who may have seen her leaving. What do you know? Are your cop mates talking about that?'

'They know there are lies being told, that's for sure. They all say they didn't see the girl leaving, but someone must have – the bouncers, people like that. They have to be lying.'

'What about the post-mortem? Do you know much about it?'

He sat, not answering, looking at me as though wondering what I knew.

'The family have spoken to me about it,' I said.

'They told you about the drugs and alcohol in her system? About the semen?'

I nodded but kept quiet and we sat in a long silence, the sound of the fire crackling, and the heat on my face.

'That girl was raped, Billie.'

I hoped my face showed nothing.

'How do you know?'

He gave me a long look.

'There's a video. Bastards filmed it.'

I was silent but I could see him studying my face.

'But you already know that, don't you?'

I had to be as straight with him as I could without giving too much away.

'That's what I've been told. But proving it is another matter. Have you seen the video?' I asked.

'I haven't,' he said. 'But my mate has and he told me what's in it. Fucking animals.'

'Do you know who they are?'

He nodded. 'And I'm not the only one. The dogs in the street know too.'

I looked at him, bewildered.

'But why is nothing being done?'

'It's not what they are, Billie. It's who they are. They're untouchable.'

'What do you mean? Why?'

'Listen, if you're serious about trying to find the truth, I'll help you. But believe me, it's safer for you to get into your car and drive the hell away from this town.'

'I don't scare easily,' I said, defiant.

'Well, maybe you should.'

Fowler looked away, his face hardening as though stirred by some bitter recollection.

I waited as long as I could, then asked, 'Is there a bigger picture here? Is that what you're saying?'

He nodded slowly, finally turning to me.

'What is it? What has it got to do with Astrid?' I asked.

'Nothing,' he said. 'She was just an innocent kid in the wrong place at the wrong time.' He paused, picked up his drink and drained the glass. 'But as I told you it's not just what they did to her, it's who they are.'

'Christ, Dave,' I said, a little impatient with this cryptic drip-feed. 'You can't just leave it like that. I need to know what I'm dealing with here.'

He pulled up the collar of his jacket and was about to stand up when he leaned across to me.

'Go see the cops, Billie. The boss. Chief Inspector Andrew McPhail. Ask him some questions about Astrid and look at the whites of his eyes. Ask him about her mobile. Then call me. We can meet tomorrow.'

Before I could answer, he was on his feet and turning to go, leaving me to the stillness and the fire and the barman standing, arms folded, gazing flatly across at me.

CHAPTER SEVEN

I was dog tired, my mind teeming with everything since I'd left Glasgow this morning. After my talk with Fowler I was intrigued, and despite my exhaustion, I knew I had to finish my day by paying a visit to the local police, even though it was just before six. I drove my car the short journey to Thurso police station and was a little surprised to see a modern white building rather than the traditional police station and house I'd been expecting in this kind of old town. I pushed through the swing doors, and though the front desk was unmanned, I could see, behind the frosted glass, officers at their desks and hear the low murmur of chatter. There was a bell on the counter so I rang it. I waited, looking at the stuff on the wall, the usual pictures of Crimewatch, Neighbourhood Watch, numbers to contact for help. Nobody appeared, and I rang the bell again. This time, after almost a minute, a young uniformed cop came from behind the glass, face like fizz.

'We heard you the first time,' he said. 'We're very busy.'

'Are you?' I said deadpan, giving him my best you-don't-intimidate-me look.

He glared back at me.

'I'd like to speak to Chief Inspector McPhail if he's available,' I said.

He paused for a moment, glanced me up and down. 'And you are?'

'My name is Billie Carlson. It's regarding Astrid Eriksson. I'm here on behalf of her family in Sweden.'

He stood back a moment and had another long look at me. Then he turned and went behind the glass partition. I waited, and through the frosted glass I saw him talking to someone at a desk and whoever it was looked back, the image distorted. Then I saw him get to his feet. A big uniform sergeant emerged, his pot belly stretching his regulation blue sweater to the limit.

'Can I help you, dear?' His voice was brusque.

I loathed when people called me 'dear'. It made me feel like a little old lady.

'I'm looking for Chief Inspector McPhail,' I said, purposely resting my eyes for a moment on his sergeant stripes, hoping to convey that he wasn't high enough up the pecking order to deal with me. 'Is it possible to speak to him?'

He sniffed then flicked a glance at me.

'Can I ask what this is about please?'

'I just told your officer,' I said curtly. 'I'm here on behalf of the family of Astrid Eriksson.'

He put his hands in his pockets, showing no signs of moving.

'Do you have some identification? Are you family? What's your name?'

Christ. It must be a slow crime day. One of the other officers came from behind the wall and had a gander at me, shuffled some papers then went back in. I pulled out my card from my wallet and handed it to him. He read it, turned it over.

'Billie Carlson, Private Investigator? Hmmm. You're all the way from Glasgow.'

I sighed impatiently but didn't answer. Eventually he pushed himself away from the counter.

'I'll see if the chief inspector is available.'

He turned and disappeared again and I heard a door creak open and shut. I checked my watch, irritated, and at least two minutes later, the big sergeant appeared again. He opened a small hinged half-door at the counter and beckoned me inside. I followed him, feeling the eyes of the two officers staring at me as we headed towards a corridor. Then he knocked a door two down, and held it open for me to pass.

'Billie Carlson, sir,' he said, introducing me, then left.

Behind the desk was a middle-aged man with a florid complexion and a shock of steel-grey hair. He was wearing his jacket complete with the silver epaulettes of his rank. He took a good look at me for a moment then stood up.

'Miss Carlson.' He leaned across and stretched out a hand. 'Is it Miss? Mrs? Ms?' he offered, half smiling.

'Billie will be fine, thanks. That's my name.'

'Okay. Billie it is then, dear.' He looked at his watch. 'You just got me as I was about to go. Late meeting this afternoon.' Then he motioned me to the chair opposite his desk. 'Take a seat. You want a coffee, tea?'

'No thanks.'

'You're all the way up from Glasgow then. Long drive that.'

'Yeah. It is.'

'So, what can I do for you, Billie? You know that the procurator fiscal's office has spoken to the family about the post-mortem. Terrible, terrible tragedy. That young girl.' He shook his head. 'Her family so far away too. They must be devastated.'

'Beyond devastated,' I said. 'They aren't able to come here – the parents are not well enough to travel – and it was her brother who asked me to come. I will be accompanying Astrid back home.'

He nodded. 'To Sweden?'

'Yes.'

He raised his eyebrows, surprised.

'I think they will be releasing Astrid's body in the next day or so. The necessary paperwork will be at the procurator fiscal's office or faxed to us. You can collect it here.' He sat back, linking his fingers across his stomach. 'Now, is there anything else?'

I looked at him and struggled to hide my disbelief.

Anything else? An image of the description of the video crashed into my mind and anger began to rise. I swallowed to control it.

'Well, yes, Chief Inspector. There is, actually. I have some questions to ask.'

He looked at me, poker-faced.

'Well, you know, Billie . . . I'm not sure I can answer questions. Is that what the family have asked you to do? Because I know nothing about that.'

'Well, perhaps you can phone them, or contact the procurator fiscal, and they'll tell you why I'm here,' I said flatly.

He took a breath and pushed out a bored sigh, but there was something beneath it and it looked like he was hiding the tension he really felt.

'What can I tell you?' He spread his hands. 'Young girl, depressed perhaps, lonely, feels she can't cope. It happens. It's just a sad case. We had a kid like that a couple of years ago, washed up on the beach. No explanation. Sad, sad thing.' He shook his head as though empathising.

I watched him closely for a moment, knowing he would be wondering why someone like me had come to question him.

'I've been asked by the family to bring Astrid's belongings back, from her flat,' I said.

'Oh aye,' he said. 'I understand she had a flat in the town.'

I waited, searching his face before I spoke.

'Chief Inspector, can I ask you about the extent of your investigation into her death?'

'What do you mean?' He looked suddenly indignant, irritated. 'Of course our officers conducted a thorough investigation. We went over everything the night she'd been out with friends, checked out her flat, but we could see nothing that would bring us to any conclusion of foul play – if that's what you're suggesting.'

'It wasn't,' I said. 'But I take it you interviewed people who were with her, friends, et cetera?'

'Of course we did, dear.'

Again with the 'dear'. I bit my tongue. He went on.

'She'd been out on the Friday night. You know what it's like, these young students getting bevvied up – and drugs.' He shook his head, arched an eyebrow. 'You know this place can be a haven for drugs and young people these days; cocaine and weed and all sorts of stuff sold in the bars. But we usually catch the perpetrators quite quickly.'

'And the post-mortem? The family told me about it.'

He shook his head slowly as though he'd seen it all before.

'Yes. Alcohol and drugs in her system. That wouldn't help her if she'd gone for a walk in the woods in this weather. In fact, that's maybe what made her go for a walk. You know, not thinking straight, not considering the consequences of going wandering on a freezing night. Young people. You just can't tell them.'

I waited to see if he would mention it but he didn't.

'And semen,' I said. 'On her body and inside her.'

He froze a little as though awkward and uncomfortable

that a woman was mentioning semen in front of him. Then he shrugged.

'Well. You know what it's like. As I say. Young people. Sex is . . . Well. Sex . . . You know what I mean.'

'Do you have any idea who she was with? A boyfriend or anything?'

'No. Nothing to suggest that. She was a quiet girl, apparently.'

'So you didn't think it was odd that a quiet girl with no boyfriend is found dead in the woods with semen inside her?'

His face reddened. 'I'm not sure I like your line of questioning here, dear. You're not a police officer, and I really don't think, private eye or not, you have any jurisdiction to come in here and start quizzing me about an enquiry on my patch. I mean—'

'Yes I do, Chief Inspector,' I snapped. 'The family have brought me into this investigation.'

'What investigation? The girl appears to have died from hypothermia, so it will likely be ruled death by misadventure. There is no investigation.'

'You mean the case is closed?'

He shrugged. 'What do you want me to say here? There's no smoking gun. A young girl gets drunk, wanders into the woods carrying a bottle of vodka and painkillers and is found dead. There's no bruising or injuries on her that would prove anything other than what the post mortem found. Do you not think we would be looking for that?' He paused, nostrils flaring, shifting in his seat. 'Because I can tell you, dear, you can't be swanning up here from Glasgow as if you're Columbo, and start accusing us of not investigating. There was nothing to see.'

'Nothing to see,' I said, nodding my head slowly, the words choking me.

We sat in fuming silence. I could see he wanted the meeting to end.

'Now if there is nothing more—'

'Her mobile phone,' I interrupted. 'Where is Astrid's mobile phone?'

I could see the question stunned him and the muscle in his jaw flinched. He was trying not to look flustered, but I've seen shit like this before. He was lying through his back teeth.

'How would I know that?'

'Well was it on her when she was found?'

'No. Of course not. It would have been listed in her belongings.'

'Don't you think that's odd, that a teenager wouldn't have a mobile phone on them? Kids are never off their mobiles.'

He shrugged. 'Well, put it this way, Billie – and I'm sorry you've been dragged all the way up here to find a reason behind this poor girl's death – what if there isn't a reason? The thing is, a girl who perhaps felt ill with depression, out of control, didn't ask anyone for help, might have made a decision to end her life and if she did – and we don't know that for sure – then maybe she decided not to take her mobile with her. Because maybe she didn't want anyone to contact her. Sad, but it happens.'

'Then it should have been in her flat,' I said, keeping my eyes on him. 'And it isn't.' I paused. 'You said the police searched her flat during their investigation?'

His eyes narrowed. 'Of course.'

'And there was no mobile?'

He didn't answer.

The silence hung for long enough for me to see he was struggling to find a way out of this. He took a breath then snorted.

'Who knows what happened to her phone? Maybe she put it in a bin on her way to the woods that night. Maybe she lost it on her way home from the pub. I can't answer that. How do you expect me to?'

I glared at him. He couldn't answer it because he knew the mobile had been in the flat. It was with Astrid the afternoon after her attack, because Jenny saw it when she showed her the video. I felt rage at the sheer lies and cover-up going on here with this big copper who, for whatever reason, was betraying every oath he ever took, and betraying himself as a human being. Why would he do this? I stood up. This meeting was over. I'd seen enough. I put my hand up.

'Thanks for seeing me, Chief Inspector. I think we're done here.'

'We are, Billie.' He looked out of the window at the rain, then straight at me. 'You should go home. I understand the family are broken-hearted. But there's nothing for you to see here. Go home.'

The last 'go home' sounded like he was trying to say 'Before it's too late.' I got the message all right, the veiled threat, and it made me so angry I had to get out of there quick before I said something I might regret. I turned away from him.

'I'll see myself out.'

CHAPTER EIGHT

I had dinner in the hotel because I didn't feel like wandering around the town in the rain to find a restaurant that might be open. As well as that, I didn't really want to be seen in town. I'd got the distinct impression I was being watched, after that glimpse of the two men looking up at the window of Astrid's flat. I thought of Fowler's cryptic words: 'It's not just what they did to her, it's who they are.' Jenny had said as much when she spoke to me and she was obviously terrified to go any further. That should have kicked off alarm bells for me that it might be best to cut and run, but it didn't. That's not how I do business, and I've got the scars to prove it. If there was a bigger picture to Astrid's death, then it was beginning to look like the shutters had come down on any investigation. If I'd been in any doubt before, then my chat with the big chief inspector confirmed that there was no appetite to look further into her death. But it was more than that. It wasn't just reluctance or weariness on the part of a small police force having to plough tight resources into what looked like a suicide. My gut told me there was something dark beneath the surface, and I knew I wouldn't be able to stop until I found it.

The hotel restaurant was quiet, apart from a youngish couple who the receptionist had told me were the only other guests in the hotel tonight. I chose a table well away from them as I didn't want to be drawn into any conversation, and ate a decent meal of heartwarming vegetable soup and pan-fried salmon. I would have relished a good glass of wine to help me unwind from a long day, but I gave it a pass as I felt I needed my wits about me. Throughout the meal I kept my head in my laptop, going over emails from Millie and Scanlon. There was another from Lars saying Astrid would be released in the next twenty-four hours, and he was making plans for the flight back home, and if it was okay to book me on it. But the message that I read and reread, and that I knew would torment my sleep later, was from Dan Harris, my private eye in the USA.

After dinner, as I lay in a steaming hot bath, having read the email half a dozen times, my mind drifted back to Cleveland, Ohio, to the wrong end of a run-down city, to a place where never in my wildest dreams did I ever believe I would be going, hunting for my three-year-old lost boy.

I'd been in the US hotel bedroom watching myself on television being interviewed by an American reporter on the search for my missing son. How had it come to this? I felt as though I'd been thrust into some awful nightmare, suddenly catapulted from Glasgow to this trailer park on the edge of nowhere in Ohio, standing wide-eyed and dazed amid the embers of a burnt-out trailer. Dan Harris had urged me to talk to the female reporter who was hovering around the scene with her cameraman shooting images of the debris. Harris said that my interview would go out on prime-time television and might jog the minds of anyone who may have seen a small boy wandering around the trailer park. Lucas had been staying here with his father, my husband, the man who took everything from me, and whose charred remains were in the body bag on a stretcher I watched being pushed into the back of a blacked-out mortuary vehicle. Lucas had to be out there somewhere. Somebody must know something. I'd watched myself saying this to the TV reporter and was now struck by the haunted, defeated look in my eyes as the cameraman homed in on my face for my final appeal.

'Please, if you know anything about Lucas, if you've seen him, please get in touch. He's just a little boy, and he needs his mummy.'

The phone number of Dan Harris, private eye, ran along the bottom of the screen along with the appeal.

My throat had felt tight as I'd watched it. Afterwards, Harris had stepped towards me and put an arm around me.

'You did good, Billie,' he said.

'You really think someone might come forward?'

I was trying to sound hopeful, but I knew how these

things often panned out in televised appeals like this – everyone from nutcases to clairvoyants would be phoning. But it was all I had. And the terrifying scenarios flooding through my head were far from hopeful. What if my husband, up to his neck in debt and trouble, simply offloaded Lucas to the nearest person? What if he'd even sold him?

It didn't take long for the first lead to come in. A couple of hours after the appeal went out, I was having coffee with Harris in a diner close to the hotel when his mobile rang and he took a call. I could tell by the way he immediately shot me a glance that this was from the appeal. He put the phone on loudspeaker and turned the sound down so the whole place didn't have to hear. My stomach turned over when the caller said he knew where the kid was. He'd seen the dead guy – 'that dude', he'd called Bob – but he said Bob had left him with Lofty, some guy down on the east side. The guy said he was there last night and he saw the kid for sure. Then he asked whether there was any money as a reward for his information. Dan said there might be and asked if he could meet us.

'I don't want no cops,' the guy said, and reeled off a meeting place.

'No cops,' Dan assured him.

Then the line went dead. Dan put the mobile on the table and spread his hands and made a you-never-know face.

'What do you think?' I asked.

'I think we drink up and go meet this guy. We have to.'

*

We headed away from downtown Cleveland, and the further we went from the main hub of the city, the more run-down it was. In its heyday, Cleveland had been a thriving steel town famed across the US and beyond, but in the past twenty or so years, with cheap steel imports, the industry that had been the life blood of the people for generations shut down. Jobs went, along with the hopes and dreams of the people as the ravages of unemployment and poverty bred a whole new generation of underclass. It was not unlike Britain in many ways, but on a much larger, spread-out scale. The rust belt, as it was known across the Northeast and Midwest, was dotted with towns like this, and the life stories of the victims were written in every boarded-up shop, broken-down skate park, rundown and derelict housing estate. We stopped on the corner of a street next to a launderette and saw a tall, reedy guy standing alone. He looked underfed, a goatee beard, no more than early twenties. His face was pockmarked and spotty, and he wore a faded denim jacket hung loosely over a sweatshirt with the Harvard University logo.

'That could be our man,' Dan said. 'He's looking right at us. You wait here, Billie.'

Dan got out of the car and I glanced around me, half expecting to be ambushed from behind the building, but all was quiet. Dan went up to the guy and I could see them talking. The guy looked edgy, shifting from one foot to the other, and wiping his nose with the back of his hands. He looked like a junkie or a meth-head, judging by the spots around his mouth. Then Dan came back to the car.

'He's our guy, all right. He's the one who phoned.'

'What's he saying?'

'Well. He's a meth-head, that's for sure.'

'I gathered that by the look of his face.'

'Yeah. But he's calm enough and sounds quite articulate at the moment. It's just that these guys are so unpredictable.' He paused, glanced out at the guy who stood watching and furtively looking around. 'He says he can take us to the area where he saw the kid. To the house. But it's really rough. I know where it is, and it's the worst part of East Cleveland. I mean nobody goes there who doesn't belong, so that's a bit of a problem for us. We can't just go walking in there, asking questions.'

'So what do we do?'

'I think it's safe enough for us to do a drive-by. You know, take this guy in the car and just case the place. We can't sit in the street or anything because that would get noticed. But our man says he can make some more enquiries from people as time goes on. The kid might not even be there by now.' He pushed out a sigh. 'It's not ideal, Billie. But right now it's all we've got.'

'Did he say who lives in the place?'

'It's a squat,' he said, giving me the look.

'A squat! Jesus, Dan!' I closed my eyes picturing my little boy, grubby in some shithole flat surrounded by meth-heads. 'There must be some way we can get in there.'

He put his hand on my arm in a calming gesture.

'We just have to play it slow, that's all we can do. What do you think? I say we should take this dude in the car and just drive past the place in the area and get a better picture for ourselves.'

I nodded in agreement. 'We have to do something. Let's go for it.'

'By the way, he wants money.'

'How much is he asking?'

'He asked for a hundred dollars, but I told him no way. I said I would give him fifty if he takes us there and shows us the place, and another fifty if he comes up with something solid.'

'Okay,' I said, not quite knowing what I was getting myself into. 'Let's do it.'

Dan got out of the car and went up to the guy again and beckoned him across. He got into the back seat, filling the car with the smell of cigarettes and stale sweat. I turned around and scanned his face for a moment. He looked like so many boys I'd seen over the years, and made me think of Johnny, the drug addict in Glasgow who had gone so far to help me find Jackie Foster's kidnapped kid, but paid for it with his life. I wondered what this guy's story was. With his sharp nose and narrow, snake eyes circled with dark smudges, he looked shifty and desperate, and nothing like as placid as poor Johnny had been.

'Is it your kid, ma'am?' he asked.

'Yeah,' I said. I stretched out my hand. 'My kid. Billie Carlson. Thanks for calling us.'

'Philip Katowic,' he said. 'When I saw you on television, I just felt so bad for you, man. I mean I have a little brother – he's older though. He'll be ten now, but he just adored me before all this shit. I haven't seen him in two years.'

I nodded, gave him a sympathetic look. There was really no answer to that.

My mobile pinged me back from my dark reverie. I picked it up from the shelf over the bath and cleared away the steam. It was an email from Tom Brodie, my lawyer friend back home who I'd asked to look into anything he could find on the Thurso police boss, McPhail. There was nothing of any interest. The only piece in the newspaper archives locally was of a car crash years ago where a woman died after her vehicle apparently went out of control and careered over a cliff edge into the sea. I glanced at the clipping, but that was all. The hot bath on top of the exhaustion of the past few weeks was suddenly overwhelming and I could barely get out of the bath. I wrapped myself in a towel and lay in the darkness of the room until I cooled off enough to get under the duvet. I drifted into a deep sleep almost immediately.

I don't know how long I was asleep, but suddenly I was startled awake by what sounded like footsteps in the corridor. I sat up in bed and peered at the light showing under the door. I could see shadows moving. Someone was standing there outside my room. I could almost hear them breathing. I thought I heard whispers. My heart began to thump. Then, the handle of my door slowly turned. I had locked it twice, and though it was just the subtlest turning of the handle, the pulse in my neck throbbed at the possibility that whoever it was behind that door had a key to my room. Then it stopped, and nothing. I kept my eye on the door and the shadows beneath the gap, and then I heard something. I strained my eyes in the dark and saw something was being pushed beneath the door. I crept out of bed, holding my breath as a piece of paper appeared. Again the whispering, then nothing. Then the sound of fading footsteps. Whoever it was had gone. I waited a good minute then I went across and picked up the paper. It was A4 paper folded in half, and when I opened it, my eyes gaped at the message typed in large bold capitals. GO HOME. That was all it said. GO HOME. I stood staring it. Was it a threat from someone or was it a warning that I wasn't safe here? Whatever it was, it completely creeped me out, and I knew it wouldn't be wise to open the door and go chasing after whoever this was and pin them to the wall. I sat back on the bed. My watch said one a.m. and I got back under the covers. As if I didn't have enough nightmares. But then I got out of bed again and crept to the window, and as I stood behind the curtain I saw the backs of two figures going up the street and disappearing around a corner. A shiver ran through me.

CHAPTER NINE

It was still dark when I woke with a pounding headache. I opened one eye and let out a frustrated sigh as I saw my watch glowing six thirty. The last time I'd looked it was two a.m. and I was still tossing and turning, my mind refusing to shut down, and every time it did, the words GO HOME came at me in raging flashes. I threw back the duvet and went to the bathroom, filled a glass with water and swallowed two paracetamol from my bag. It would take the edge off the headache, but it was going to be a long day. I stood by the window, transfixed by the soft rain blurring in the street lamps, the soaked pavements and the road, black and shiny and as empty and desolate as I felt inside. I guessed it would be way too early for the hotel to be serving breakfast, so I switched on the kettle and headed for the shower. I stood under the warm spray, letting it run down my face and body, hoping to pull myself up from the exhausted, jet-lagged, weary feeling, and by the time I stepped out I was feeling marginally better. I heard my phone ping with a message as I came out of the bathroom, and saw it was a text from Fowler. Either he was an early riser or he'd had a sleepless night too. It read: 'If you are available this morning I'll pick you up and take you to see something that will interest you.' Intrigued, I messaged back 'Sure,' and remarked that he was up very early. He texted back – 'Insomnia' with an emoji face doing an eye roll. As I was getting dressed, drinking tea, the thought crossed my mind if it was wise to get into a car with a man I had only just met. Paranoia rising from recent encounters in my work made me ask what if he was part of this? But I'm driven by instinct, and my gut told me Fowler was genuine. If he wasn't, I'd soon find out. But first, I had one thing to do that – given the note pushed through my door last night – I couldn't put off.

By the time I left the hotel room the town was beginning to wake up, cars and delivery lorries winding their way through the streets, shops opening. The nearby fishing village of Scrabster provided a lot of the local work. But much of the employment across the area was in the now defunct Dounreay nuclear plant that was still in the process of trying to wind down after the infamous clusterfuck more than thirty years ago when a leakage incident left radioactive waste strewn across the area for miles. The clean-up was an operation that could take years. I drove across the town to the baker shop and could see lights were on but nobody was out front yet. I got out of the car and let myself into the entrance to Astrid's flat and climbed the cold damp staircase. I pushed the key into the lock and opened the door slowly, slapping on the light in the hallway as I stepped inside. I could feel my heart beating, a feeling of dread that someone would be in the flat. If they were, it was too late by now. I picked up a hockey stick propped against the coat stand and crept along the hall. I nudged open the kitchen door with my foot and switched the light on, listening hard for any noise. There was none. I stepped inside. Nothing. Then I backed out and did the same in the bathroom and bedroom, gingerly stepping into each room half expecting someone to jump out and attack me. Finally, I went into the chilly living room and had a quick scan around. At first glance it didn't look like anything had been disturbed. Then I went into the bedroom and looked at the bedside drawer. It had been pulled open and closed tight. That was not how I'd left it, and I pulled up the photo on my mobile to make sure. I took another picture. Then I pulled it open. The few things that had been in it, underwear and a vest, were still there, but not in the same place. I pulled on surgical gloves and put my hand in the drawer, rummaging around at the back, and my fingers touched what felt like a small package. I stopped immediately, pulled my hand back. Then I opened the drawer fully. There were three small packages of white powder. Then, to my shock, at the very back, something the size of a brick inside thick bubble wrap. And another one. I didn't need to touch it to know it was cocaine. At least two kilos. I took several pictures, then gingerly picked up the package. Someone had been in here and planted this after I left. Or had it been here all along, and I hadn't fully opened the drawer? I kicked myself for not doing that, but what could I have done if I had found it? And if the police had been in here why hadn't they found it? Could they have planted it? Could it have been drug dealers? Someone had shoved it there, either to taint a dead girl's reputation or to blackmail her into keeping a stash of cocaine under the threat that they would expose her in the sex video. Astrid was no threat to anyone. She was just a kid too far from home. I picked up the bag along with the packets and carefully put them into a ziplock bag I had in my jacket, and took a few pictures. Then I walked around the living room, looking for anything else I needed to take that belonged to Astrid. If someone had been in here since my visit yesterday and planted the drugs, this was my last chance. I would have to hand back the key and leave it behind. I took a few snaps around the living room, then found a plastic carrier bag in a kitchen cupboard and put in a few things I thought might mean something to Lars – a couple of pictures, books, pens. That done, I stood for a moment taking one last look, trying to imagine Astrid on that final day, tired, terrified and threatened, lonely and desperate. It wasn't supposed to end like this for a young girl with big dreams, and my heart bled for her. I couldn't bear to be in this place a moment longer. I picked up the plastic bag and headed for the door.

Downstairs the baker's was open, and cakes and sausage rolls and breads were stacked on boards alongside the window full of pastries. The landlady was serving a customer and I waited until she'd finished before I went up to the counter. She was looking at me as though she was expecting me to say something, and I wondered if she knew someone else had been in the flat. I was seeing all sorts of conspiracies here, the look on her pale, jowly face, avoiding my eyes.

'Here's the key to the flat,' I said, placing it on the glass-topped counter.

'Did you find what you were looking for?'

I gave her a flat glare, then narrowed my eyes. 'What do you mean?'

'Oh, nothing. I just thought you were looking for something.'

'I was picking up the belongings of a young girl who died. That's what I was doing. Is that a problem for you?'

She shifted on her feet and looked away, embarrassed or afraid I was going to make a scene.

'No. No problem at all. If that's you finished then that's fine.'

'Yes. I'm done.' I turned and left without another word.

As I got into my car, my mobile rang and it was Fowler.

'Morning, Billie. You okay?'

'Not exactly. But I'll tell you when I see you.'

'Something happen?'

'Kind of. But I'll tell you later.'

'Listen. Just thinking. Instead of me picking you up in Thurso, how about you driving to Scrabster and meeting me? I want to take you along the coast here a few miles, and anyway it might be best not to meet in the town and be seen with me. You get my drift?'

'Sure. I understand. Where in Scrabster?'

'I'll be parked just as you go into the road that takes you to the harbour. Then we can go in my car.'

'That's fine, Dave. I'll be there. What time?'

'An hour?'

'Perfect. I'll grab some breakfast before I head out.'

The line went dead.

As I got into the hotel foyer, the aroma of bacon cooking made me hungry and I went straight to the dining room. The place was deserted apart from myself and the couple I'd seen yesterday. I smiled in greeting to them, then asked, 'How you doing? Were you out in the fleshpots of Thurso last night?'

They grinned back at the irony.

'Well, not quite. We went to the pub down the road, but it was deadly quiet and we ended up coming back here and watching a movie on our laptop.' She smiled to the man. 'We're on the move today anyway, travelling to Orkney.'

'Are we the only guests in the hotel?'

'Yes, that's what we were told when we booked in.'

'It's just that I heard some noises last night in the hotel corridor. Like people talking or moving around.'

They shook their heads, glancing at each other.

'Never heard a thing. What time?'

'It was well after midnight. Might have been my imagination though.'

'It was really quiet – that's what we were saying; that a hotel like this in the middle of a place like this is kind of creepy when there's no guests. Actually, we'll be glad to be on our way.'

I smiled. 'Me too.'

I took a seat away from the windows and ordered some scrambled eggs and bacon with tea. My mobile pinged with an email, and I saw it was from Lars. They were releasing Astrid's body later today and he had been consulting with the undertaker who was going to transport it to Glasgow Airport. Astrid would spend a night in a funeral parlour in Glasgow before the afternoon flight to Stockholm tomorrow. He asked if it was okay to book me on the flight. I sat back and took a breath. It didn't leave me much time. I answered that I'd be ready and would head down to Glasgow later today and bring Astrid home tomorrow as promised. Once I'd eaten, I went upstairs and picked up my bag, then came down to the reception and settled the hotel bill. I gave a little shudder as I stepped out of the hotel and climbed into my car.

CHAPTER TEN

It was only a few minutes' drive to Scrabster, where the harbour dominated the area and stretched along the coastline festooned with fishing boats, trawlers and containers that had been brought in by cargo ships from the North Sea and beyond. At the end of the harbour, the ancient Holborn Head Lighthouse, whitewashed and splendid in the sunlight, stood at the edge of the rocks, a silent witness to a million life stories that had come to these shores over the generations. I slowed down on my approach past a couple of big, sober-looking harbourside houses and saw a car facing, flashing its lights. I pulled into the side of the road and got out and crossed to where Fowler was in the driver's seat of an old silver Land Rover Discovery. He didn't get out of the car and I climbed in. He turned to me as he eased the car out onto the road.

'How you doing, Billie?'

He looked fresh and more rested than when I saw him last night, and seemed genuinely glad to see me. It made me wonder if he was lonely all the way up here living on his own and if he was buoyed up just by having different company. I hoped there was more to it than that and that he had something to tell me. But the truth was I was glad to see him, as I needed a friendly face after last night.

'I'm good,' I replied, which was a bit of an exaggeration. I looked away from him out of the windscreen, then glanced back at him and half smiled as I said, 'Well. That's not really true. There's some dodgy stuff going on here, that's for sure.'

He nodded, seeming glad that I was confirming something he already knew.

'You bet.' He paused as he turned the car around away from the direction I'd come. 'I'd like to take you on a little drive, if you're okay with that, and talk to you along the way about some things.'

I nodded. 'What kind of drive? I mean where?'

He shot me a quick glance, then the lines around his eyes crinkled, his face smiling as he let out a chuckle.

'Don't worry. I'm not going to abduct you! We're not going far. About half an hour along the coast. It's very picturesque, but this is not a sightseeing trip.' He paused, raised his eyebrows for approval then said, 'Anyway, I'll tell you as we go. So what's been happening from your side? How did you get on with the cops?'

I shook my head, pushed out a sigh.

'Not very well. They were all creeping around the station like something weird, then I was taken to see McPhail the chief inspector in his office. I asked a few questions but he just fobbed everything off. They're not remotely interested in Astrid's death. They just want to wrap it up and get her out of here. In fact, they already have. Her body is being released later today and is being driven down to Glasgow. I'm going to be there too. So, wherever we are going and whatever we are looking at I'll have to be back and on my way by about four or five. That okay?'

'Yep. That's fine. That gives us plenty of time.'

I didn't answer, waited for him to start talking as we headed down the coast. But he didn't, and we drove in silence. I gazed out at the scenery. Eventually he spoke.

'So, did you go out on the town last night?'

'You're kidding! I ate in the hotel. But something strange happened. Someone tried the handle of my door in the middle of the night.'

He took his eyes off the road for a second and turned to look at me, eyebrows raised.

'Seriously?'

'Yep. There were only two other guests – a young couple – but their room was not on my floor, so I was the only one on that floor. Not that it bothered me, I was dog tired and just wanted to have a bath and go to bed. But after I fell asleep, I was wakened by a noise, like shuffling outside my door, and I thought I heard whispering, like there was more than one person. Then the door handle turned. My door was double-locked. I do that everywhere, even in my own home. Perils of the job, I think.'

'What did you do?' He glanced at me then back at the road as we rounded a bend.

'I just sat there frozen, wondering if someone was going to burst right in. But there was nothing. Then I heard a rustling noise on the floor, and I could see something being pushed under my door . . .'

He glanced eyes wide. 'Jesus!'

'Yeah. Very creepy.'

'What was it?'

'A piece of A4 paper. When I picked it up and turned it around, it had the words "GO HOME" on it. That's all. But it was enough to make me worried.'

'No wonder!'

'A couple of minutes later, I went to the bedroom window and peered out, and I saw two guys walking up the road then disappearing around a corner. I suppose they might have come from anywhere, but this was one in the morning and I'd put good money on it being them who shoved the paper through my door.'

'Had to be,' he said. 'Nobody is out in Thurso at one on a Monday morning. Nobody. Did you get much of a look at them?'

'No. They had anoraks on and hoods pulled up. Could have been any age. One looked tall and skinny, the other was shorter and squat, from what I could make out.'

He said nothing, and bit the inside of his cheek, concentrating.

'But that's not all,' I said.

I told him about going back to Astrid's flat and finding the bags of cocaine, as well as small packets, the kind of stuff a drug dealer would have in the house. And I described how I'd taken photos before of the drawer when I'd thought it only had a few clothes in it, proving that someone must have been in there after I was gone. If it was there earlier and I just hadn't spotted it maybe whoever put it there was checking on it or taking some to sell on.

His brows knitted.

'Wonder what that's all about,' he said. 'If it had just been the packets of cocaine, then it could have been that someone – maybe the guys who raped her – was trying to smear the poor girl's name, so that if police had to go back and do a thorough search they would find she had coke in her possession.' He shook his head. 'But the kilo bags? Why were they planted in her drawer at this stage, and by who? Could that also be in case cops came around again, and they would find proof that Astrid was actually dealing drugs? Seems far-fetched. Or maybe they were blackmailing her. Maybe the coke had been somewhere else in the flat so that you wouldn't have found it when you were first in getting her things, but suddenly they've moved it, thinking you'd not be back. I can't figure that out. Or maybe they were just stashing it there, you know, if they'd stolen it from their bosses?'

'I can't get my head around it, Dave. I've no idea.'

'Who owns the flat she was renting?'

'Seems to be the bakery shop down below. A torn-faced woman.'

He chuckled. 'That's Isa. She owns the building and the flats are rented out.'

'But she's hardly going to be stashing two kilos of cocaine.'

'No. She's a widow, lives by herself, but her nephew, Rab Mason, is a bit of a toerag and he used to rent a flat in there a couple of years ago. Maybe it's the same flat and he still has a key.'

'Is he into drugs though?' I asked.

Dave shrugged. 'Who knows. He was away for a while working on the fishing boats, and was staying in the Faroe Islands at one point. I don't even know if he's back.'

'Could he be mixed up in drugs and blackmail? And rape?'

'I've no idea. But he's someone to bear in mind. By the way, what did you do with the bags?'

'I took them.'

Dave swerved coming off a bend a little too fast.

'Christ! You took them? The kilo bags as well?'

'Yeah.'

'Shit, Billie! That might not have been a good idea.'

'I'm taking them to Glasgow where I'll get someone to look at them. I'm sure it's coke, but I need to be certain.' I paused. 'I don't really know right now what good it will do proving it's coke, but the idea that someone was in there and planted drugs stinks big time. And maybe me sniffing around is beginning to upset people.'

He took a breath and pushed it out through clenched teeth.

'I think you're right. And that message you got is not advice, Billie. That's a threat. And that's before they even know you snatched the cocaine. Jesus! That's dangerous.'

'I know,' I said. 'It was an impulse thing. It's one of my traits.'

I tried to smile as he turned to me, and he puffed.

'It could get you into trouble,' he said. 'It might be as well for you to bail out of here pronto. But before you do that, I want to show you something in a bit and tell you some things about this place and just what exactly is going on.'

We drove in silence for a bit and I gazed out of the window along the coastal road at the lush green fields sloping down to the craggy coastline. The sky was bright blue with patchy clouds, but the greyness and rain from earlier had gone, giving way to a breezy freshness, the sea white-tipped and choppy against the rocky shoreline. Sheep were dotted across the hillside and sturdy Shetland ponies grazed in small dyke-walled fields. Once or twice I looked up and saw soaring birds with the longest wingspan I'd ever seen. I could see why this was a place where people came to escape the cities and grind of life because on a day like this you wouldn't want to be anywhere else. In the distance I saw a couple of ships on the horizon, and smaller fishing boats far out to sea. It was a different world to the one I would be back in before the night was through.

'It's beautiful, isn't it?' Fowler said. 'Everywhere you look is more breathtaking than the next place. That bird you were looking at – a gannet. They're huge. You won't see many of them in Glasgow.'

'No,' I said. 'It is really beautiful though, the whole area.'

'But you wouldn't want to live here, would you, Billie – too far away from the bright lights.' He grinned.

'Yes. Definitely too far away for me. I can see the attraction though.'

After a long moment, he pulled into a lay-by overlooking a sandy cove. We got out of the car and stood in the fresh breeze.

'It's lovely here,' Dave said. 'Great spot for surfers. But it's more than surfers you get.' He turned to me. 'This is where a lot of the drugs come into the UK.'

I looked at him and we didn't speak for a moment as he stood gazing out, his face set.

'This place and the bay along the road that we'll get to shortly is where millions of pounds' worth of drugs are smuggled in every year.'

As a cop, I knew about dealers and drug barons using the sea and coastal routes to bring in drugs, and now and again there had been some historic busts from Felixtowe and the Cornish coast, to Irish and Scottish shores, as drug dealers continually tried to outwit the National Crime Agency, operating across Europe who tried to keep up with them.

'I know about the coastal routes,' I said. 'But I never worked on the drug squad so anything I know would be anecdotal. But right here? How is it done?'

'It's well organised, and the drugs barons come up with new ploys all the time. Here's what often happens. Along the road is the place called Bettyhill. It's a quiet cove and as secluded as this. But that's where a lot of the action is. Plenty of people have boats around here – fishing, sailing boats, little cabin cruisers like the one I have. And then, often, the big ships that come through the Faroes or Northern Europe have set off from places like Africa or even Columbia. The checks at Faroe aren't brilliant and this stuff is so well disguised. Container ships arrive with cargoes of tons of equipment – everything from engineering materials to furniture – but it only takes one of these containers to contain thirty million pounds' worth of cocaine. It either comes here on a container ship, or by another means where a vessel will stop somewhere out to sea – the mother ship, the dealers call it – and someone from here will go out and load up their boat with the drugs, then store it here. You get the picture?'

'I get the picture,' I said. 'So, if you know this, where are the cops? Inverness, drugs squad? I mean, there has to be some intelligence coming in somewhere.'

He shrugged. 'If there is, and there should be, it doesn't get acted on. But this is happening across coastal areas everywhere in the UK. I'm only showing you this because I think it may be related to what happened to that girl. And especially now that you tell me about the bags of coke in her flat. I'm sure it's all related.'

'But who would do that? And why her?'

He motioned me back into the car and we drove off. The road was quiet – secluded farmland mostly and one or two small houses – then he pulled into the left onto what looked like a dirt track road and into a wooded area. Through the trees I could see a stone-built cottage in the distance. I swallowed the little surge of fear I couldn't help having, and told myself that this was a man I could trust.

'Up here,' he finally said, pointing to the farmhouse. 'We'll not go right into the grounds because there are security cameras, but do you see that house?'

I nodded. 'Yes, is it a farm?'

'No,' he said, driving slowly up the dirt track, then taking an even smaller road for a few yards before pulling in. He stretched into the back seat and picked up a set of binoculars, put them to his eyes. 'It's not a farm. It belongs to a guy who's been smuggling drugs here for the past three years. He's known to the locals as the Irishman. Or just "Irish". He's some sort of wildlife photographer; he told people he's making films for a documentary, you know, about the puffins and wild birds.' He lowered the bins and handed them to me. 'Have a look.'

I put the binoculars to my eyes and scanned the landscape from the hillside across to where the house was. I could see a barn of some sort, corrugated tin roof, double metal doors, that were heavily padlocked. Close to it was the house, which looked just like any hillside cottage, blinds closed and no sign of life. Along both sides of the guttering I spotted the security cameras.

'It looks empty, locked up,' I said.

'It is. The Irishman isn't here just now. But he'll be back soon.'

I handed him back the binoculars.

'So, who is he really? He's not a wildlife photographer making a documentary, is he?'

'Correct,' said Fowler, nodding. 'He's part of the drug-smuggling operation. It's massive. Cocaine. Much of the cocaine that moves in the UK now is run by the Irish drug gangs. He's their man on the ground, the guy who brings it in from whatever ship or yacht it arrives in. Then it's stored in his barn until the truck arrives to move it on. That's his only role. To anyone who knows him, he's taking pictures and making films of wildlife over a period of weeks, months. He's integrated himself into the community and the locals all know him. His name, or the name he gives, is Brendan O'Leary. He's full of the chat and very popular. But people have no idea who he is – well, if the police know you'd have to ask yourself why they don't do something. Irish is the man who makes sure the drugs go to Glasgow initially, where they will be cut and then collected by other dealers across the UK.'

'So how do you know?'

'Because I know,' he said, turning to look straight at me.

I looked back at him, cocked my head a little.

'Come on, Dave. You'll have to do better than that,' I said, spreading my hands. 'How do you know? You can trust me.

You wouldn't have brought me all the way out here if you didn't know you could trust me.'

He took a long breath and pushed it out slowly.

'I've been watching him. For a long time.'

'But have you physically seen the cocaine?'

'No. But a guy I know did, a . . . local lad who was doing some building work for him got nosy, and one day he was working in the barn and came across a well packaged bundle. He opened it a little and saw what it was. The boy, Joe, a bit of a crazy horse himself, was stupid to do that. The Irishman walked in and caught him red-handed.'

'Jesus. What happened?'

'Joe disappeared. But I knew him really well, have done all his life, and he came to see me the night just after he'd seen the stuff. He told me what he saw, and I said to him he had better make himself scarce because he wouldn't be safe here any more. He said he was leaving in the morning. But he never did.'

'What do you mean?'

'He disappeared. Nobody saw him again. Until his body washed up on the rocks about two weeks later.' He paused and shook his head. 'Suicide, they said. Joe lived alone after his mother died and he was left with the farm which had become run-down. He drank a lot and was a bit of a loner, but he was harmless, a good lad with a good heart. One thing I know for sure is that he never committed suicide. No way. The Irishman got rid of him.'

'What did you do about it? Did you go to the police? Tell them what Joe told you?'

He shook his head. 'No. I have no proof. Nothing. The police at the time were quick to assume suicide as the body had been in the water and there was no forensics to examine really. But his head was bashed in. Okay, it could have been hit against rocks while he was in the sea, but it was never really looked at hard enough by the cops.'

'But there must have been some way you could've talked to your old colleagues, maybe even in Inverness, away from here? You could've let them know what Joe told you? Even gone independently to the NCA?'

As soon as I said it, I regretted it because he looked hurt, and I could see the sadness in his eyes.

'Don't you think I know that, Billie? I feel riven with guilt every day because maybe I could have done more. I should have driven him away that night he came to me, but he said he was leaving in the morning and I left it at that. I feel terrible that I didn't do enough.'

'Sorry,' I said. 'I didn't mean to say it like that. I understand what you mean. I know what it feels like to think you could have done more, believe me.'

We sat for a long moment, my window lowered, listening to the sound of the ocean in the heavy atmosphere of guilt and regret that I knew too well. But I couldn't see the connection with this story and Astrid's death. Eventually I had to ask.

'But what has this got to do with Astrid? I mean, she was drugged and raped, then apparently took her own life or was so reckless she died in the icy woods. But I'm not making any connection to everything you are telling me.'

He nodded slowly and we sat in silence, then he turned to me.

'Okay. I understand. But here's what I know and why I think they want you out of here.' He paused. 'The longer you're here and the more cages you rattle, the more worried people will get. By people, I mean those who stand to gain from the drugs coming in. There's another shipment coming in soon. There's a thing that goes on here every year – it's an international car rally, souped-up cars being brought in from all across Europe, shipped in containers. It's huge business here. But every year, the rally has a secret. In all the cars that come in legitimately, one, maybe even two, will be loaded with cocaine, and the Irishman will see to that. The cars will be brought to his place, the cargo unloaded, then off it will go to slaughter – that's what the dealers call the distribution or whoever is going to sell it on. You being here, looking into Astrid's death, is the wrong time because this rally is happening in a couple of weeks. If the video or anything got out it would bring newspapers from all over, and the people running the show don't want that. The rally must go ahead because it's good business for the local area – huge business. But more than that it's a hidden drug business and they want to avoid anyone trying to look too closely at things.'

This was a lot to take in and my head was buzzing. I could see Dave wasn't finished.

'And,' he twisted his body to face me, 'some of the hotels around here and further on in the area are just money-laundering; some built from scratch involving huge sums of money thrown at construction. They're owned by Donny Mason. The hotels launder the money and get a massive kickback for doing it. So everybody wins, except for anyone who gets in the way. And right now, you are in the way, Billie. Astrid was too. Because despite how cruel and barbaric it was what those boys did to her, the people running the show don't want anything to upset the apple cart. They want it covered up. And that's exactly what they've done – covered it up. Rab Mason, who used to rent Astrid's flat from his aunt, is Donny Mason's son. If he's one of the rapists he will have had to answer to his father and other people higher up for what he did. But perhaps the only way to keep this from coming out about Astrid was to blackmail her with the threat of exposing the video. As far as the cocaine in her drawer is concerned – who knows – maybe they stole it from someone. I suppose the last thing they would have expected was her to end up dead in the woods, therefore blowing everything sky high.'

I sat for a moment, still trying to process everything he was saying.

'But it seems incredible that cops would be involved in any of that. I mean, the boss – the chief inspector?' I said.

He shrugged. 'Maybe. But he wasn't always the chief

inspector. Years ago, about twelve or so years ago, he did something and I believe he's been blackmailed ever since.'

'What did he do?'

'McPhail is married, but he was having an affair with a woman from Scrabster, and they were in her car together. Who knows what happened – maybe they had a fight or something – but the car crashed and it went over a rocky cliff and plunged into the water below. He got out, but he couldn't get her out, and she drowned. He somehow managed to scramble up the rocks onto the road, and he was found, staggering and bleeding, by Donny Mason, the guy who owned two of the local hotels. They'd known each other, and Mason helped him get off his mark. But that wasn't the end of it. These things never end well. He was a cop, and he left the scene of an accident. But the subsequent investigation didn't link him to it at all. They didn't even have him in the car. Mason helped him get away and go off down south for a holiday and basically stay out of the way until his wounds healed. Nobody suspected a thing. But from then on McPhail was in Mason's pocket. At that time Mason only owned the two hotels, but he was the kind of guy with no scruples on how to make money, so when the drug gang approached him to launder for them, he bit their hand off. Soon, he owned three hotels, then one in Inverness, and various lodges in the area. It's all drug money. But nobody can prove it. And when the drugs come in, your Chief Inspector McPhail doesn't bust a gut chasing the smugglers down. He knows who's behind it. He could stick them all in, but he won't. He's being blackmailed, because Mason knows his secret of the car crash that could ruin him. So when there's something like the death of a student, or the mystery death of a loner like Joe, he turns a blind eye. He just gets it cleaned up quickly and moves on.'

'This is horrendous, Dave. I got a lawyer friend of mine to search for newspaper cuttings on McPhail, but there weren't any specifically on him. Though there was something on a car crash over the cliffs years ago and a woman was trapped and died.'

'That's the one I'm telling you about,' he said.

'It's hard to take in. Poor Astrid is completely innocent and her death is part of a bigger picture she could've known absolutely nothing about.' I looked out at the farmhouse. 'So where is the Irishman now?'

'Who knows. Somewhere with his cronies, or organising the next import. But he's coming back in a week or so because the rally will be going on, and he'll have to be here for the pick-up when the cars come in.'

'But why don't you just go to the NCA with this? I mean, you must want to go by instinct, as a cop.'

'I do. But once I do it then it's out of my hands. I want the Irishman.'

'But why? Why is it so important to you?'

He didn't answer and we sat in silence for what seemed like an age, his head down and I saw his jaw twitch. Then he looked up and I saw the crushed look in his eyes.

'Because Joe was my son.'

CHAPTER ELEVEN

We didn't speak much during the journey back along the coast to Scrabster, and because of the bombshell Fowler had just dropped on me about his son, I was silent as I tried to wrap my head around the entire scenario. How unjust and unfair that an innocent girl like Astrid had lost her life for no reason other than to keep things quiet. Even if she did take her own life, which I couldn't believe, if she hadn't been drugged and raped she would still be here, enjoying her life, fulfilling her dreams. I was probably as close as I was going to get to finding out why Astrid died, and when I saw Lars in Sweden at least I would have something concrete to tell him, however upsetting it would be. But it wasn't enough for me. Astrid died because she was in the wrong place at the wrong time, an innocent victim of the ruthless scum who raped her. For me it was as simple as that. And she deserved justice. And the wider picture of the murky drugs operation, of blackmail, secrets and murder, was something I couldn't walk away from. I'd come to find out what happened to her. My job, the job I was sent here to do, was done. But it wasn't, not for me. The people behind this operation should be hunted down, and every one of them made to suffer. I'm not a cop any more, but I cannot shake off that sense of injustice.

Once we got closer to Scrabster, Fowler asked me if I wanted to come to his cottage for lunch. He said he had fresh seafood chowder on the stove that would set me up for my journey back to Glasgow. The more I talked to him the more I felt he was a lonely figure, especially after he told me what he did, and I got the feeling he wanted company – even that of a relative stranger – for a little longer. I agreed, and a few minutes later he turned off at the edge of the village and up a steep hill onto a dirt track where I could see a white cottage standing alone facing out to sea. The garden was neat and ordered, and as his car pulled up a Border collie that had been sitting on the step came racing towards the car leaping and barking.

'That's my Jess,' he said. 'She's off her head, never gives me a minute's peace, but I love her to bits.'

He opened the door and got out and the dog was jumping all over him, then she saw me and came bounding towards me.

'She's a beauty,' I said, ruffling her lush steel-grey and white coat, and was struck by her pale blue, almost white, eyes which were full of curiosity and trust.

He opened the farmhouse stable door and the dog and I followed him inside. The aroma of chowder filled the room, and the remains of a fire glowed in the hearth. It was an old and traditional cottage, one large square room with a small hallway and rooms off it, and perhaps hadn't changed much in design from the days when an entire family would have lived here, cooking on the open fire, and existing from farming and fishing. He went across and prodded the fire with a poker and as flames shot up, he threw on another log, then went to the range stove. I crossed the room and stood at the window, looking out to sea, the sky an icy blue now, blending to darker grey on the horizon, with the sea rough. Everything changes so quickly on the coast.

'What a great spot to live in,' I said. 'Have you been here long? I mean, like when you were working in the force?'

I felt a little awkward trying to make small talk given what we had just been talking about. He turned from the pot, rolling up his sleeves before washing his hands at the sink and drying them on a towel that hung on the wall. Then he stood with his back to the stove, looking at me.

'It's the family home. I was raised here, along with my brother and sister. They're long gone to Australia though, emigrated as teenagers, and our mum died when we were young, so I was the only one here to help with the bit of farming my father did. He had sheep, and a couple of fields further up, but once he died I just rented the fields for grazing.'

'What about when you joined the police? Were you based here or Inverness?'

He stretched up to the cupboard and brought out two

deep bowls, then to the bread bin and picked out a loaf. He spoke as he sliced it.

'Both. In the beginning I was in Thurso as a rookie, but then moved to Inverness, through the ranks from uniform to detective. I was a sergeant but didn't go any further.' He turned to me and half smiled. 'Too big in the mouth, I was told. But there were things even back then I didn't like. Then . . .' He paused. 'Well, then life took over.'

He turned to look at me, and I stood with my back to the window, waiting for him to speak.

'I was married for a while, but you know what it's like on the job – you're never home.' He paused. 'And, well, there's the drink. I was a big boozer back in the day, and it didn't help. I still get lost in it sometimes.'

I knew well how alcohol could creep up on you, but I wasn't ready to tell him how I'd been there too, when you sometimes drink thinking it will help you cope. It doesn't. It does the opposite.

'You split up?' I ventured.

He stirred the pot, the steam rising, making me hungry. He looked back at me.

'She bailed on me.'

'Oh, sorry,' I said, not knowing what else to say.

'Writing was probably on the wall for a while but I was so wrapped up in work and booze I didn't notice.' He paused for a moment, then turned to the pot and ladled out the chowder into the bowls. 'She buggered off with an estate agent from Wick.' He shrugged. 'That was twelve years ago.

Last I heard they were living on the Costa del Sol.' He carried the bowls to the table and motioned at me to sit down. 'He's welcome to her,' he said as he brought over the loaf. 'She was a bit of a ballbuster, to be honest, and she hankered after that kind of life, you know, material things, which was never going to be my thing. So I'm fine with it. At least she didn't clean me out in the divorce.' He smiled as though he'd reached a place in his head where he was at peace with all of that.

We sat down at the table and he tore off a piece of bread and dunked it in the chowder.

'Dig in,' he said, looking happy and comfortable in his own space.

I did, and the chowder, with chunks of salmon, cod and mussels, was the best I've ever tasted. We ate hungrily, the food and the heat of the fire warming me through.

'So, what about Joe?' I asked. 'I don't want to pry, Dave, but the way you told me it was a real surprise.'

He put his spoon down and sat back, taking a deep breath through his nose, his mouth turned downwards. For a moment I thought he was struggling to talk about it, then he swallowed and spoke.

'I didn't know Joe was my son.' He shook his head. 'His mother never told me. We'd had an affair, well, not anything that was ever going to last – I was married at the time, and she was too. So, when she had the baby I didn't even think much of it. I assumed it was her husband's. It was only after Joe died, I was contacted by a lawyer in Wick who told me Joe's birth certificate was in his estate, and my name was on it. Joe left the house to me. He must have known I was his father for a while and yet he never cracked a light about it, even though he did some work for me and we'd always got on well together. What I keep asking myself is why didn't I see it. He didn't look like me, he was his mother's double. But he was a troubled lad all his life and maybe it was because she never told him, and maybe even when he found out about it, he didn't want to tell me. I didn't even know when or how he found out. That's the hard part. If he'd told me before, I would . . . well I don't know what I'd have done, but I like to think I would have tried to look after him, or at least look out for him. The idea that he went to his death not ever having told me, and me not knowing,' he shook his head, 'it sticks in my gut. And that's why I won't let this go.'

I listened, not saying anything, moved by his emotion. I could see the hurt all over his face, parts of his life squandered through drink and bad choices, and no kids of his own as he grew older. Yet all the time he had a son that he never got the chance to cherish and influence and help along the way. I know what it feels like to grow up, to become a teenager without that watchful eye of a parent.

'That's so hard,' I said. 'I can see why it makes you feel so bad.'

'I feel I was robbed,' he said. 'And I'm a bit angry at his mother too, though she was married and obviously couldn't say, but after her husband died, she could have told me. I was still married, so maybe she wanted to keep a distance. But I feel it's years wasted. I feel useless. And now it's too late.'

I nodded, not knowing what to say. It wasn't my place to comfort him. I could have told him that I know what hurt and suffering means but it was not something I wanted to go into right now with someone I barely knew. But I could feel his sorrow.

'So you want revenge on these people, Dave?' I asked. 'Is that what's driving you? Motivates you?'

He shrugged, blew out of pursed lips.

'Joe was robbed of his life, Billie, and that's just not fair. He was a boy who never asked for anything. And these people, the Irishman and his cronies, they only care about money, profit – and the people who run the hotels laundering their money, that's all they care about too. It's all about money and greed, and a boy lost his life because of that. I can't let it go.'

'But what are you going to do?'

'I don't know. I'm working on how to find out where their cargo goes when it leaves here. I'm told Glasgow, but it could be anywhere. Joe said something he overheard. There's a warehouse down in Glasgow the stuff goes into.'

'Then you need to get the cops involved.'

He shook his head. 'Hopeless here. I know they'll just do nothing. It's not that they're all corrupt, but McPhail is, and he's the last person I would go to. I have a couple of people I could take this to in Inverness but I'm at the stage where I'm not sure who at the top level I can trust.'

'Then get the NCA. Go down to Glasgow and tell them what you've told me. They'll listen and they'll act.'

'I might,' he sighed. 'I want the Irishman though. It had to be him who killed Joe, and I want to make him pay.'

'Then get the NCA to deal with it. If these gangsters are as big as you say with this level of operation, you can't even think about taking them on.'

He nodded, but said nothing, and I knew what was on his mind. We sat for a while finishing the food, not talking, just the hiss of the fire and the atmosphere in the room now somehow heavier than it had been.

Eventually, after we drank coffee, I made moves to leave. He got up and looked out of the window where the brightness of the earlier sunshine had faded, and the sky had turned into heavy slate grey.

Fowler drove me back to my car. I got into my Saab and he followed behind. A sudden squally shower swept up from the sea as though someone had thrown a switch. We pulled into a lay-by outside Thurso and he got out of his car and came to mine. I lowered the window and looked up at him, the icy rain on his windswept cheeks. He shook my hand and our eyes locked and for a moment I somehow felt a strange closeness to him.

'Sorry I offloaded all that personal stuff on you, Billie,' he said. 'I shouldn't have done that. But I wanted to be honest with you, explain everything.'

I waved my hand in a 'no worries' gesture.

'Not at all, Dave. I'm glad you told me, because it's much clearer now what's going on here, and why. I'm going to talk to one of my closest contacts in the force in Glasgow and see where we can take this. And maybe I can call you again and see what happens? When is this rally?'

'It's in ten days or so.'

'So, you think there will be a cargo coming in on one of the cars?'

'For sure. The Irishman is coming back next week as he's ordered some food and stuff from the local farmshop. He's not coming here to watch cars racing, I'm certain of that much.'

He turned his head to look across the horizon.

'Storm's coming. You'd best get moving, see if you can beat it down the road.'

He shook my hand again and held it long, then he backed away. I drove off and watched in the rear-view mirror as he stood looking after me, a big bear of a man, a lonely figure with only a heart full of revenge to keep him going.

CHAPTER TWELVE

I drove back along the coast towards Thurso, my eyes drawn to the sea and how quickly it was changing, strong gusts buffeting my car. In the town I kept to the main road and exited towards the A9 south, checking my dashboard clock at three, guessing it would be nearer eight or nine by the time I got to Glasgow. The road was quiet apart from a couple of lorries passing on the way north, possibly to the ferry terminal, or headed further afield, and there were a few cars behind me. Once I was away from the town the buildings were sparse, only the odd farm dotted well back off the road. The Land Rover behind me overtook and I saw one more car behind me. I sped up hoping I didn't get caught behind any lorries or farm trucks on the way down. In my side mirror I could see the car behind suddenly going faster and thought it must be in a hurry. I drove on, pulling a little to the side to let it pass, but it didn't, and by this time it was close on my tail. I felt a nervous dig in my gut as I accelerated then slowed down. The car did the same, only this time getting so close it was almost on my bumper. I saw two figures in the car, but the visors were down. I told myself it could be some boy racers getting their kicks, but my instincts were telling me different. The road ahead was straight as a die and quiet and I checked again to see how many vehicles were behind me other than the one that was now racing up close. There were none. A bolt of fear shot through me when the car behind me honked its horn hard. I slowed down a little, but now the car was right on top of me, so close it touched my bumper and jolted my car. I glanced at my mobile on the passenger seat and thought if I could phone Fowler and tell him he would jump in his car and come. But this was happening so fast and I was almost paralysed with fear. I knew I was in trouble. I considered doing a quick handbrake turn and heading back to Thurso where at least there were people and traffic, but then suddenly I was bumped again. Then, before I knew what I was doing, I saw a tight road to my right and I could see some woodland on the horizon. I turned sharply into it, almost losing control of my car. I had no idea where it was, but if I got off the road and put my foot down, I was confident they wouldn't catch me. The Saab was old, but it still had plenty of fire in it in an emergency. I hit the floor and raced away from them, hoping I would find a house or a backroad to Thurso. But they were racing up behind me and pulling out to overtake on the narrow road. I knew what they were doing but I couldn't stop them. If they bumped me hard I'd land in the deep ditch, so I gripped the steering wheel tight, trying to concentrate. Then they suddenly overtook and pulled up sharp at a lay-by, swiftly turning their car to block my way. I hit the brakes. I felt the blood drain from me and my hands shook on the steering wheel as I saw them getting out of the car and coming towards me. One was squat, fat and balding, the other was tall and skinny, with a stupid grin. They looked high, either from the chase or the prospect of whatever they thought was coming. I looked around for anything I could find to defend myself with and picked up a metal thermal bottle filled with water, and stuck it in the inside pocket of my jacket. I was breathing fast and my head felt light as they came towards me. I pushed the central lock button and heard it click. I didn't look in their direction.

'Get out!' the tall skinny one said, his small eyes black as dots, his thin lips hard.

I glanced at him, then away, and kept still. Then the squat one came up behind him.

'Get out the fucking car, bitch,' he spat. 'Or we'll fucking drag you out.'

I tried to swallow but there was nothing there. I was trapped. I tried to stare straight out of the windscreen, but from the corner of my eye I saw the fat man reach into his jacket and bring out a gun.

'Out!' he said, smacking the gun on the window so hard I thought it would shatter. 'I'll not tell you again.'

I took a breath and turned to face them.

'What is this? What do you want?'

'You fucking know what we want.'

I spread my hands in a bewildered gesture and shook my head. Then the fat guy cocked the gun.

'Three seconds. Three . . . Two . . .'

My trembling finger reached to the central lock button and it clicked. I braced myself and released my seat belt. The door was yanked open and the skinny one grabbed a handful of my hair at the temple, the excruciating pain making me shriek, and dragged me out. I had to steady myself on the car.

'What the fuck is this? What do you want?' I managed to croak, angry with myself that my voice sounded pleading.

The fat man took a step towards me and I looked into his pale face and caught the stink of bad breath when he drew his lips back in a snarl, revealing brown stained teeth.

'The coke that's missing.'

'What coke?'

'The fucking coke you took from that whore's flat.'

I took a long look at him, defiantly. 'I didn't take any coke. Why don't you ask the landlady down in the baker's? Maybe she's sprinkling it on the cakes to liven things up a bit.' I knew it was stupid as soon as I said it.

I felt a hard punch on my cheek from the skinny one who laughed as he did it. He was high all right, and after he punched me, he touched his grazed knuckle with his tongue and grinned. I saw stars. But also I glimpsed a tattoo on the back of his hand. A scorpion.

'Just fucking shoot her, man. We'll get the coke and torch her car,' he goaded his mate.

I said nothing and tried to catch my breath. I could feel my cheek starting to swell, and the pain was making me dizzy, nauseous.

The fat man pulled me by the hair again, gun pointed into the back of my neck, and pushed me towards the boot of my car.

'Open it.'

I knew the coke was in there in my small rucksack, and I would only have a few seconds left by the time I unzipped the bag for him to find it. I pinged open the boot and stood looking inside, then turned to them.

'Open the bag,' skinny one said. 'Empty it out.'

The rucksack was one of those soft material travel jobs with loads of zips. I reached in, opening one or two of the zips, then pushed my other hand under the rucksack towards the back of the boot, praying that it would be there. It was. The wheel wrench. I hadn't put it back where it should be the last time I'd had to change a tyre, so I knew it was lying loose beneath the bag. I could feel my hand grip the cold metal. I leaned in and hunched over, to make sure I had a good grip. I began to fake a retch.

'I'm going to be sick,' I said, half turning. 'Please. Give me a minute.' I retched again.

'Hurry the fuck up then and throw up in there, don't be making a mess of my fucking boots,' the fat man said. The skinny one sniggered, wild eyed.

From the side of my eye, as I continued to retch, I saw the fat man lower the gun, his hand drop down by his side, and the skinny one reach into his pocket and pull out a pack of cigarettes.

'Nice arse,' the skinny one said. Then I felt his hand push between my legs, and I really did feel sick.

'Temptin', isn't it?' the fat man said. 'But leave it.'

The skinny one removed his hand, and I saw him shove a cigarette between his lips then fumble in his pocket for a lighter.

I had one, maybe two seconds at most. I kept hunched over, but spread my legs for maximum balance, the way I'd been taught at police training. Then I counted one, pushed the bag away, and at two, swivelled my body around swiftly and brought the wheel wrench across the fat man's head with every scrap of strength I could muster. He dropped like a stone, a look of surprise in his eyes as blood pumped out of the side of his head as though he'd been shot. Before the skinny one, his mouth gaped open, had a chance to take it in, I jumped back and swung the wheel wrench across his body. He leapt back as it hit him on the ribs and buckled over. I glanced at the fat man who lay still, blood trickling from the side of his head. Then I started running. But for some stupid, desperate reason, I didn't run in the direction of the road where I'd been, but towards the woods. What the hell was I thinking about? I could hear the skinny guy shrieking after me.

'You are so getting it, bitch. I'm fucking going to enjoy this.'

I jumped over a fence and fell face down into the soggy earth, then clambered back up and started running across the field towards the clump of forest. I glanced over my shoulder to see him running just as fast but I had at least forty yards on him, still clutching the wheel wrench. I sprinted, my legs heavy, and headed for the darkness of the trees. As soon as I was in I threw myself down and crawled below a thicket of high spruce trees until I was well inside, dark and soaked, and I lay, trying to stop my body from trembling, trying to catch my breath. I turned at one point and saw a small deer peeking out from the dense under-growth. It stared at me, unblinking. I was deathly quiet and automatically put my hand to my lips as though to silence it. Then I heard him shout.

'You'll no' hide here long, hen. I know every corner of these woods.'

He sounded close but not close enough for me to hear his footsteps. I crawled on my belly, further in. The deer flinched but didn't flee.

'You might as well come out, or I'll just start shooting. You've hurt my fucking mate bad, you bitch.'

I felt suddenly strengthened. I had only one to beat now. I could do this. I had to. For Lucas. What if one day he came looking for his mummy and found I had been murdered in a forest by some spaced-out psycho? I could never let him suffer like that. I had to be there for him, and one day I would tell him of this day, these moments. I lay still, barely breathing. Then I heard the squelchy ground as he walked. He was that close now. It was dark where I lay, but peering through the trees I spotted him, his back to me. He had the gun in his hand, down by his side. I looked around for any gap where I could get out of there fast. I glanced at the deer. She stared back at me, her liquid eyes full of fear as though she sensed danger. I eased myself onto all fours, crouched down, then picked up a piece of wood. I stared at the deer, then threw the wood hard in her direction. Startled, she turned and bolted, and as she did, I saw him jump back. But before he had time to react and look around, I was out of the thicket and on top of him. I jumped on his back and furiously hacked at his legs with the wheel wrench as he screamed in pain. I hit him between his legs and he doubled over. I fell on top of him, and as he lay writhing in agony I chopped at his hand with the wheel wrench in a frenzy until he let go of the gun. I scrambled to my feet, standing over him, the gun in my hand, a sudden surge of adrenalin and anger. I cocked the gun and leaned over him, aimed it between his eyes. There's a dark part of me that is capable of killing someone. I didn't know there was until I was faced with the murdering paedophile who was going to kill me. People could pick away at the bones of that as they did at the time, and suggest I could have shot him in the foot or the leg or anywhere to stop him. But I had shot him square in the chest. I don't ask myself any more why I did that. But I have never regretted it. I could do it again now, I thought as I looked at this whimpering shit-faced wreck of a human being who raped Astrid, who along with his lowlife scum mates was responsible for her death, and may even have been involved in the death of young Joe. Who would miss a bastard like this? Few people, maybe his family, but they would know what he was. If I pulled the trigger right now it would send a message to all of them. But the bigger picture of the millions of pounds of cocaine being smuggled – even though it wasn't what had brought me here – flashed into my mind and I could see the chance that I could trap all of them. The police pragmatic part in me kicked in. I booted him one more time hard between his legs and for good measure aimed a kick at the side of his face that sent blood sputtering out of his mouth as he groaned.

'Your time's up, you skinny prick,' I said, as I turned and ran back across the field.

When I climbed the fence, I could see the fat man was still on the ground. I didn't stop to see if I had killed him. If I had, I could live with that. The icy rain drenching my face felt good after the struggle. I could see their car was blocking my path, and I quickly jumped in, pulled it onto the side and into the ditch with a thud. Then I got into my own car. The fat man lay behind my car, but there was no way I was going to touch or move him. I put my car into reverse and felt the bump as I drove over him. Then I turned my car around and sped away. I didn't look back. I didn't care. I knew that later I would lie in bed and ask myself if I was thinking straight at this point, because I had just driven my car over an injured man. What did that make me? No better than them? But that was for later. I could live with this. I bombed out of the side road and back onto the A9 and pushed my foot to the floor, my head beginning to throb. My hands, that had been shaking, suddenly stopped and I gripped the steering wheel as the driving rain lashed the windscreen. I didn't stop until I got two hours down the road, and then it was only because I was beginning to feel light-headed and weak. I pulled into a roadside café and wiped the excess dirt from my face. I grabbed my medical kit from the glove compartment, pulled on oversized dark glasses to hide some of my swollen cheek, and slipped into the toilets to clean up. In the bathroom I looked at my face in the mirror, the swelling, the dark but focused look in my eyes, and bit my lip hard to keep it all together. I splashed water on my face and dried it with a paper towel then gingerly put antiseptic cream on the graze on my cheek. Then I went outside, kept my head down and bought some juice and a chicken sandwich which I ate quickly in the car. Feeling a little better, I took a deep breath, picked up my phone and called Fowler.

'Dave,' I said. 'Listen. Don't speak. Just listen.'

There was a pulse beat of silence then he spoke.

'Billie, what's happened?'

'I got attacked,' I said. 'Two guys. They ran me off the

road. Somewhere a few miles out of town. I took a side road but they came after me.'

'Jesus. Are you hurt?'

'Yes. But I'm okay. I got away.'

'I can be there in fifteen minutes.'

'No. It's okay, I'm on my way down the road.' I swallowed, feeling a sudden tightness in my throat. 'But I think I killed one of them.'

'Oh fuck!'

CHAPTER THIRTEEN

From the motorway I could see the illuminated church spires in Glasgow's West End reach up into the blackness. I was home. I was safe. I'd lived to fight another day. I'd felt so far away from Lucas up north – even before anything happened – and just being home made me feel closer to him even though he was really thousands of miles away. This is where our lives are, his and mine, and the comfort of that was overwhelming. Sheer exhaustion, adrenalin levels dropping, as well as the delayed shock of the last few hours, all kicked in at once. I choked back tears. But I quickly snapped out of it as my mobile rang on the passenger seat and I saw Scanlon's name. I'd called him on the way down and told him the short version of what had happened, and he'd said he'd come to my flat as soon as I was home.

'You home yet?' His voice chipper, steady, was music to my ears.

'Nearly. Will be at my flat in ten.'

'Great. I'm on my way.'

Relief and gratitude flooded through me. Tonight, more than ever, I didn't want to go home to an empty flat.

I parked outside and went into my building and the sensory hallway lights clicked on. I opened the door to my flat, feeling the instant warmth of the central heating. I dropped my rucksack on the floor and switched on the rest of the lights as I walked through the place. I needed brightness, not shadows tonight. Then I went into the kitchen and took a bottle of wine out of the rack and pulled a bottle opener out of the drawer, but I stopped. It could wait. I wanted a drink, at least one, maybe several, but that's not what I needed right now. I needed to slowly unwind, to decompress, come to some kind of terms with what happened, and what I would do next. I filled the kettle and switched it on. The wine could wait for Scanlon. Soon after the kettle pinged and I'd poured water into a mug, the door buzzed, and I pressed the key to let him in. I stood in the living room waiting. I heard his footsteps in the hall, then he walked through the doorway into the living room where I stood with my back to the window.

'Pizza guy's here!' he said, armed with a large cardboard box.

I tried to stop my lip trembling. The smile dropped from his face and he placed the pizza on the table and strode towards me. He wrapped his arms around me and pulled me in, hugging me close, his hand stroking the back of my head as I allowed myself to bury my face on his shoulders, feeling my chest hurt as I tried to hold back the tears.

'They were going to kill me, Danny.' My voice came out muffled, buried in his shoulder.

'Sssh. Don't talk.'

We stayed that way for a while, silent, Scanlon stroking my hair. Then he drew back a little and winced as his eyes narrowed at my swollen cheek. His fingertips reached out to gently touch it.

'Christ, Carlson! That looks bad. Maybe you should have it looked at.'

I eased out of his embrace.

'No way. It's just swollen. Do me a favour, will you? Can you bring me a bag of frozen peas from the freezer and I'll try that?' I stepped back and sat at the table, looking up, attempting a smile. 'And while you're at it, can you open that bottle of wine on the worktop? I really need a drink.' I opened the lid of the pizza box and breathed in the tantalising aroma. 'I'm starving!'

Scanlon's face broke into a smile, and he ruffled my hair.

'Good to have you back, Carlson.'

He turned and went into the kitchen, and I could hear him opening cupboards and then the pop of the cork on the wine bottle. He emerged a moment later with the bottle and two glasses and poured a decent glug into them. Handing me a glass he sat down, his eyes scanning my face, my hair, reaching across and picking a bit of dried mud out of it and looking at it, snorting, bemused. Then he raised his glass, but didn't say anything.

'To Lucas!' I said, and felt my throat tighten. 'He got me through this day.'

I wasn't ready to talk about anything that had happened on my US trip, and Scanlon instinctively seemed to know that. I knew he would be eager to find out, and I was dying to offload it all to him, but not right now. He would leave it until I was ready. He smiled, then reached across and touched my face.

'To Lucas,' he said. Then he shook his head, smiling. 'What are we going to do with you, Carlson?'

He handed me a slice of pizza and we both took a swig of our wine.

'So,' Scanlon said, mouth full of pizza, 'tell me the full lowdown of what happened up the road.'

'You're not going to like it,' I said.

'That much I know. But I'm all ears.'

I finished a slice of pizza and began to tell him.

Scanlon listened intently, watching my expression as I went through everything from the moment I arrived in Thurso. He shook his head when I told him about Fowler and the claims he'd made. He told me I had to talk Fowler into coming down to Glasgow and speaking to the National Crime Agency, and I agreed I would. Then I described the final part, being chased by the two thugs and run off the road. I told it slowly, halting to get a grip of the emotion as I relived being hunkered down in the trees not knowing how I was going to get away, but determined I would.

Scanlon poured another glass of wine, but I was still sipping my first.

'I wanted to kill him, Danny,' I said, shaking my head. 'I know I could have done it. And do you know what? I'm not even alarmed by that thought. I'm okay with it. I shouldn't be, but I am.'

He nodded slowly. 'Understandable. In the heat of the moment I might have felt the same.'

Then I told him the last part.

'I drove over him – the other guy, the fat one. I think he was dead, but I didn't even check. I just drove over him to get out of there as fast as I could.' I took a breath and pushed it out through pursed lips. 'And maybe I'll feel bad about it once all the fright and the panic of the moment wears off, but right now, I'm not even sorry.' I looked at him, and his expression was solid, listening, not judging. 'I might have killed him, in self-defence, but I drove over him as he lay there. Shit! I don't know what that makes me, but I'm not sorry. Maybe it hasn't hit me yet. But the thing is, nothing kicked in. Nothing that would normally have told me to move him out of the way, or to phone for an ambulance, or even to check his pulse. Nothing. I had no feelings about him. I was just cold, scared, and angry probably more than anything. But there was no compassion anywhere in my mind about him. And even now, I don't feel it.'

'Are you worried about that?' he said, his voice soft.

'No. I'm not. I've just zipped it up and put it in a box

somewhere in the back of my mind. Maybe it will come back to haunt me. Maybe it should. But I'm not going to let it, Danny. I'm not going to let the bad guys win. Ever again.' I shrugged, took a swig of my wine, and looked at him, then away.

I knew he wouldn't judge me, but I also knew that deep down the cop in him would be disturbed by my revelations. But if he was, he didn't show it, perhaps because he cared too much about me even to point out where I had failed. Then to my surprise he shrugged and let out a long sigh.

'Okay. Quite a story. But here's the situation, Carlson. If this bastard is dead, then he's going to turn up somewhere at some stage. I can't imagine his mate, if he ever did get up and out of that wood, would phone the cops to say his friend had been killed. More likely he'd phone one of his bosses and tell him what's happened and they would have to move the body – that's if he's even dead.'

I nodded but said nothing.

'And,' he went on, 'if he is dead, his bosses will get rid of the body, because they won't want a police investigation into him in case any of it leads back to them. So, I wouldn't worry about it coming back to haunt you through the cops.'

I looked at him, wondering if he was going to advise me what to do.

'So, what do you think? I just sit tight and hope it goes away?'

He looked at me, sat back and folded his arms, stretching out his long legs and blowing out of one side of parted lips. I sensed he was choosing his words. Eventually he spoke.

'Okay. Here's what I think.' He cleared his throat. 'I'm going to pretend you didn't tell me any of the stuff you just did – well, about the guys who attacked you and you driving over one of them. Let's just wait and hope it goes away. I'm sure it will, though his bosses might come after you. But the fact that they attacked you, and really, they would have probably killed you, should be reported to the police. But that will open up all sorts of shit for you, so my advice is to forget it.'

I nodded, but said nothing. If he'd told me to go to the police I would have said no anyway.

'But the drugs stuff – the things about the rally – that really needs investigating. So that's up to you. I think you should get Fowler to come down and then step back altogether.'

I nodded again, waited for a moment then spoke. 'Okay, but there's the coke. I have it in my overnight bag. It looks like at least two kilo blocks. As I told you, I took it from Astrid's flat. I think I should pass that on – for analysis. How do you think that would go?'

'Well, you'll be questioned closely. You know that, don't you?'

I shrugged. 'Like I'm not used to it!' I half smiled. 'I don't mind that. But if I hand over something that will be material evidence in a drugs investigation, I want something back.'

His brow went up, enquiring.

'Like what?'

'Clothes. I took Astrid's clothes – the jeans she had on that night, and underwear, the night she was raped. I took other things from her house that could be used to get her DNA. And there must be DNA from the rapists on her jeans or pants. If forensics could get that, then maybe we could swab these guys.'

He nodded slowly. 'Maybe. That's if they don't completely disappear – which is also entirely possible. If you're talking the kind of drug-smuggling operation that involves millions, then anyone down the food chain like that pair of Neanderthals will be got rid of now that they've fucked up.'

'But we can cross that bridge later. My deal is that I'll hand over the coke, if forensics examine Astrid's clothing.'

'Okay. I know who to ask, so we'll see.'

We sat for a while sipping our wine, and by the time I'd got halfway through my second glass I was beginning to feel overwhelmed with tiredness. I yawned and Scanlon grinned.

'You're knackered,' he said. He drained his glass, stretched his hand across the table so it was over mine. 'But are you okay? I mean, I'll stay over if you want – in the spare room – just in case you feel bad later, once all this trauma kicks in.'

I slipped my hand from under his and leaned over and brushed my hand over his hair.

'I'll be fine, but thanks,' I said. 'And if I'm not, then, well, I'll get through it.'

He took my hand from his face and we stood up.

'Okay, Carlson. I'll let you get to your kip.'

I puffed out a sigh. He put his arms around me and held me, his voice soft in my ear.

'I'm here for you. I'll always be here for you.'

'Stop it,' I said, giving him a dig. 'You'll make me cry.'

'I mean it, though.'

'I know you do.'

I eased myself away and we looked at each other. Then he kissed me on the lips and I let it linger as I kissed him back. It was fleeting, but we both knew we wanted more. We looked at each other again, part desire and part embarrassed. Then he smiled.

'Okay. But you're going to have to stop trying to molest me, Carlson.'

I chuckled as I stood back.

'Away with you,' I said, and watched as he winked and turned towards the door into the hall. I listened as the door opened, then heard him shout.

'I'll call you in the morning. Get some sleep.'

Then he was gone, and I stood watching from the window, still feeling the softness of his lips on mine, as he went down the steps into the square and disappeared down the street.

CHAPTER FOURTEEN

I was dropping with exhaustion by the time I came out of a hot bath and went to bed. But still sleep wouldn't come, and I had no option but to let my thoughts run. I don't have anywhere to go in my head that will give me an escape from the darkness that sometimes engulfs me. People talk about being able to take yourself to your 'happy place'. Even my own shrink, who was a lifeline in the beginning after Lucas vanished, told me I had it within me to control my thoughts, that it was down to me to decide if I could be happy and positive or negative and miserable. It sounded like psychobabble at the time, when it was taking every scrap of strength to get out of bed and face each day. Time will lessen your pain, he told me. He was wrong about that, but I have tried hard to control the way I handle the blackness. For me, it's not thinking my way to anything like happiness, but it's about knowing I'm doing something that might lead me down a path where one day Lucas will be there waiting for me. I can do it if I know in my heart I will find him. That's what took me to the States last week, that's what drove me into the squalid side of a city and a ghetto, a human jungle, where predators ruled, and everything was for sale, even a small child.

Philip Katowic had stressed to us that he couldn't promise the boy would still be there. But he had seen him with his own eyes, he said, just two days ago, and he was sure from the picture on the news that it was the boy we were looking for. Dan Harris drove away from the run-down, boarded up shopfronts where we picked Philip up, and headed into an area more sparse, derelict and gloomy. As we went further from the city, we saw burnt-out cars and small fires glowing on street corners. I tried to gauge Harris's thoughts, but his face showed nothing and his eyes were fixed on the road. I scanned the backdrop of houses, many boarded up. Outside one block there was a bunch of youths standing around a bonfire and blaring out music. Kids in hoodies raced up and down the road on scooters or bikes. As we drove through, the streets were empty of traffic and all eyes turned towards us.

'Don't stop anywhere here, man,' Philip said from the back seat. 'This is their hood. Any shit, you know drugs and stuff, that comes in and out of here is theirs. You won't see no white faces around here, and these dudes aim to keep it that way, you know what I'm sayin'?'

'Sure,' Harris replied. 'I don't plan on stopping. Am I going in the right direction?'

'Yeah, man. You just keep on going right down this way, and then you come to the big junction in a mile or so, and you cross into where you see the blocks of houses. But don't stop anywhere unless I tell you. Okay?'

'Sure,' Harris said. He shot me a sideways glance. 'You okay, Billie?'

I nodded, keeping my eyes straight ahead.

'Yeah,' I replied. 'I'm from Glasgow. Parts of it are not that much different. I've seen places like this before.'

His lips pulled back and he turned a little to me.

'So this isn't your first rodeo?'

'No,' I said, shaking my head staring out of the windscreen. 'Not by a long shot.'

As a uniformed cop I had walked the beat in some of the roughest housing schemes in Glasgow, where lowlife bottom feeders stood on street corners hawking drugs to junkies bouncing up the street for their fix. These parasites hooked in children in the playground so that some of them were beyond saving before they even had a chance to grow up. No, I wasn't scared going into this shithole, but I felt sick inside. If Philip was right, my Lucas was in there somewhere. My whole being ached to see him, to hold him, but deep down I hoped Philip was wrong. Wherever he is, I prayed, let it not be here. We drove another few minutes and could see we were on the edge of the next neighbourhood. Streetlights were few and far between, and in the steady drizzle it was hard to adjust our eyes to the darkness. We pulled off the main road into a street strewn with debris, old chairs and sofas. Someone had set light to an armchair outside a row of derelict buildings. Youths stood around the blaze, wide eyed, spaced, one or two looking in our direction then back to the fire. All white people, mostly young, I thought. From the top floor of one of the buildings we heard a commotion, then a gunshot, and suddenly a body came flying out of an open window. It crashed onto the grass below. From around the bonfire there was jeering, and a couple of guys ran across, but from what we could see cruising slowly past, the body wasn't moving.

'Oh, man!' Philip said. 'Did you see that shit? Fuck me, man! That is not good. The cops will be here soon for sure.'

'Should we just carry on?' Harris asked.

'Sure, man. Keep going. It's a good distraction. Means that none of these assholes are looking at us now, so we just go ahead.' He paused. 'It's just down here. Let me phone my buddy though, Lena. She said she would introduce us. She saw this boy too.'

My gut was beginning to feel like someone was twisting it, and I could feel my mouth dry as we approached another block of derelict flats at the far end of the street.

'Hey, Lena?' Philip spoke into his mobile. 'I'm out here, girl. I got these dudes with me.'

I strained my ears to hear what was being said, but I couldn't.

'Okay, that's cool. We'll be outside in two.'

Philip was leaning forward between the driver and passenger seat and I could smell the staleness of him.

'She's gonna come out. Take us in there. You okay with that?'

'Yep,' Harris replied. 'Did she say anything about the boy?'

'No. She's just taking us inside.'

'Do you think he's there?' I asked, anxious.

'Don't know. We'll see.'

I looked at Harris and could see his expression was flat, like he was suspicious. My palms were sweating and I rubbed them on my jeans. Could I really just be a minute away from seeing Lucas behind this door with the wood kicked in at the bottom, in the only flat with a single light bulb burning?

Harris turned to me. 'Billie, when we go in here, can you just let me do the talking?'

'Dan,' I said, hearing the nerves in my voice, 'if my son is there, I'm picking him up and I'm walking out of that house with him. No matter who does the talking.'

He put a hand out in a 'simmer down' gesture.

'I know, I know,' he said. 'You're nervous. I get that. But we don't know what is going to happen when we walk through that door, so please, just try and stay calm. Let me do the talking.'

'You packing, man?' Philip asked.

'Why?' Harris asked.

'Nothing really.'

'I'm packing. But I'm not looking to go in here and have to shoot my fucking way out again.'

'No, man. No, it's gonna be okay. Just trust me. Lena will help us.'

The entrance door opened and a girl came out and stood smoking a cigarette in the shadows. She was short, a skinny blonde girl who looked no more than twenty, wearing a denim jacket and black jeans. We pulled the car up at the kerb and she beckoned us. I felt my legs shaking as I opened the door and got out. I walked a step behind Harris, and Philip walked ahead of us. When we got up to her she eyed Harris, then gave me a long look, but didn't say anything. Her eyes were black, with tired, dark smudges under them. She looked very calm and I wondered if she'd had a recent hit.

'Follow me,' she said.

Harris glanced at me and didn't look that sure of himself which made me even more nervous.

'Who's in here?' he asked.

She looked at him, her eyelids a little hooded.

'Just follow me, man.'

We walked behind her down a stone hallway that smelled of urine and stale vomit. Tin cans were strewn around and a bag of rubbish littered along an alley leading to a back door. The apartment opposite had no door on it and we glanced in the long hallway, grimacing at the stench wafting off it. Then we got to the door, and Lena pushed it open. We followed her inside the cold, damp, silent hallway. What had I hoped for, the sound of Lucas's voice? It smelled of cigarette smoke and rotting food. Lena pushed the door and it opened into a living room. I stood in the doorway as Harris walked in and my eyes quickly scanned the room, my heart pounding in my chest, desperately searching for a small figure, a bundle under a blanket, anything that was a sign of a little boy. But there was nothing. My heart was sinking fast. The only person in the room was a rake-thin white man who could have been in his thirties or forties, his face ravaged with deep-set lines and hollow cheeks. He sat on a chair, his back to the window and looked at us.

'These the people I told you about, Ray. The boy?' Philip said.

Silence. I could barely breathe.

He nodded slowly, looking a little distracted.

'Yeah. That little boy. He gone now.'

Anger rose in my chest and I could feel my face burn. I took a step forward but Harris put his hand out to stop me.

'Listen, man,' Harris said. 'If you know anything, then please tell us. Was this little boy here, the one from the television?'

He nodded slowly, his mouth turning down at the sides.

'He was. He was here all right. Little boy. Blond hair. He gone now.'

Harris stepped forward.

'What do you mean, he's gone? When was he here? Today? Yesterday?'

'He was here for two whole days, but Williams took him away.'

'Where? Who's Williams? Where did he take him?'

He looked up, his eyes glazed, at Harris, then at me.

'Listen, man. You need to get your damn wallet out if you want more information. I'm not a fucking public service, you know.' He picked up a fat joint from the small table next to him and lit it. The joint glowed red as he took a long tug on it, smoke swirling.

Harris stood in front of me as though sensing I was about to explode.

'We can do that, no problem,' he said. 'But I need something solid. I need to know more. When did he come here?'

'Day before yesterday, I think.' He looked up at Lena. 'That right, Lena?'

She nodded, but didn't say anything.

'Yeah,' he said. 'Day before yesterday. Little boy. I don't know his name though. He was just a little white boy.'

'Who brought him here?'

'Williams did. He brought him.'

'Who's Williams? How did he find the boy? Where did he find him?'

'Down by that trailer park, I guess. Where the fire was.' He spread his hands. 'Now I don't know nothing about that, but Williams said it was burned down bad and that the daddy was inside. That's what he said.'

'Why was it burned down? You know why?'

'I don't know stuff like that. I don't even know the man. I just know Williams brought this boy here because he was wandering around by himself, and he knew that his daddy was in that fire.'

'How did Williams know that?'

'I don't know. Fuck! How would I know? I guess Williams – he works for some shitty people, you know. I mean, if you owe money for something, then Williams is the collector. That's all I know.'

'So where is he now?'

He took a breath and sighed, shaking his head slowly.

'Can't say for sure.' He looked at Harris. 'What about that wallet, man?'

Harris looked at me, went into his pocket and pulled out two fifty-dollar bills. He handed them over, and the guy slipped them into his jeans.

'Tell me more.'

'I need more money, man.'

Harris took another fifty from his pocket.

'You need to tell me something solid. Where is this Williams? What happened? Why didn't he take the boy to the cops?'

He took a long moment, seemed to slow down his breathing.

'We don't do cops round here, know what I mean? Williams? Man, he sure knows ways to make money out of anything. Said he was going to New York. That's what he told me anyhow. He said he can get good money for this boy in New York.'

'What?' I heard my voice burst out like a shriek. I stepped

forward so I was almost in his face. 'What the fuck is going on here? You know something. You know more. This is my son you are talking about here. Where is he? You're fucking us around.' I leaned forward and grabbed him by the T-shirt and twisted it, almost lifting his stick-thin body off the chair. A fat skinhead with a tattoo across his throat who had sat opposite saying nothing until now, got up and shot across to me, pulling my hand.

'Hey! You just cool down, lady. You watch your fucking step now. You hear? You could get yourself hurt doing shit like that.'

'Fuck you!' I could feel tears in my eyes as Harris gently put his arm on mine and eased me back. I stood trembling with rage, and glanced at Lena who looked at me, eyes unblinking.

Harris put his hands out in a surrender.

'Listen, man. We need some more information. Billie here, her son has been stolen from her by her ex-husband. She's not looking for any trouble. She's been searching for her boy for a year and a half now and she came here because I'm working for her and someone saw her ex-man with the kid down at that trailer park a few days ago. That's why we're here. Please. You need to help her.'

He gave a lazy-eyed look.

'I ain't gonna help no goddam broad who puts her hands on me, that's for sure.'

'She's sorry. Aren't you, Billie?'

I looked at him, my eyes brimming with tears.

'I'm sorry. I . . . I'm sorry,' I managed to say.

We stood in the silence of the freezing room, the filthy torn net curtain billowing in the draught from the broken window.

Eventually Harris spoke. 'Look, do you have any way of contacting Williams?'

'Gonna cost you.'

'How much?'

'Hmm. Another hundred will get you a phone number.'

Harris pulled out another two fifties and handed them to him. Then the man opened his phone and read out a number which Harris punched into his phone.

'Do you have anything of the boy that we could see? I mean a toy, or some clothes?' I asked, aching to see something, knowing deep down it was hopeless.

'Nope.' He shook his head. 'I guess Williams took everything.'

Harris looked around one last time. 'I think we're done here.'

He headed for the door and with Philip walking behind him. I followed him just behind Lena. In the hallway, suddenly Lena took out a mobile from her jeans pocket, stepped back towards me and touched my arm.

'Listen. Don't tell anyone,' she whispered. 'This didn't come from me.' She seemed to be scrolling down, then handed me her phone.

'This your boy?' she asked.

My legs almost buckled and I staggered against the wall.

Harris overheard and turned back. On the screen was a photo of a grubby little boy with blue eyes and long straggly blond hair. He was wearing blue jeans and a shabby, dirty, yellow T-shirt. He looked lost, forlorn, afraid, tears in his eyes. But he was my Lucas.

'I took that,' Lena said. 'Yesterday. Before he left. I don't want no money.' She paused, her eyes locking mine, and I saw her swallow hard. 'I . . . I had a boy too. But he's gone now. But I know how you feel. I'll try to help you.'

I stood, Harris holding me by the arm, tears streaming down my face, looking at the picture. Harris took it off me and scrolled down and I saw him sending it to his mobile. He took out another couple of hundred dollars, folded them and stuffed them into her hand.

'Thank you. Here's my number.'

I looked at her as Harris led me out to the doorway, then I looked over my shoulder, and mouthed 'thank you', as she stood there, her eyes steady and unblinking.

CHAPTER FIFTEEN

My crying woke me. In my dream, Lucas was standing in the rain at the bottom of a long dark road, his face lit up by the streetlamps. He wasn't smiling, and his arms were outstretched, pleading. I was trying to run towards him, but my legs felt like lead and no matter how hard I tried I couldn't lift them off the ground. I kept telling him to wait, that I was coming, that I would bring him home. But then suddenly his head dropped to his chest as he turned away, and he was gone. For the first few seconds when I woke I was still sobbing, because it had been so real, even though I knew it was a dream. Sometimes when I dream like that about Lucas, the heaviness in my chest stays with me the whole day and I cannot shake it off. I wiped my eyes with the back of my hand and lay there, taking long slow breaths, telling myself that it was just a dream, that there was hope, that I had seen a picture of my son and that he was waiting for me somewhere. I picked up my phone and brought the image up on my screen and lay there in the dark, studying every tiny line in his body. His little arms had lost their baby chubbiness, his lips were full and red, his blue eyes wide and wondering. He'd grown in the past eighteen months. He was no longer the little two-and-a-half-year-old toddler, but a little boy now. And I'd missed that part of the change. But he was out there, somewhere, and I'd seen him. The thought of that alone made me kick back the duvet and pull myself out of bed. I opened the curtains and stood for a moment, transfixed by the traffic around the square snaking its way down towards Charing Cross. Then I stood in the shower, the steaming hot water cascading over me. I thought about Scanlon, and how last night I hadn't even told him about seeing the photograph of Lucas, and I knew he'd be hurt at that, because Scanlon had shared so much of my heartache since my baby was taken from me. But he would understand when I explained to him that this was mine alone; this knowledge that I had seen my son was something I hadn't wanted to share or discuss last night, not when I was having a conversation about a desperate battle with the thugs who attacked me. He would understand. And also, part of me was afraid to talk about it in case it would somehow jinx things. Harris would be chipping away at it, trying to track down Williams, he told me, as he'd driven me to the airport, despite my suggestion that I should stay on in the US, that we should both go to New York and hunt for Lucas. 'Leave it to me,' Harris had said. 'When the time is right, I'll tell you. Then you can come. But we are getting there,' he assured me, as he hugged me hard before I left. I believe him because it is all I have. As I came out of the shower, rubbing my hair with a towel, my mobile was ringing in the bedroom. I picked it up and saw Lars Eriksson's name on the screen. It brought me back to the day ahead.

'Hello, Billie. How are you?'

'I'm okay, Lars,' I said, which was an overstatement. 'You?'

After a couple of beats he answered. 'Ah, you know. It's difficult. Trying to get my parents through this, day by day.' He paused. 'They are looking forward to seeing you.' Another pause. 'I just wanted to say that I received a call from the funeral people and they confirmed that Astrid is now there and will be on the plane today. You are okay with that?'

'Sure,' I said, as enthusiastically as I could. On so many levels, it was the last thing I needed right now, but I had made a promise. 'I'm looking forward to seeing them too, Lars – though such tragic circumstances.'

'Yes. I know.' Another pause. 'How did things go up in Thurso?'

I took a breath and let it out slowly.

'It's a very long story. But I'd rather talk to you about it in person than over the phone.'

'Yes,' he said, softy. 'I do understand. But can I ask you this one thing?'

'Of course.'

'The death certificate has said she died from heart

failure due to hypothermia. It doesn't say suicide, but the implication is that she took her own life, that she went to the woods in the cold with no regard for herself. Do you think that?'

Lars seemed distraught, even more than he'd been when he'd phoned me in the beginning. I got the sense this was all beginning to take its toll, dealing with Astrid's death, his own heartbreak and shock, and the trauma of handling his stricken parents. I had to choose my words carefully.

'Lars, there's a lot to talk about with Astrid, and it's best to wait till I see you. But no. I don't think she in any way tried or wanted to take her own life.'

There was a long silence, then Lars spoke. 'Okay. We can talk tonight. I will pick you up from the airport. I so much want to see you.'

'Me too,' I said, sensing the emotion in his voice. 'It's been too long, Lars.'

He hung up and I stood for a long moment in my bedroom thinking of how difficult it was going to be to tell him the truth about Astrid's final hours.

I packed a bag for my short trip to Sweden and drove down to my office, partly to touch base with Millie, but also because being there kept me grounded when everything around had been chaos for the past few days. I needed to be in the buzz of the city, to nod to the news vendor outside my office, the people in the café nearby, all the stuff that keeps me sane when the walls are closing in. But in all of that, I felt positive today, and I knew it was because of the picture on my phone. As I walked from my car to the building, my mobile rang and I fished it out of my pocket. It was Fowler.

'How you doing, Billie?'

'A lot better since I left the Highlands,' I said cheerily. 'How are things?'

I wanted to ask if there were any reports about a body found in a back road, but thought it best not to. Fowler seemed to read my mind.

'Well, there's no stiffs lying anywhere overnight, so that's a good thing – well, in terms of any heat from the cops coming your way.'

'Good,' I said, 'so nothing on the grapevine?'

'Nope. Whatever happened to that guy, they must have moved him. I'd say his mate must have either bundled him into the car – alive or dead – and got off his mark, or he phoned his bosses and they sorted it. Whatever. But there's not a word being said about an incident. And I would've heard if there was.'

'So, what do you think?'

'Not sure at this stage. I'll keep my ears and eyes all over it. But if there is some suspicion that you're rattling cages and stealing drugs, then I hate to say this, but don't imagine they won't come after you down the road.'

'You mean here, in Glasgow?' I knew as I said it that it had already been on my mind, but I'd pushed it away.

'Yes. I told you that the drugs go to some place in the city for cutting and further distribution. I'm working on where that is. But that means there's an operation down there, so they won't want people like you anywhere near it. So be very careful.'

'I will. For sure.' I paused. 'But, Dave, I talked to a very close cop friend of mine, a detective, and told him what happened and also about the rally, and he said you should come down and speak to the National Crime Agency. I told you that myself. You really should consider it.'

'I am. I'm thinking seriously about it.'

'Are you safe up there? I mean at the moment? Do you think these guys saw us earlier down in Scrabster and in that Bettyhill Cove, and maybe got suspicious? If they came after me like that, then they could come for you.'

'I know. I've thought about that too. Might not be a bad idea to blow town for a few days.'

'Okay. Let me know what you decide. I'm going to Sweden today with Astrid's coffin and I'll be there for a couple of days. But when I'm back, I could talk to some people if you want to give the information you have to the NCA.'

'Yeah. Okay. I'll see how it goes.'

'Be careful, Dave.'

'Of course. I'm a farmer. I sleep with a shotgun under my bed.'

'Good idea.'

'Take care in Sweden. It'll be a hard trip for you.'

'Yes. It will be. I spent a good chunk of my life out there, and it's sad to be going back in these circumstances.'

'Yes. Well, maybe I'll see you when you get back. Good luck.' He hung up.

It was seven in the evening by the time my flight was landing in Sweden, and from my window seat I could see the lights of the city shimmering like a million stars. So many memories, so many things in my life from the day of my arrival as a forlorn twelve-year-old who had lost her parents. And now, accompanying Astrid, the sister of my friend. We never know what is in front of us, as my mother used to say, and it's a good job we don't. It was probably one of the most profound things she ever said. She always had little sayings like that, from her Irish background, words of wisdom handed down from ancestors who knew a thing or two about struggle. I wished so many times as I grew up that I could have known her better, talked to her in my teens, listened to her advice. I miss her still, every day. As the plane touched down, I thought of my mother, and my father, of me as a child walking and playing, always together with them. Then as the teenager who left Sweden to come back to her homeland full of hope and excitement. But right now, as the doors opened and I stepped out of the plane into the icy Stockholm night, there was a weird feeling that here, I was also coming home.

I walked through the arrivals hall scanning the waiting faces, wondering if I would instantly recognise my friend after so many years. Then I spotted him. Tall, slender, blond, just as I had imagined him, only older. His face smiled as he saw me, and when I got close, he walked towards me, arms outstretched. He embraced me and we stayed that way for a long moment. Then he eased me away, and told me we had to go to the area off the concourse apron and sign a document to accept Astrid's coffin. After we did this, we stood on the empty, blustery tarmac, the landing lights illuminating the plane I had just got off. Then the luggage compartment opened and the silent, respectful baggage men stood, heads bowed, as the coffin was brought out and the funeral directors eased it into the back of the waiting hearse. I took hold of Lars's hand and sensed his pain.

'My little sister is home,' he said.

CHAPTER SIXTEEN

It was getting late by the time we got to the bar/diner in Västervik after the three-hour drive from the airport in Stockholm. I had asked Lars not to ask about my investigation in the Highlands yet, as I didn't want him driving with the shock and heartache of what happened to Astrid. He agreed, but all over his face was the realisation that he was about to be told some awful truth, so the journey down was difficult. It was surreal to know that somewhere on this highway, in all of this traffic, there was a hearse carrying her body. She would be taken to the funeral parlour tonight and the funeral service was planned for tomorrow afternoon. We spent much of the journey with Lars asking me about my life, and even though I didn't want to, I poured out everything that had happened in the past few years. He was shocked, angry, sympathetic, reaching across to hold my hand when I choked up telling him about Lucas being taken by his father, and how every day I waited for news. He spoke about growing up after I left,

going to university and becoming a teacher, his relationship with his university sweetheart breaking up, and how
he had never got beyond dating since it happened. We
talked about the old days, my first time in school when I
arrived, this twelve-year-old girl who spoke some Swedish
but was struggling for the first few months to integrate.
He reminded me of how he saw me in the playground and
had been plucking up the courage to talk to me, and when
he did, we instantly became friends. How can something
so close and powerful in your life become so distant? I
wondered. We both spoke about how we should not have
lost touch in these past years, and made a vow that it would
never happen again. Eventually we got to the bar/diner
where Lars said we would eat and have a couple of drinks
as his house was just at the edge of the town.

We drove into the harbour, the streetlights twinkling
on the water, and everything felt so familiar as images
flooded back, and it was as though the years I'd spent here
as a teenager were only yesterday. Lars parked close to the
Burger Shack where, despite the cold, a few young people
wrapped up in heavy jackets and gloves sat outside smoking and drinking beer. It could have been us a few years
ago, carefree teenagers, when nothing could touch us.

Inside, the bar was minimal but pretty, with wooden
chairs painted blue and red and orange, and big solid pine
tables. It was busier than I expected given the time, the
late-night burger clan noisy with jugs of beers. The fresh
garlic and cooking aroma from the kitchen made me

realise how hungry I was. We sat at a table close to the window and I gazed out at the harbour where sailing boats nudged alongside cabin cruisers and the kind of small dinghies we learned to sail in all those years ago. Lars ordered some beers and we both decided on grilled chicken steaks with fries. When the beers arrived, we poured them into tumblers then we looked at each other and for a moment didn't speak. Lars, his pale blue eyes full of hurt and sadness, raised his glass.

'To Astrid,' he said, and I saw him swallow hard, his Adam's apple moving in his slender throat.

'To Astrid,' I said, my lips pulled into a sympathetic smile.

He took a long drink, and then sat forward, his elbows on the table, his eyes locking with mine.

'So, Billie,' he said. 'I'm ready.'

I nodded slowly and blinked my agreement, then I began.

'It's so hard to tell you this, Lars. There's no easy way to start or to describe what I found out in Thurso, but I will try.'

He nodded. 'I understand. I knew it was not good.'

I swallowed a mouthful of beer and took a breath.

'From what I have gathered, and this is through talking to a friend of Astrid's . . .' I paused, Lars scanning my face. I had to just say it. 'Astrid was drugged and raped by two men the night before she went into the woods and died.'

The words were like an explosion, the fallout hanging in

the air. The chatter of the couples a few tables away erupted in laughter as someone telling a story had reached a punchline. The colour drained from Lars's face. He looked at me, then down at the table, shaking his head.

'I was dreading something like this,' he said, his voice soft and desperate. 'I sensed in my heart that it was bad.'

I reached across and put my hand over his.

'Do you want me to go on? You don't have to know all the details because it's going to be painful.'

He waited for a few moments, staring at the table, then he looked up at me.

'I have to know,' he said in a whisper. 'Please, go on.'

'Okay. I think it is best that I tell you everything from what I have been told – how the evening began, Astrid out with her university friends at a bar in the town. It's better that way, I think.'

He didn't reply, his eyes a little distracted as though he was trying to process what I'd already told him, trying to imagine what happened to the sister he'd waved off to university just last year. Suddenly I could see his age in the tiny lines around his eyes, the dark shadows beneath them. There was less than eighteen months between us, but tonight he looked somehow older – perhaps because he was weary with shock and grief. We picked at the food on our plates for a few minutes and then I continued.

'It seems she was talking to a couple of guys at the bar. Her friends were dancing to a live band, and she was chatting to some guys who had come in. Often on the Friday nights young people come from all over. It was a kind of party atmosphere.

'The girl I was talking to said that when she came back to the bar Astrid had gone. Her friends tried phoning her mobile and they asked the bouncers whether they'd seen her. The bouncers said they hadn't, but they must've been lying because she left with these two guys.'

He shook his head. 'But that is so out of character for Astrid,' he said. 'She would never do anything like that – not even here in Västervik. Maybe she knew the guys, but even so, she would have told her friends.'

'Yes. It seems she was drugged. Probably with a date rape drug.'

Again, his head went down. I waited for a moment then I told him how her friend had come to the house the following day, wondering why she hadn't replied to her calls or texts.

'That was when the truth of what happened to Astrid came out. When her friend arrived there, she said Astrid was distraught, shaking and crying. Then she told her she'd had sex with these boys but she couldn't really remember it, but she knew that something had happened to her because physically she could see she'd had sex when she woke up in the morning. But then there was the bombshell – Astrid showed her a video.'

'A video?' His hands went up to his face. 'Oh God, no!'

'Are you sure you want to hear the rest?'

He closed his eyes, nodding. 'I have to.'

'There was—there is, a video. The boys must have sent it to her mobile, threatening her. There was cocaine found in her flat. We don't know why it was there, but I found it when I went to collect her things. It's possible that someone planted it there.' I stopped. 'I'll come to the cocaine part of the story in a minute. But I think they may have been blackmailing her.'

'They raped her and then blackmailed her? Oh God. Why didn't she call me?'

I sighed. 'I think it was all so overwhelming, Lars. It was happening so fast and she was terrified and wouldn't have known what to do.'

'Why didn't she go to the police?'

'Because she was afraid, her friend said. She couldn't remember it happening. She didn't know who to trust. Her friend pleaded with her to go, but she said she couldn't. She told her she wanted to be left alone, that she had to sleep.'

'So her friend left her?'

'Yes. She wanted to stay, but Astrid told her to go.'

I told him it seemed she must have had alcohol in the house, that her friend said Astrid had an ankle injury from falling off a horse recently, so she may have had painkillers and mixed them later in the day with alcohol – before she went out. This must have made her confused, because when she was found, she wasn't dressed for the weather with only a thin jacket on as she'd walked into the woods in the snow.

'My God, Astrid! I cannot bear to think of her so desperate, walking around alone, frightened, in such danger.' His eyes filled with tears. 'Why did she not phone me? I would have come and got her immediately.'

I held his hand.

'She wasn't thinking straight, Lars. She was so distraught, and then, with the pills and the alcohol . . .'

Lars pushed the food around his plate and sipped his beer. We were silent for a while, then as we ate as much as we could of our meal, I told him what had happened with the police and how vague they'd been. And about Fowler and the attack by the two thugs who chased me. I told him about the wider picture in all of this, of the cocaine and the rally. And the possibility that there was a cover-up.

Later, I lay in the small spare bedroom in Lars's apartment three floors up in a newly refurbished building where I could glimpse the harbour. When we'd come in from the restaurant, we were both tired and talked out, and I sensed the two of us felt the need to be alone. I declined the offer of a glass of wine, and he showed me to my room. Before he said goodnight, he stood in the door frame, the tall willowy figure he'd been now with sagging shoulders, and a lost look about him that I didn't recognise. I stepped forward and hugged him, the warmth and strength of him filling me with love. He had been like family to me in those formative, difficult years. Then he hugged me back, and I was alone in the quietness of the room, just the lights of the harbour on the water, and I slipped under the duvet and lay staring at the ceiling. Eventually I closed my eyes, but instead of sleep, memories of my past here came flooding in, of that first night when I arrived as a twelve-year-old child, lost, bereaved. I've never felt so alone before or since, not even after Lucas was taken. I lay on my side and pulled my knees up to my chest, and remembered how I used to do that when I'd woken up hearing my mother weeping in the night after my father took his own life. It was a desperately sad thing to hear your mother weep like that and know that nothing you can do will make it better. I would hug my knees, hoping it would stop. Then eventually I would get up from my bed and pad to her room and climb in beside her. I would slip my arm around her, and even now I can still feel the satiny nightdress she had on, can still feel the contours of her body as I curled myself up to her, as much to comfort her as myself, because I didn't know how we could possibly go on from this. And she would stop crying eventually, her hand clutching mine, holding me close, and we would sleep like that, two souls broken by grief.

CHAPTER SEVENTEEN

The daylight streaming into the bedroom window woke me, and I could hear the traffic and movement outside as the town of Västervik began its day. The house was warm and smelled of new timber, the room bright with yellows and cobalt blues. I hadn't looked around last night, but now a small framed photograph caught my eye on the wall above a chest of drawers. It pulled me up short. There were seven young people in the picture, teenagers, sun-burnished, blond, in shorts and T-shirts, all gathered in a place I knew too well across the harbour, where we used to swim. Those faces, all of us, happy and grinning, one or two making silly faces, adolescents who hadn't found out yet that life is a struggle, that it's not just fun and plans. How happy we had been. I scanned the faces one by one: Lars, his arm around my shoulder, me with my blue eyes smiling, Jenna, Erik, Johann, Lizzie and Thomas. I moved along, then I saw Elias, smaller, younger than us, but always following us, and not for the first time I felt a pang of regret. An image came into my head and I turned away from the photograph. I couldn't think of that today, not when I was about to say goodbye to Astrid.

I was glad to see Lars smiling as I came into the kitchen. He was mixing up pancake batter and pushing oranges into a juicer. The smell of fresh coffee filled the room.

'This is lovely,' I said, sitting up at the breakfast bar, watching him work. I looked up and caught his eye. 'Are you okay this morning, Lars? Did you get some sleep? I know it must have been difficult.'

'I slept.' He nodded, then turned the cooker ring up high. 'But not great. I'm okay though, Billie. I have to be for my parents. I just want to get them through this day. Everything I feel inside can wait.'

'I know,' I said, not quite knowing what to say. 'So tell me about your work teaching secondary children. I hope they are not as wayward as we all were.' I paused. 'Oh, by the way I saw the photo in the bedroom. That took me back. Beautiful memories. What times we had.'

He turned and smiled over his shoulder.

'We did,' he said. 'I thought you would like the picture. I dug it out a couple of days ago when I was going over old photos – we must find time before you go to look at some more, maybe after the funeral today we can have some trips down memory lane. But I loved that picture – so . . . us. All of us.' He grimaced. 'Yes, and of course, Elias. I still think of him, of that day.' He poured the pancake mix into the pan.

I nodded. 'Yes. Me too. But I would be lying if I said it was always in my mind. It was so shocking, so hard, that for a very long time my mind blocked it out. But it comes to me sometimes. There will always be guilt.'

He turned around with the pan in his hand.

'I know. But there shouldn't be.' He smiled. 'Come on. Things are sad enough today. Let's have some breakfast.'

We ate well, pancakes, syrup, chocolate sauce for Lars – always the chocolate sauce.

'So tell me about your work.' I said.

'It's great. It took me a while to find out what I really wanted to do, and if you'd asked me when that picture was taken if I was planning to be a schoolteacher I would have laughed at you. Yet here I am. I spent years in finance and made some money, but it was like an epiphany moment – I decided if I was going to stay here, I could teach. Maybe because of all of us and remembering how we all were. Who knows? But I love it.'

'I'm so pleased for you, Lars.'

The funeral was in the small chapel in the crematorium. It was cold and only a couple of dozen people were there. I recognised two of my old friends and we embraced long and hard. They lived in Stockholm now and had to go straight after the ceremony, but we stood together as a clergyman led the small service, and I watched as Lars's parents, so much older now, mourned their only daughter. His father was still handsome, with lush grey hair and little rimless spectacles, and his mother was beautiful with high cheekbones and flawless skin. Outside afterwards we hugged and Lars's mother asked me about my aunt Lilly, my dad's sister, and whether I was planning to see her at the nursing home. I felt a twinge of guilt, and made up my mind that I had to make some time to visit.

We went back to the small hotel for sandwiches and drinks with family friends, and despite the warmth and that these people were the salt of the earth who I'd grown up with, I felt that I had grown so far away from this place now, that life had taken me on a different journey. I had my aunt's house that I would inherit, but I could never imagine coming back to live here. It reminds me of what brought me to this place as a child, and how much I had lost. That had been the reason I had decided to opt for university in Glasgow rather than here. And it was still the reason I didn't think I could live here.

In the afternoon Lars drove me to the nursing home, and I felt uneasy about seeing Aunt Lilly after all these years. The home was pleasant and bright, with an area laid out like a small village, with shops and a post office and wooden benches so that the residents would not feel institutionalised. I was led by a nurse to a room at the end of a corridor that had a few chairs and a sofa but was empty apart from one woman. Then I saw her. Aunt Lilly. She'd had a stroke last year, and I could see a Zimmer frame and wheelchair close by. She sat in front of a television watching a daytime show which she stared at blankly, the sound turned down.

'Aunt Lilly?' I said, venturing closer. 'It's me. It's Billie.' I did my best to smile.

Her brows knitted, and for a moment she looked irritated, a look I had seen so many times before, then she slowly turned to me and I could see the stiffness on one side of her face, her right hand still and rigid on the edge of the chair. I could see the slow recognition in her eyes, but no smile, even if she could only have smiled on one side. A proud and good-looking woman, she would be furious that I was seeing her like this, so vulnerable, so unglamorous. She'd always been fastidious in her dress and grooming, but she looked old now, tired and defeated. I felt sorry for her. I stood, trying to smile, hoping she would say something. Eventually her lips moved a little and I could see she was trying to say my name. I sat on a chair opposite her, so we could properly look at each other.

'Billie,' she said, her voice deeper than I remembered, and slower the way she pronounced it. 'Bi . . . i . . . leee.' Then her face did crack a bit of a smile. She looked confused and signalled with her hands to ask why I was here.

'I am here for the funeral of my friend's sister, Astrid,' I said. 'She died in Scotland. So I am here to be with Lars for the funeral. It was today.'

She nodded, but it was hard to see if she felt any empathy as her expression was blank.

'How are you, Aunt Lilly?' I asked.

She rolled her eyes a little and I caught a glimpse of the old caustic Lilly, the judgmental, cold figure full of ridicule, who cared for me and kept me, but showed me nothing that resembled love or even understanding. She shrugged one shoulder.

'I am here.' The words came out slowly, softly. 'This. My life.'

'Are they treating you okay?'

She nodded. Then she looked at me.

'How you?'

'I am fine,' I said, exaggerating the reality. 'Sometimes my life is hard, but I am okay.' I didn't know if she knew about Lucas, as we hadn't spoken in years, but I wasn't going to tell her now.

We sat in silence. I realised we had nothing to say to each other, and even though she'd given me nothing in my childhood to remember fondly, I still felt a pang of sadness for her and for what she had become. I wondered if she had many friends, anyone who visited. I never remembered her being sociable, and often wondered why not and what kept her so distant from people. I would never know now, I supposed. After a while I stood up. There was nothing for me here.

'I must go now, Aunt Lilly. I'll leave you in peace.'

I reached out to touch her hand, and her face showed nothing. It was blank, the way I had remembered her. Then, as I turned, she pushed out a hand towards me and caught mine, clutching it so tight it almost hurt. I turned to look at her, and to my surprise, tears filled her eyes. Her mouth moved, the part of it that could, and as I leaned in I could smell fading perfume that I recalled she wore.

'I'm sorry, Billie,' she said in my ear.

She gripped my hand and squeezed it, and tears spilled out of her eyes. I looked at her and for the first time I could see her pain, the face she'd never once shown me. I didn't know what to say so I stood, her hand holding mine, until she relaxed her grasp. Then there was a knock on the door and a woman with a trolley laden with coffee and drinks broke the moment. I pulled away, and tried to give my aunt a look that said I understood, but I didn't understand now any more than I did when I was twelve years old.

Later in the afternoon Lars and I sat on a bench in the harbour drinking steaming coffee from polystyrene cups. We were killing some time before I was due at the airport for my flight home. It was cold and the light was beginning to fade on the silent deserted quay, and the whole atmosphere somehow summed up the mood at the end of a long, emotional day. We sat for a while not saying anything, but I sensed Lars was thinking the same thoughts as me, looking out at the dark water where we had spent so many summer nights as teenagers. And the one memory that haunts everyone who was there the night Elias drowned.

'You thinking of Elias?' Lars said, and from the corner of my eye I saw him turn his head towards me.

I looked at him. 'Yes. Just being here, looking out towards the bay, it brings it all back. I used to torture myself thinking, if we could have done more, should we have tried . . . What if . . .'

'I know,' Lars said. 'I'm the same. For a long time I think we all felt like that, because you know, I think we all know that we are a little guilty. What if we hadn't been drunk that night? Could we have saved him?'

We fell into silence again, and I knew both of us were recalling the moments and the hard truths we have all had to live with ever since.

It had been the usual start of the weekend, a raucous Friday after school for our gang of sixteen-year-olds who were counting down the days to the long summer holidays in two weeks' time when we'd be free to spend our days and nights together. We had been barbecuing in the garden of one of our friend's homes and drinking from a secret stash of beer and vodka. Elias, who was only thirteen, was with us. He used to hang around with us even though he was younger and didn't drink or get involved the way we did. We kind of felt sorry for him as his parents had split up and his sister had gone to university, so he was alone. He was a nerdy kid who spent a lot of his time reading and didn't have many friends his own age. Lars had been close with his sister and we knew him well so he hung out with us and we kept an eye on him. We were tipsy by the time we got to the harbour, and were messing around, pretending to push each other into the water. Then we decided to go to the quiet place we knew, where we could dive off the pier and race towards the boats on the far side. The larking around went on for a while. Elias was a fine, strong swimmer, and he was playing the game too. We were all diving in and swimming under water to see how long we could hold our breath. The harbour restaurants and bars were crowded and nobody paid any attention to us. Then it happened. We looked around and suddenly Elias wasn't there. We called out his name again and again, but nothing. And then one of the boys shouted to look and we saw a hand waving above the water. We dived and swam, our hearts bursting to get to him, and some of the boys dived under and they could see his foot had become snagged in a chain and a rope on the anchor of a small fishing boat. I dived and swam under water towards him, dived down to his ankle and tried to free it, but my chest was bursting. There was blood on his ankle and the bone was swollen. Elias looked at me, panic in his eyes. By the time I got to the surface, I could hear the wail of sirens as ambulances and firemen rushed to the harbourside. I watched, shivering, as they dived under with their cutting gear. We all gaped, but with that awful sense of foreboding that it was already too late. Eventually they managed to cut the chain and pulled Elias to the surface, his limp body held up until they were able to get him onto the jetty. We stood in a circle around him as the medics pumped his chest, willing him to breathe, but he lay there, lifeless, his narrow chest naked, his slim body wet and still. And eventually they gave up. We were distraught, weeping. All of us were in shock and none of us were sober. Police came and we were questioned, and newspaper articles followed about the drunken teenagers who'd let a young boy die. We were hated all over town. Over that summer we became different people. Our friendships were strained, each of us blaming ourselves and sometimes each other. We grew up that summer; we grew into guilt-ridden teenagers who would get on with their lives because they had to but who would always wonder if they could have done more. Because deep down each of us knows we could have.

CHAPTER EIGHTEEN

At the airport, Lars took both of my hands in his and pleaded with me not to leave it so long until I returned. I told him I wouldn't. But over the last couple of days, going to the old haunts, remembering, my mind was conflicted between thoughts of never coming back yet also wanting to return. Looking at Aunt Lilly and knowing I would one day inherit a house here, I had always assumed I would sell it. But standing here with Lars, part of me knew that I could never really walk away from this. Much of what I am today is rooted in who I was when I came here. I knew, though, as we stood and embraced, that I was in no hurry to return. If I ever did, it would be with my son, to show him, to teach him who he is and where he comes from. I would never come back until I could do that.

By the time I got into Glasgow Airport, my phone was rattling with message after message and several missed calls. I scrolled through them as I walked along the arrivals hall, headed for the exit and hailed a taxi. Two of the calls were from Fowler, and three from Scanlon. I sat in the back seat of the taxi and browsed through my emails from Millie. Then I saw a WhatsApp message from an unknown number. I clicked on the blurred image then watched as the video downloaded. Jesus! I watched in horror as Astrid was violated by two men wearing ski masks, pouring alcohol over her and laughing as they high-fived across her body. I fell back, realising I'd been holding my breath. Then I sat up again, my heart sinking. I needed to look at this. I had to examine it meticulously for any clues of background, clothing worn by the males, everything, especially the expression and movement of Astrid. From what I could see, the background wasn't her flat so they must have taken her somewhere. Freezing the frame, it looked like a shed or something. There were work tools in the background and a bench. It was clear what was happening, although there were no male private parts or her genitalia showing. They only showed Astrid's face in a couple of shots and she wasn't screaming or fighting, but she was clearly drunk or drugged and incapable of doing anything to stop them. I'd seen defence lawyers drive a train through this kind of evidence, if a rape victim claimed it was intercourse without consent. There was no fight, but she couldn't fight. Poor Astrid. The little trusting girl I'd known since she was a baby being cruelly assaulted like this. I watched it again, and then I suddenly saw it. My stomach lurched. I froze the video and looked closely. One of the men had a tattoo on the back of his hand. A scorpion, tail raised, poised to strike. The skinny thug who'd terrorised me and attacked me in Thurso had a scorpion tattoo. There couldn't be too many people in a small town with a tattoo like this on their hand. 'Whoever you are, you bastard, I will hunt you down,' I said aloud.

'What's that, darlin'?' the taxi driver said, eyeing me in the rear-view mirror.

'Sorry,' I said. 'Just thinking aloud.'

I looked at the unknown number and checked it with my recent call log, and saw that the WhatsApp message was from Jenny. There were no words attached, nothing, and I resisted the urge to call her or to answer it. It was enough for me that she'd had the courage to send it.

It was after eight in the evening by the time I got into the flat, and rummaging around the freezer pulled out a ready meal of baked fish. When I'd finished, I called Scanlon.

'You're back! How was it? Are you okay?'

As always, just the sound of his voice was enough.

'It was emotional, Danny. Astrid's family are heart-broken. And shocked – well, I only told Lars what happened to Astrid. He could scarcely take it in.' I paused, not wanting to go over it all again. 'I'll tell you all about it when I see you though.'

'Okay. Listen, I spoke to a couple of people about what we talked about up north. They want to see you, and they definitely want to talk to Fowler.'

'Yeah, thought they might. What about Astrid's clothing and stuff? Are you going to be able to get forensics to look?'

It took him a moment to answer.

'I haven't asked yet. I thought it would be better coming from you – maybe a bit of leverage, that you're giving them info and you want something in return?'

'I want some kind of justice for what happened. From what I gather, there are some rotten cops up there.'

'Well, if things go well, it will be part of the one investigation. Once you start peeling shit like this, it will all come away, and so will their cushy lives.'

I trusted him, and I knew he was, like me, burning with a sense of justice, but I also knew the pitfalls of throwing everything in with the cops.

'Who did you talk to?' I asked.

Another silence. 'Your old pal.'

'Christ, Scanlon, you talked to Wilson? What's he got to do with anything?'

'You know he likes you, Carlson.'

'Could have fooled me.'

'No, he does. He respects you. Especially after your help with the Foster girl and the traffickers.'

'Hmm,' I said, not convinced. 'But what has he got to do with drugs in the Highlands, or any drugs investigation? I thought you were going to talk to the National Crime Agency boys.'

'Wilson's mate has been made head of that now up here, so he's the best man to get in with. The way the NCA works is that they involve cops from wherever the investigation or intelligence gathering is. So, Wilson is already earmarked for the case. He wants to meet you ASAP.'

I heaved a sigh. The prospect of tussling with Wilson again and having to hand everything over to him didn't thrill me. But I had to admit I did have respect for him, even if he was an irascible old bastard. He had been one of my first DCIs, and I'd learned a lot from him – including how cops framed villains sometimes as a means to an end. He doesn't know, but I witnessed him planting cocaine in a gangster's home we were turning over so the thug would get jailed. I said nothing, not even to him.

'Okay, I'll meet him.'

I didn't tell Scanlon about the damning video as I didn't want to have a phone conversation about it.

'Wilson is going to call you tomorrow. What about Fowler?'

'I haven't talked to him yet. I just got here a couple of hours ago, and I've a few missed calls from him. I'll catch him now.'

'Good. He definitely wants a meet with him.'

'I think he'll be up for that. But I need to talk to him first.'

'Okay. What you doing now?'

'Going to bed. I'm shattered. All that emotion drains you.' I paused. 'By the way, I went to see Aunt Lilly in the nursing home. It was weird.'

'How so?'

'She was just strange. She's had a stroke and I felt sorry

for her.' I stopped, as there was no point in going into this tonight, I was surprised I'd even brought it up. 'I'll tell you when I see you.'

'Maybe tomorrow. Afternoon sometime or early evening?'

'I'll call you, once I've seen Wilson.'

'Good to have you back, Carlson.'

I felt my face smiling.

'Good to hear your dulcet tones, Scanlon.'

I hung up, took a sip of wine and pulled up Fowler's number.

'Dave. How you doing?'

'Billie, are you back now?'

'Yes. Just got here a couple of hours ago. What's happening, any developments up there?'

'Yeah. I had to get out of Dodge fast yesterday. I'm in Glasgow now.'

'Really, what happened?'

'I got a wee message, courtesy of, I believe, the Irishman.'

'What? How?'

'I got a visit from your favourite cop in Thurso. He gave me the gypsy warning that I was to be careful where I was stepping these days. McPhail and I go back a long way. I knew him when he was just a rookie cop like me.'

'What did he mean by a gypsy warning?'

'He said I had been seen with you and asked what the hell you were all about, coming up sticking your nose in everywhere it didn't belong. I told you, he's in it up to his neck.'

'Christ, was that it?'

'No. I'm afraid not. I woke up with my dog barking later that night and the barn was on fire. So some bastard paid me a visit.'

'My God! Did you call the cops or the fire brigade?'

'Nah, no point. I managed to put it out myself with a pressure hose. Bit of damage, but worse things could happen. So, I decided to get the hell out of town for a bit. My mate has a flat in Glasgow and he's in the Canaries for a month, so I'm staying here.'

'Where is it?'

'City centre, near Argyle Street.'

'Good. I'm not far from there. We can maybe meet tomorrow if you're up for it?' I paused. 'Dave, my friend talked to the cops and they want to chat with you.'

'I'm okay with that. But let's talk first. I need to know how the land is lying.'

'By the way, what did you do with your blue-eyed collie? Did you bring her?'

'I did. Couldn't leave her there.'

'Good stuff.'

There was a silence. Then he spoke. 'Incidentally, you don't have to worry about killing anyone.'

'Seriously? How so?'

'The one you drove over. His name is Gordon McKay. I'm told he was injured but is out of hospital. Head and leg injury. He won't be talking to the cops.'

'Well, that's something.'

'Yes, but it doesn't mean he's going to forgive you. So, you'll need to watch your back. You've made some enemies all right. These guys are just fodder; the people who pull their strings are the danger, so just be careful. There's two kilos of cocaine unaccounted for so someone will want to get that back.'

It should have made me shudder, but it didn't. I felt safer in Glasgow than on a back road in the Highlands, even though recent scrapes with some hoodlums in my home city told me different.

'I'll bear that in mind. I'll call you tomorrow, after I've met this old cop boss of mine.' I paused a moment, bursting to tell him about the video.

'And I have some exciting news to tell you. But I don't want to talk on the phone.'

'Really? I'll look forward to that. Take care.'

He was gone before I had the chance to answer.

I was in my office by nine thirty, just as Millie was taking her coat off. She turned to me, surprised.

'Almost beat me to the punch there, Billie.' She placed her handbag on the desk and went to the coffee maker, holding out a mug questioningly.

'Yes, please,' I said, 'I'd love one. I feel as though I've been jet-lagged for weeks.'

'Probably because you have been. How did it go in Sweden?'

'Grim enough, but I'm so glad I went. For Lars.' I sat back

and looked up at her. 'I haven't had the chance to fill you in on Thurso, Millie. It all got a bit hairy up there.'

She glanced around at me as the coffee maker gurgled.

'Yes, I did notice the bruise on your cheek.' She shook her head and gave me a reprimanding look. 'One of these days, Billie. One of these days. I keep telling you.'

'I know. But I can't believe the shit that's going on up there. From drug smuggling to police corruption. And poor Astrid. She was raped and blackmailed. That's how she ended up dying, desperate and alone in those woods.'

Millie shook her head. She poured two mugs of coffee and handed one to me, then sat down at her desk. 'You want to tell me about it? And you haven't mentioned anything about your US trip yet. You were gone to Sweden before I got the chance to ask you. But you know I don't like to pry.'

I took a sip of my coffee and puffed out a breath. Then I picked up my mobile and brought up the picture of Lucas. I got up and crossed to her desk, holding it in front of her. Her eyes widened, then her expression seemed to crumble a little and she bit her lip.

'Oh, Billie. My God! You saw him?'

'Not in the flesh. But someone who did see him took this picture before he disappeared again, with some guy.'

'Christ! What guy? Where to? I mean. Are cops over there not doing anything?'

I shrugged. 'Children go missing all over America every five minutes. All I can do is keep plugging away with my private eye. It seems some guy has taken Lucas to New York. But we don't know for sure yet. It's just a mess.'

'I'm so sorry. I wish to hell there was something I could do.'

'I know you do. It's enough to know that.'

Her landline rang and she immediately became Millie my front-of-house woman, sharp, clipped, in charge.

'Carlson Investigations. How can I help you?'

I turned away and went into my office. Another day, another client, another last hope for some poor bastard. I knew the feeling.

DCI Harry Wilson was sitting on a leather Chesterfield sofa in the Starbucks café on Buchanan Street pedestrian precinct. It was busy with lunchtime trade and most seats were taken up by punters on laptops or with heads down scrutinising mobile phones. He looked up when he saw me, and I acknowledged him and crossed the room. He didn't get up. Not that I expected him to.

'I hate these fucking places, Carlson.'

I grinned. 'Good to see you too, Harry.'

I plonked myself on the big easy chair opposite him, conscious that he was scanning my face.

'Christ. What's with the bruise?'

'If I told you, I'd have to kill you.'

He puffed, did an eye roll. 'Aye, very funny. Where did you get it?'

'Up in Thurso. These Highlanders. It's not all sea shanties

and breathtaking scenery, you know. There's some bad bastards up there.' I paused for effect. 'And that's only in the police station.'

He half chuckled, then stood up.

'What d'you want? Coffee? Skinny mocha or whatever shite that is?'

'Just a flat white, Harry. I'm a woman of simple needs.'

He almost smiled as he turned and walked towards the queue.

When he returned, carrying a tray with a couple of cups of coffee and some kind of biscuits wrapped in cellophane, I remarked, 'You know, Harry, the way you carried that tray there, not spilling a drop ... you could make it as a head waiter.'

'Aye, would probably live longer too.'

I eyed his florid complexion, his tired, slightly bloodshot eyes, the beer belly stretching the buttons of his shirt under his jacket. He was knocking on, and probably looking to his retirement at fifty if he didn't stay in the force. But despite all the crap he liked to dish out, and the protesting he'd always done with me, he was a good cop. Well, if you put to the side the odd framing of a criminal who probably deserved it.

'So,' he said, glancing around him, making sure nobody was within hearing distance, 'what's going on up there in Thurso? Got a call from your mate Scanlon.' He glanced at me a twinkle in his eye. 'Are you doing a line with him, by the way?'

I gave him my best sarcastic, piss-off look.

'We are close mates. None of your business anyway, even if I was.'

He put a hand up. 'Just wondered.'

From the look in his eye, he would have heard the tittle-tattle about me and McCartney, one of his detectives I'd had something of a fling with a while ago. But I knew he would never venture there with me. He sniffed, swallowed, then leaned forward.

'These scumbag drug dealers,' he said. 'It's so hard to nail them down. Because the NCA is getting better at their job, you know, detecting drugs at airports and stuff, these fuckers bring it in on boats. We know it goes on, but the drug gangs are so well organised. Anyway, I talked to my mate who's moved back up from London from the National Crime Agency to head the organised crime team in Scotland. They work very closely with the serious crime squad when investigating or tracking drug shipments, as you know. If everyone gets on board with this investigation, they can bring in Europol and Interpol and track this all the way.' He sipped his coffee and took a breath. 'But that might be difficult as, according to your information, the drugs are in a rally car, and there are lots of vehicles coming in for the rally. But with inside information there's a real chance to bust this. He's right up for it. So, tell me all about it. If you want, and I hope you do, we can meet him later to talk.'

I nodded. Then I began by telling him why I'd gone to

Thurso in the first place. I told him about Astrid, and the rape, and that I had her clothing which needed to be handed over to forensics, and even a video of the rape. I said that I didn't want to give up the video until the forensics came back from Astrid's clothes. I didn't want anyone tipping Thurso off that there was a second video of the rape, in case they had been doing anything dodgy. Wilson told me it's really their case and that I should hand the video over, but I explained to him that after my trip there, and with what Fowler had told me, I wasn't sure who I could trust. He agreed to help me with the forensics.

I told him about leaving Thurso. And when it got to the part at the end when I got attacked, I decided to come clean with him and tell him everything. He laughed out loud and almost looked proud when I told him about driving over the guy who I thought was dead.

'Fuck me, Carlson! What would you have done if he'd died and the cops had traced it back to you?'

'I'd have pleaded self-defence and called you as a character witness.'

He laughed, his belly shuddering in his too-tight shirt.

'You're off your fucking head.'

CHAPTER NINETEEN

I walked down to meet Dave Fowler in a café under the Hielanman's Umbrella – the famous Victorian-style glass-walled railway bridge at the far end of Argyle Street. He'd been out walking his dog after his long drive last night. He was already inside when I passed the window, and through the condensation from the fryers steaming up the window, I saw him at a table, his dog lying on the floor at his feet. He looked up, his ruddy complexion even redder from going from the cold outside to the heat of the café. He broke into a smile when I came in.

'And there was me thinking that it was all posh cafés and bistros in the big city,' he joked, glancing around as I sat down opposite him.

'I like these places,' I laughed. 'You get to see real life in the greasy spoons of the world.' I picked up the menu. 'How're you doing?' Then I bent down and ruffled the collie. 'Hello, girl. You're a beauty, aren't you.' I looked up at him, the dog licking my face. 'I love dogs. I say hello to them all the time in the street.'

'Aye.' He smiled. 'They're a lot easier to get along with than people, that's for sure.'

The waitress came across in a blue nylon overall holding a pencil and pad, and we both ordered coffee and toast.

'How's your digs?' I asked, by way of small talk. I wanted to gauge how he was feeling before I discussed anything about seeing Wilson.

'Flat's great. The dog is settled in already. I took her for a walk in Glasgow Green this morning. I'll tell you, it's a lot different to when I was last here. Some of the people bouncing around! Jesus! Out of their tree junkies.'

'Yes, there's a lot of that down there. Used to be worse though.'

The coffee and toast arrived and he broke a piece off and fed it to the dog and we both watched as she gratefully wagged her tail and scoffed it.

'I went to see a DCI this morning. I used to work with him. His name is Harry Wilson. He's very keen to meet you.'

'What's he like?'

I half smiled. 'He wouldn't win a cuddly bear contest, but he's very good. He knows his game. Doesn't always play by the rules, you know, to get the bad guys.'

'I'll drink to that any day.' He sat back and took a long breath, as though he was remembering a time when he didn't play by the rules. Then he ran a hand through his hair, lowering his voice. 'I got a good tip last night from my contact about the Glasgow connection. Needs checking out though – very softly.'

'Really? What, you mean a place where the cargo comes to?'

'Yep, so it would seem. A lot of it gets cut there and then sold in batches, but some of it will go uncut, you know, pure cocaine. That'll be for the bigger dealers – the London and Manchester mobs.'

'What about Dublin? You know, the Irishman's connection?'

'That stuff will probably come in through the Irish coastline anywhere from Cork to Donegal, but the stuff coming in through Thurso is for the UK.'

'Do you have an address for the place? Is it a warehouse or what?'

'I do. It's a packaging place, or that's what it is on paper.'

'How did you manage to get this kind of information, Dave? I know the cops will be asking when we meet them.'

He looked at me, then beyond me, and took a moment to answer.

'There's a wee guy up there, does some work for me sometimes, and he was a big pal of Joe, the boy I told you about ... My ... my son.' His jaw tightened. 'The two of them were close enough and he works as a kitchen porter in one of the big hotels I told you about – just money-laundering projects, all of them. The wee man works in the gardens too so he gets to hear and see a lot. He never really

asked that many questions in his head with the comings
and goings as there are a lot of tourists, but after Joe, he
started to keep his ears and eyes open more. He called over
to my house when he heard about the fire and we had
a cup of tea and a good chat. He told me everything he
knows.'

'And these guys talk openly about a place in Glasgow
where the stuff is moved to?'

'The pricks running the show won't be talking, obviously, but you always get some eejit down the food chain
who is either bragging about something he's getting away
with or is stupid enough to let slip.'

'So what about the pair of thugs that attacked me – any
update on them?'

'No,' he said. 'But they might come after you. The coke
you took from Astrid's flat was either stolen by them or one
of their bosses, who's fleecing his bigger boss. But nobody
just lets a couple of kilos of coke out of their hands, it's too
valuable. So, whatever happens once the cops get involved,
you should step back from it and let them take over.'

I agreed. 'I can see that. But what about Astrid? The drug-
ging and raping? These guys have to pay.' I paused. 'I've
brought back some of the clothes she was wearing and I've
told Wilson that the deal is they'll get information from
you once forensics have examined Astrid's clothes, and he's
agreed. I'd like to nail these guys.'

'Yes. But you sure as hell can't go to Thurso to hunt them
down, Billie.'

'I know.'

'I'll be getting the wire once this McKay bastard gets out of hospital and then it's a matter of time. The cops up north will have to be railroaded into looking harder at Astrid's death. So you'll need something more solid than a belief she was raped.'

'I have the video,' I blurted out.

'What? When did you get it?'

'Last night. On my way back from the airport I switched my phone on and there it was on a WhatsApp message. It's sickening.'

'Jesus! Who sent it?'

'Astrid's friend Jenny. She told me she didn't have it, but she must be feeling guilty, and sent it. No message. No words. Just the video.'

'Brilliant!'

I told him about seeing the scorpion tattoo on one of the guys' hand in the video and that the man who attacked me in Thurso had the same tattoo in the very same place. So either McKay or Mason was one of the men shown in the video.

Fowler shook his head slowly.

'Bastards! My cop mate up the road told me the police definitely took the mobile from her flat. One of the cops on the case initially told him that. But it seems to have vanished.'

'How can that happen?'

'Who knows,' he said. 'Maybe the police saw the video

and someone spotted something that could identify the rapists.'

'Do you really think the cops would get rid of evidence like that? Of a girl being raped?'

'Depends who leaned on who.'

'Jesus! I'm not giving up this video until I know more,' I said.

My mobile rang and it was Wilson asking when we could meet. I turned to Fowler.

'The cop I told you about. He wants a meet.'

He shrugged. 'Sure. Any time.'

I spoke into the mobile.

'Whenever suits you, Harry.'

By the time I got back to the office it was late afternoon and my head was buzzing with listening to Fowler and the cops go over everything he'd told them about the smuggling operation. Wilson had introduced his DCI mate as the new head of the NCA in Scotland, and McCartney was there too, but we barely acknowledged each other. They'd spent time discussing criminal gangs and the set-up across Scotland and across the UK. I felt I didn't need to be there for all of that, but it was interesting to hear the level of detail Fowler had about the hotels up in the Highlands. He said so many of them were all just a means to launder dirty money, and that he had documents and details of the main players.

*

I just wanted to go home early for once and put my feet up. Millie had left the details of a new client on my desk, a businessman who was trying to catch out his unfaithful wife in an affair with her personal trainer. He was asking whether I would come and see him, instead of him coming to the office. Whatever, it could wait until tomorrow. I told Millie to call him back and arrange a meeting place.

It was dark and the traffic was beginning to thin down at the top of Blythswood Square when I drove up towards my flat. I got out of the car and lingered for a moment to give directions to a man in the street who was looking to get to St Andrews Square down in the Merchant City. While I was talking to him, I was conscious of someone standing across the square looking in my direction. As I pointed to the man how to get to Merchant City, I glanced over his shoulder and again, the man on the other side of the square was looking across. Given that this was the red light area, all sorts of people came around here, from pimps to prostitutes to punters, but if he was a punter, he would have been in his car, and this time of the evening was a little early for cruising. The guy thanked me and headed down West George Street, and I climbed the stairs to my flat and let myself in. I decided not to put any of the lights on when I got into my flat, but in the dark of the hallway I suddenly felt wary and uneasy. I told myself I was just overtired and maybe everything that had gone on in recent days was coming back to bite me a little. That happened sometimes and I knew how to handle it. I walked softly into each room, listening out, but there was no sound. Then I went into the living room, kept the lights off, and stood well back from the window, but in a place where I could have a broad view of the square. I saw the man walking briskly towards my building and I stepped back behind the drapes. He slowed down when he got to outside my flat, and stopped with his back to me. He then looked at his watch and stood around for a few moments, taking out his mobile phone. Still he didn't look round. Then he put his phone back into his pocket and walked away. Nothing had happened, so why was I freaking a bit? I knew why, but it didn't stop me from feeling uneasy. I felt as though I was hiding in my own home. I went into the kitchen at the back of the flat, stuck on the lights and the television. I was a little paranoid, but with good reason after Thurso. If the heavies were still after the missing cocaine they might have come all the way down here.

Later, I was putting off going to bed because I knew I wouldn't sleep, and I found myself wandering around my flat in the quietness, just the low murmur of the television on in the kitchen. I rarely did this, ramble around from room to room, because mostly I was busy preparing to go out or had just come home from working. Down-time isn't really my thing – especially here where every room sparks images of my whole life. Coming back on the plane from Sweden had brought a raft of memories from years ago when I was a student returning for the first time to the flat where I'd lived with my parents until I was twelve. Some things stayed the same, almost like a shrine to my past life. In my parents' bedroom, my mother's paintings hung on the wall, and my father's books and music were in the piano stool in the corner. Of course, over the years I'd changed some things – painted the walls, renewed some of the furniture – and when Lucas arrived, so much had been transformed. But on nights like tonight I could almost hear the laughter of my parents as they would remain at the dinner table drinking wine long after I had gone to watch television or read a book. It was such a safe, happy, constant existence. Yet so much had happened since. I pushed open the door of Lucas's bedroom and looked around at his bed, still with the pile of soft toys laid out, the handprint paintings on the wall, the little shoes he would never again wear in a row below the big sash window. I sat on the white rocking chair where I used to sit some nights and read to him until he fell asleep on my chest. Who was reading to my son now? I wondered, and the thought made my throat ache. Was he getting bathed and fed some toast and milk before bed? What did he think about in whatever new home he'd found himself in? They say children his age have no long-term memory or real sense of time, but I cannot allow myself to believe that, because if that was true then Lucas would not remember any of this, would not remember me. I lay back and closed my eyes, as my thoughts drifted back to Cleveland, to my motel, to the girl called Lena with the black lonely eyes who promised she would help me find my boy.

*

Dan Harris had taken a call from Lena the morning after we had been to the shithole in East Cleveland. She had some information, she told him, and she wanted to meet. Dan told me he was wary, because she'd seen him throwing money around and could just be making sure some more of it went her way. People in that kind of jungle, he said, knew who they could play, and he'd seen the way Lena had looked at me, and she might have decided she had caught a big fish. I should have been more wary, but all rationale had gone out of the window for me the moment she'd shown me the picture of Lucas. Lena didn't have to do that. I didn't want to say I trusted her, because that would have sounded naive, but I told him I wanted to meet her, and since Dan was working for me, he had no choice.

We met her in a diner next to a petrol station at the edge of downtown Cleveland, the kind of place where it seems you're out of step if you can't eat six stacked pancakes for breakfast. The clientele looked to be truckers hunched over food at the bar, or old men in check flannel shirts and baseball caps and a few couples sat at tables by the window whiling away their day. Lena had cleaned up and looked fresh, her hair was shiny and washed and she wore a clean sky-blue sweatshirt hoodie over tight faded blue jeans and new trainers. She was at a table close to the toilets, away from the other diners. She looked up when Harris and I walked in and shifted in her seat as we approached her table.

'How you doin', Lena?' Harris said, looking down at her. 'Thanks for getting in touch.'

He would know he had to hide his scepticism in front of her. I managed a thin smile to her as I sat down.

'Thanks for calling.' I scanned her face, her eyes dark and deep, looking for signs that she was high. She didn't seem to be, so whatever she was on, she looked as sober as us.

The middle-aged waitress came up, took the pen out from behind her ear and stood poised for a big order. She looked crestfallen when we only ordered coffee.

'What, no breakfast? Not even pancakes?'

Even in the midst of all the stress and darkness it was a surreal moment that almost made me smile as I raised my eyebrows at Harris. He looked at me and then at Lena. Pancakes were compulsory.

'You wanna eat something, guys?' Harris said.

Lena glanced at me, and then at the waitress who was standing, legs apart, as though if we didn't order breakfast we might not get out of there alive.

'Yeah,' I said, 'I'll have some scrambled eggs and pancakes. Might be a long day.'

Harris looked up at the waitress.

'Make that for three,' he said, shrugging as though he had no choice.

'Coming right up,' the waitress said. 'You won't regret it, I promise.'

Even Lena smiled for the first time, and I saw how young she was and that whatever her story was, there was another one underneath that haunted face we'd seen last night.

After the waitress had gone, we sat for a moment and I wondered who was going to start first.

'So, what you got, Lena?' Harris said, matter-of-fact.

She shot me a glance, sipped from a glass of water and placed it down.

'I got another phone number for Williams,' she said.

'You have?' Harris said. 'Good. You called him?'

She nodded. 'Yeah. I had to call him, because he said he was going to New York and I had a contact for him that he had to see.'

'What d'you mean?'

'It's a dude I know up there. I lived there for a while.'

'What kind of dude?'

'One that will make sure he's all right, you know, with the kid an' all?' The inflection in her voice went up a little, as though it was a question.

I watched her, picturing Lucas being dragged from pillar to post.

'Lena, what dude though? Not someone like the dude we just met last night in that shithole?'

She took a moment to answer. 'No. He's no drug man. He ain't no dealer either. Okay, he's a crook, small time, but he has a good heart. And he don't live in no shithole either. He's got family, two little kids, so that boy, your boy, will be all right there. To be honest, I don't think it's good that Williams be digging around all over New York with a kid in tow. You know what I mean?'

I nodded.

'And do you think Williams will contact your man?'

'Who knows? I can't say. But all I can do is give you Williams's number and the phone of my friend up there. I called him and told him the background, and he said if Williams comes to him, he'll take care of the kid no problem, and he'll look after him good too.'

It was far from reassuring, but right now it was all we had to cling to, and I was so grateful. But Harris's face looked less than convinced.

'So, when you talked to Williams, was he already in New York?'

'He was on the train, I could hear it.'

'What train?'

'I dunno. The Amtrak, I guess. Has to be. They got four or five of them a day that goes to New York.'

'Last night? Today?'

'This morning that was. Early. Around seven, I'd say. Took me all evening to get his number.' She paused and looked at me. 'But look now, I'm pretty sure that was a burner phone Williams has, so he might ditch that very soon. I know what he's like. If he makes some deal with someone up there then he won't want no trace of it, so he'll likely throw that burner in the bin. You understand?'

Harris nodded slowly. I was still locked in the image of Lucas on the train, wondering what he was wearing, what he'd eaten, what bed he'd been lifted out of so early in the morning to catch a train to some distant place so far from home.

'Okay, Lena, that's helpful. But could you do this one thing for us?' I asked, more in hope than anything else.

'Sure. If I can.'

'Can you make a call to Williams again on that number, you know, like have some excuse to phone him and talk to him again? Just, well, just so I can hear his voice? Maybe get him in conversation for a little bit, maybe even ask if the kid is okay?'

She pushed out a breath.

'Yeah, I can do that. But I have to be very careful. I mean Williams is no idiot. If I call him too much without a reason he might wonder what is going on, know what I'm saying?'

We both nodded.

'Maybe you could say something about your friend, and that you touched base with him and he said any time Williams wants to drop the kid there then he will babysit him. And he doesn't want to be paid.'

She made a face that seemed to agree.

'That might work. Williams won't want to pay for no babysitter.'

CHAPTER TWENTY

I met Scanlon in the Naked Soup, a little café off Great Western Road that had turned soup-making into an art form. They also served particularly great coffee, and it was close to Scanlon's flat in Kelvinbridge. He'd bought his flat there long before it became a chic place to live with diverse communities – Asian, Afro-Caribbean and a hotchpotch of nationalities, some who'd come here a generation ago, others who'd come as refugees and made their homes in Glasgow. It was cold, but the sun had come out and even at this time of the year you could almost feel that spring was not a million miles away. There was warmth in the sun and we sat at a table outside with the patio heater on, wrapped up, determined that winter wouldn't beat us inside.

Scanlon had just gone for a run out past Gartnavel General Hospital and was showered and fresh. His eyes looked a clear blue colour in the sunshine, making me acutely conscious of my own red eyes, which were baggy and tired-looking.

I hung my bag over the back of a seat and sat down.

'You look like you've stepped out of some health spa promotion. Makes me feel like chopped liver.'

He lifted himself out of his chair and leaned over, hugging me.

'You always look great to me, Carlson, you know that.' He kissed me on the cheek, then pulled back, scanning my face. 'Sure, you could do with a night's sleep or two.' He grinned, knowing I wouldn't mind the dig.

I sighed. 'You bet I could,' I said, rubbing my face, conscious of the bruise at the side of my cheek. I saw him noticing it, but he said nothing.

The waitress came out and we ordered lentil and ham soup and two coffees, declining her offer to sit indoors if we were cold. I'd decided that I could handle a full conversation with Scanlon about what happened in Cleveland and hoped I could trust myself to get the story out without choking on my tears. I thought the best way to introduce it was just to show him the photograph on my mobile and take it from there. After the waitress left, I took out my mobile, brought up the picture and pushed the phone across the table. He enlarged the photo, and I watched as his expression changed from one of shocked surprise to real compassion because he knew what the photo would mean to me. He looked from the screen to me.

'Jesus, Carlson! You saw him? You actually saw Lucas?'

'Not in the flesh. Only the photo. But it's him. It's really him.'

'I see that. Christ, it must have been some moment. Look at the wee guy though.' He looked at me, then at the phone again. 'He's got bigger.'

'Of course.' I nodded. 'That's what gets me so much, Danny. That he's growing and I'm not there.' I chewed on my lip.

He handed me the phone back and squeezed my arm.

'Yeah, but it's a breakthrough. A real breakthrough. You're getting closer.'

I told him everything that had happened in Cleveland and he listened intently, shaking his head, puffing at some of it, but, in his usual upbeat way, he said I should be more reassured than ever.

The waitress appeared at my side and set down the cartons of soup and plastic spoons along with some home-made brown bread. Scanlon spread some butter on a couple of chunks and handed one to me.

'C'mon, eat up, before we freeze to death.' He smiled.

While we ate, I filled him in on the meeting with DCI Wilson and Fowler, and mentioned that McCartney was there. I noticed how he tried to look unfazed by that, but he couldn't fool me. I knew it niggled him that McCartney had a bit of history with me. Whether it was jealousy or just that he cared for me, I knew it rankled with him. I didn't tell him that McCartney had called me this morning to see if we could meet for a drink or a meal later. I'd put him off because I had an inkling where that might lead, and it was the last thing on my mind at the moment.

*

On my way back to the office, Millie called to say that the client who wanted me to spy on his wife had phoned back asking for a meeting later this afternoon. He'd asked whether it would be possible to meet him in his flat across the river next to the Clyde Arc – the modern bridge over the river, known locally as the 'Squinty Bridge' because it doesn't go straight across the River Clyde, but diagonally. The flats were just one of a host of luxury homes that had sprung up in recent years, starting with the Anderston Quay flats by the riverside and stretching across the water to Kinning Park. They were all modern, chic, with bright balconies overlooking the Clyde – a world away from the derelict land it had been. And on any given evening, with the bright spotlights of green, red and blue reflecting on the water and the span of the bridge, it was hard to believe this was Glasgow. I told Millie to call him back and tell him I'd be there at four. Just then my mobile rang and it was Fowler.

'How did you get on with Glasgow's finest detectives?' I asked, only half joking. 'Charming, aren't they?'

I heard him chortle.

'Aye, they're pretty much as I remember your typical Glasgow cops any time my work in the more genial Highlands brought me down here.'

I laughed. 'Yep. They're not a barrel of laughs, but they're pretty sharp.'

'Agreed. All of that. And I didn't come here to be doing the hokey-cokey anyway.'

I felt my face smiling at his banter and wondered what he must have been like as a cop who didn't like the whiff of corruption coming from his bosses in the north.

'I take it they were glad to get all the information you were able to provide them with.'

'They sure were. I gave them everything I have, as well as some documentation on the money-laundering. Looks like they're going to set up an operation. I'm not sure whether I'll have a role in that, but I'm just glad to help.'

'They'd be stupid not to include you in some way.'

'Well, I'm not a cop now, Billie, so I don't expect they'll be briefing me every day. But we're meeting in the morning to go out and have a recce at that place where I'm told the drugs are brought into after they leave Caithness.'

'Great. They must love you for that.'

He was quiet for a few moments and I wondered if he was phoning just for a chat or had something else to say. Then he said, 'Oh, and I filled them in on the background of those two bastards who might be the ones who raped the young Swedish student. Your man Wilson told me that forensics were working on the clothing and DNA, so that's a start. But it's no use unless we get DNA from them.'

I thought about this, and how virtually impossible it would be to get their DNA without being detected. There was no way I could go back up there and risk meeting them.

'Anyway,' he said, 'you fancy having a coffee and I'll tell you what I plan to do about that?'

'Sure. You mean now? How long are you here for?'

'I don't know. Until things die down up the road. Or maybe as long as these guys need me.'

I checked the clock on my dashboard, and I had an hour to kill before I went to see the client down by the river.

'Okay. I'll meet you in the café at the end of Lancefield Quay. It's a budget hotel but has a terrace outside on the edge of the river.'

I recognised Fowler's old Land Rover Discovery in the car park as I drove in and parked next to him. He was sitting in the hotel conservatory, his dog at his feet. The dog got up and trotted towards me.

'She likes you,' he said, a smile on his leathery face. 'It's not everyone she'll go to.'

I ruffled the dog's head and sat down, and as the waitress came up I ordered a green tea. Fowler ordered sparkling mineral water.

'I've a client to see across the water from here,' I said. 'In the next hour.'

'Do you not see people in your office?'

'Yes. All the time. But now and again people ask to see me either at home or in a meeting place.'

'You okay with that?' he asked, seeming surprised. 'Maybe it's just my suspicious cop brain, but in your line of business you must have pissed off a few people over the years. I'd be careful about venturing into a place on my own.'

'I've done it loads of times,' I said.

But now that Fowler had raised the spectre, I was thinking he was right. Especially after my battle with the thugs in Thurso.

'Cheers for that, Dave. You've made me nervous now!' I laughed, but it was the truth.

'Sorry, Billie. But I'm serious.' He stopped, putting a hand up. 'Look, it's none of my business and you've managed all these years without my advice, but you know what? This crap from the other day with these bastards up the road. That was dangerous. They were trying to kill you, and they would have if you'd not fought like a tiger.'

'I know.'

'Just a thought,' he said. 'Is it not a bit strange that you get a call to meet someone away from the office after what happened? Maybe I'm giving too much credit for those hoodlums up there to be able to have joined-up thinking, but I'd be really careful.' He paused as the waitress set down the drinks. 'Not that it's any of my business, but what kind of client is it? I mean, you don't have to tell me.'

'No problem,' I said. 'I don't mind telling you. And I'm grateful for your concern, Dave, really, I am. The client is some guy who wants me to spy on his wife who he thinks is cheating. That's fairly routine for me. So this is the first meet, to just hear his story and see where I go.'

'And he couldn't come to your office?'

I shrugged. 'So he said.'

I was already thinking Fowler might be right and was

toying with the idea of phoning Millie and asking the client to come to the office. I should be vigilant – especially after that guy lurking across from my flat last night.

'Funny you should be thinking that way,' I added. 'I've been a bit like that myself today.' I told him about the guy last night. 'To be honest I was a bit freaked about it. I put it down to tiredness, you know, with my trip to Sweden and all and after my ordeal in Thurso. But I'd almost forgotten about it until you made me a bit suspicious just now.'

'Sorry. But I'm a bit obsessed these days, and even more so now, hence the reason I got out of town fast after what happened to you. I might be wrong, but you should be careful . . .' He paused a moment, broke off a piece of biscuit and passed it to the dog who was staring at him. 'Tell you what, if you want, I can come along with you. I'm not trying to muscle in on your way of doing things, but if you feel it would make you more at ease, I can come.'

'Protection?' I said, narrowing my eyes. 'Do you think I need protecting, Dave?'

'No, no,' he said quickly. 'You're more than capable of looking after yourself. But you know, I'm here, I'm at a bit of a loose end, so if you want a bit of backup, I'd be happy to be there.'

I looked at him for a long moment, and I could feel there was a genuine concern from him. He wasn't the big kind of blustery guy he'd seemed when he'd walked into the hotel bar up in Thurso, especially after he'd opened up about the relationship and the loss of the boy he now knew was his son. I wondered how much that had changed him as a man, as I had no idea what he'd been like before that. I found myself warming to him.

'Okay,' I said finally. 'Maybe you're right. It might be a good idea to have a bit of backup, but the guy's probably just some jilted husband mortified that his wife is betraying him.'

'Better safe,' he said.

CHAPTER TWENTY-ONE

Less than an hour later, we were on our way across the bridge as the darkness began to fall and there was the usual steady build-up of traffic going from one side of the city towards the other, or leaving town. I checked the address from the note Millie had given me and directed Fowler to the block of flats. It was a big, newish, pale-fronted building, four storeys tall. There were a few cars in the car park but it was fairly empty. I knew from experience that a lot of flats along this area were money-laundering operations, all bought as a means for drug dealers to move money around without raising suspicion. We pulled up outside the double-doored entrance and I turned to Fowler.

'You want to wait here or what?'

He looked at me, then at the building.

'Up to you,' he said. 'If you want, I'll stay here, but if you go into the flat and something dodgy is waiting for you, then I won't be able to help from here.'

I thought for a moment. 'Okay. I usually interview a

client on my own, and there isn't any way I can explain your presence, so how about you come in with me, and wait maybe a floor below or something?'

He nodded. 'Sure, sounds good.' He took out his mobile, then glanced at me. 'So, if something funny is going on, or you are the least bit uncomfortable, then push my number and let it ring twice.'

I looked at him, grimacing.

'And you'll what,' I said, 'burst in the door, all guns blazing?'

He smiled, but not with his eyes.

'Aye, something like that.'

I puffed out a nervous breath. He touched my arm.

'It'll be fine, Billie.' He shrugged. 'Sorry, maybe I'm just being overcautious.'

'I hope so,' I said.

I opened the door and got out of the car, and Fowler climbed out of his side, telling the dog to sit tight, and she curled up and lay down, gazing up at him adoringly.

'It's on the fourth floor,' I said as I pushed the secured entry button.

A voice answered, but it sounded muffled.

'Mr O'Shea. It's Billie Carlson,' I said.

There was no answer but the door buzzed and I pushed it open. I glanced at Fowler and we went inside. I could see him scanning the foyer.

'No security cameras inside, and I didn't see any outside. That's a bit strange in a building like this,' he said.

'Maybe they're there and you just didn't notice.'

I went across to the lift, pushed a button and the doors opened.

'I'll take the stairs,' he said. 'What's the flat number?'

'Three, on the fourth floor,' I said.

'Good luck,' he said as the lift doors closed.

I waited a long moment to give him a chance to get to the third floor, then pushed the button for the fourth floor. I could feel my heart beating a little faster and wondered if it was because Fowler had put the frighteners on me, or if it was because I hadn't been faced with anything that might be threatening since the attack a few days ago. I told myself it would be fine, that it was just routine, and that I'd be out of here in half an hour tops, with a new client and another sorry mission that would no doubt end in misery for him.

The lift doors opened and I stepped out into the dark grey carpeted, silent hallway and scanned the doors to see which way the numbers went. Number three was at the far side, and as I walked the few steps towards it, I listened hard to see if there was any sign of life or activity behind any of the doors. There wasn't, but then most people who have a plush gaff overlooking the river would be out working to pay for the mortgage. I got to the navy-blue door with the brass number three on it, and assumed whoever was inside was already eyeing me through the spyhole. I gave the door three loud knocks. I waited, a little anxious, then heard the security chain being slid across. The door opened a few inches and I came face to face with my new client. He had hair that was too black not to have been dyed, and a bizarre droopy jet-black moustache that had been clipped and manicured to hang down each side of his mouth in a point, like one of the Village People. His pasty, pockmarked complexion had deep-set lines and he looked at me with the blackest eyes I've ever seen.

'Billie Carlson,' he said. Only the lips in his concrete face pulled back a little.

'Yes, Mr O'Shea?' I answered, still transfixed by his face.

He closed the door, and I heard the chain being freed, then the main lock being turned. The door opened, and he stepped back.

'Come in,' he said, as he opened the door wide.

'Thanks,' I said.

I stepped over the threshold into the small entrance hall and my attention was immediately caught by the big ceremonial sword hanging on the wall, its blade glinting against the ceiling light. I was still gaping at it, alarm bells raging through me, when he suddenly reached up over me to the door and pulled three solid bolts and the security chain across. The chill ran from my chest to my knees, and I found my fingers automatically wrapping around the mobile in my jacket pocket. Calm down, I told myself, then turned to him.

'What're you doing?' I asked, gesturing with my hand towards the door. 'What's with all the locks?' I hoped my voice didn't sound as freaked as I felt.

He drew his lips back slyly and he looked at me.

'Precaution,' he said.

I gave him my best flint-faced look.

'Precaution for what?'

'Burglars,' he said, flatly, his black eyes locking mine.

I glared at him.

'Well, I'd hope we can get through our chat without any burglars. So, I'd prefer you to take the locks off, if you don't mind.' I squared up to him, but I felt my face flush. 'I don't like being locked in.'

He stood for a moment, and his lips parted a little to reveal stained teeth.

'You afraid or something?'

'No,' I snapped, 'but this is not how I do business. So you've got two seconds to take the locks off, or you find yourself another investigator.'

I was shaking inside, but I cold-stared him for a good five beats until the lines at the corners of his eyes wrinkled a little and he let out a snort of disdain. Then he reached across me and pulled back the locks and turned the key in the main lock.

'Happy now?'

I was relieved, but far from happy, and I just wanted out of here pronto.

'The living room is this way,' he said.

He turned away from me and took a step down the hall. And as he did, I pushed the speed dial that I'd set for Fowler. I turned and reached for the handle of the door, but his hand was suddenly on top of mine, his strong hands crushing my fingers on the metal.

'Where you going?'

'The interview is over,' I said. 'Get your fucking hands off me.'

I tried to free my hand but his grip was like a vice. Then I felt his face close and his mouth pushed against my ear as he rasped with rancid breath, 'You're not as fucking smart as you think, Carlson. You've made some powerful people very angry. And I'm here to sort you out.'

He prised my fingers off the door handle and jerked me back, punching me hard on the cheek. His other arm drew tight around my neck so I could barely breathe. I kicked hard against his shin, but he didn't even flinch as he manoeuvred me into an armlock and dragged me down the hall. Then just as he lifted his boot to kick open the living room door, I heard a thud behind me. He stopped in his tracks, but as he was about to turn around, there was another thud and a mighty crack. His grip loosened a fraction and I turned my head enough to see the door had come off one of its hinges and teetered like a tooth hanging by a thread. It was Fowler. Then he was like a rampaging bull as he raged through the gap and thundered down the hall with a mighty roar. He dived, and all three of us fell on the floor in a heap. The impact slackened O'Shea's grip around my neck, and I swiftly wriggled free from under Fowler, who was now furiously punching his face. I scrambled to my feet and stood frozen as the pair of them wrestled in the hall, O'Shea pushing Fowler hard, grabbing him by the hair and thumping his head against the wall. For a couple of seconds, Fowler looked dazed, and before he could recover, O'Shea pulled out a knife and plunged it into his shoulder. It was happening so fast, I didn't know what to do. Fowler was struggling to his feet while O'Shea continued to lash out, stabbing his arms. I was about to punch in 999 on my mobile when suddenly O'Shea was on his feet and coming towards me. I backed out and stumbled through the doorway. He tried to grab hold of my hair, but I was too fast for him, and I staggered into the hall.

'The stairs!' Fowler bellowed. 'Don't use the lift.'

I glanced around quickly and spotted the emergency exit, pushing it open, but O'Shea was suddenly on me. He grabbed me and threw me against the railing at the top of the stairs. But Fowler stormed through the door and threw himself against O'Shea. I slipped from his grasp as Fowler punched him, but O'Shea lashed out with the knife, catching him on the cheek. Then Fowler grabbed him and wrapped his arms around him and the pair of them wrestled and pushed each other against the railings like a couple of feuding bears. And then it happened, almost in slow motion. I stood, my jaw dropping, as they rolled onto the railing, O'Shea trying to heave Fowler off his feet and over the edge, the knife pushed close to his throat. But from somewhere, Fowler found the strength for one last push and he reared up, forcing O'Shea onto the handrail.

And as he lashed with the knife, catching Fowler below his ear, the big man, his eyes blazing, his face a bloodied mess, managed to lift O'Shea's body off the ground. I stood in disbelief, as O'Shea went over, his body bouncing off the railings in dull thuds, all the way down until his skull cracked open on the stone floor. Fowler stood, his chest heaving, his hands covered in blood as he touched his neck and face.

'Fuck me!' he said.

I phoned 999.

'My name is Billie Carlson. There's ... There's ... I've been attacked. I'm on the fourth floor in a block of flats at Mavisbank Gardens on the river at Kinning Park. There's a man over the railings. We need an ambulance.'

I didn't want to say any more. I hung up and turned to Fowler as he sat down heavily on the top stair.

'Jesus Christ!' I said, sitting beside him, suddenly feeling a surge of emotion catching my throat. 'You saved my life, Dave.'

He didn't answer, but sat staring straight ahead, blood running down his cheek and dripping off his chin. Then he turned to me.

'That was close, Billie. Closer than I ever want to be.'

He sat with his elbows on his knees, and I reached across and put my hand on his bloodied hand, and we sat that way for a long time until the screaming of police and ambulance sirens got closer and closer.

We didn't say anything as we heard the main door of the

flats buzz open and the sound of police and ambulance radios fill the air and echo up to the fourth floor. We heard someone say, 'Oh fuck', as they stood over the body with a pool of crimson on the pale grey tiles. Eventually someone called out.

'Hello?'

'Up here!' I said, standing up to see police and paramedics taking the stairs two at a time.

It was around twenty minutes later, as the paramedics treated Fowler on the spot with dressings and antiseptic on some of the minor cuts, stitching up a couple of the deeper puncture wounds, that I heard the distinctive voice of DCI Harry Wilson on the ground floor.

'Carlson!' he shouted. 'You up there?'

'Yeah.'

A few seconds later, the lift doors pinged and then the exit door opened. I stood up, a bit wobbly, as Wilson came onto the stairwell and looked from me to Fowler.

'What in the name of actual fuck, Carlson!'

I shrugged as Fowler glanced up at him but said nothing.

'Do you know who the stiff is on the floor?' Wilson asked.

I shook my head. 'No, but it was either him down there or me. And if it wasn't for Fowler, it would have been me.'

Wilson shook his head. 'Holy fucking Christ, Carlson! Every fucking time!'

CHAPTER TWENTY-TWO

I was still a little shaken by the ordeal as I sat in the office that DCI Wilson had commandeered up at the police HQ in Pitt Street. He'd instructed uniformed officers to take Fowler and me there rather than asking us to give our statements in the stairwell of the block of flats where the body was being bagged and removed by the mortuary crew. Wilson had made it clear to Fowler that, although there was no question of criminality over what he had done as it was self-defence, we would both need to provide detailed statements of what happened. No surprise there, and I was glad to get out of the building and away from the scene that I knew would weave its ugly way into my future sweaty nightmares. After we had separately given our statements, we sat drinking coffee and nibbling on biscuits with Wilson and DCI Mick Thomson from the National Crime Agency who was running the investigation into drugs and the Highlands. There was a gentle knock on the door and a young detective came in and handed

Thomson a piece of paper then backed out. We watched as the DCI ran his eyes over it, then he looked up, holding the paper so we could see the mugshot which looked like a younger version of the guy who'd tried to strangle me.

'Thomas Cranshaw. Known as Tucker,' he said. 'Manchester hoodlum – Salford. An enforcer for the Morton crew out of that particular shithole. Got out of Strangeways two years ago after an eight-year stretch for dropping some teenager off a bridge for trying to stiff the gang on a drug lift.' He glanced at us. 'So you got a break there all right. No loss to the world when an arsehole like that gets his ticket punched.' He sipped his tea and snorted, then looked at me. 'But it looks like he was on an ordered job to get you to keep your nose out of their affairs, Billie.'

I nodded, not surprised. Although it was less than a week since I'd bailed out of Thurso leaving one of my attackers for dead and the other lying in a field, the news would have travelled fast to whoever was running the drug-smuggling operation that I'd been trampling all over their turf. And that I'd stolen around two kilos of their cocaine.

'Do you think their plans will still go ahead after this? I mean the drugs, the rally?'

The DCI folded his arms. 'Yep, for sure. The cargo will already have been bought and paid for, stashed in whatever vehicle they are planning to bring it in on. Plans will be too far advanced for them to pull out. Big dealers will be waiting for this stuff across the country from here to London. So they'll not pull out now. Tucker might have been one of their best men, but they'll not shed any tears for his loss. Maybe they'll send a wreath to his funeral, but guys like him are just fodder. They'll move on.' He looked from me to Wilson. 'But you're on their radar now, Billie. Big time. So you'll need to watch your step. There are enough lowlife pricks in this city alone that would cut your throat for the price of a month's supply of free coke. Even though you don't have the coke any more, they won't know that. They'll be after you.' He paused, glanced at Wilson. 'By the way, forensics checked the coke you took from that lassie's flat. It's ninety per cent pure Colombian marching powder. Worth a fortune. Couple of million at least.'

Wilson sat forward and looked across at me.

'We'll get you some protection, Billie. It's not something I would routinely do but what's happened involves you in this drugs investigation.' He raised a finger. 'But you need to butt out now. This is not your case. So you need to stay away. Seriously.'

I glanced at Fowler, then at the DCI, then back at Wilson.

'I know it's not my case. I'm out of it. You're welcome to it. But the case I went to Thurso to look at – the death of the young Swedish student Astrid – that is very much still my case. And you know it has to be connected, right back to the chief cop in Thurso, even if that was never the intention from the start. I'm sure the hotelier's son is one of the men who raped Astrid. There's a cover-up and it looks like the cops are involved – maybe they're up to their eyes with the smugglers and looking the other way when the cars come in for the rally.'

'That's as may be,' Wilson said. 'But we'll deal with that.' He eyed the DCI who blinked in acknowledgement.

I could see that Astrid's death and how it came about was not their number one priority. But it was mine. And I wasn't going to let it go.

'Sure,' I said. 'But what about the DNA from Astrid's clothes? We need to track down who that belongs to – and you can be sure it will be the two bastards who tried to do me in on that field.'

I was bursting to tell him I had the rape video on my phone, but I wanted to hold it back as I didn't want Wilson passing it on to Thurso just yet because I didn't know who I could trust there.

Wilson nodded. 'You're probably right. Forensics will have the information in the next twenty-four hours. It's a question of getting hold of these two in Thurso. They might not even be there any more. They've probably got off their mark.'

'Or been bumped off,' Fowler chipped in. 'I've talked to a couple of people up there and they haven't been seen for days. But they could be in Inverness or somewhere, lying low for a bit.'

I folded my arms, defiant. 'They raped a young girl, and she's dead because of it. In my book that means they killed her. And I'm going to find them.'

There was a stony silence, and I could see Wilson take a

breath and push it out slowly through gritted teeth as he glanced at the DCI. They both knew there was nothing they could do to stop me. And Wilson especially knew that I would keep chasing until I got a result. Eventually, Thomson looked at me, spreading his hands in a fait accompli gesture.

'Look, Billie, I hear what you're saying, and it would be ideal if we could all plough in and enlist the help of the troops in the north. But from what you're saying there may be dodgy dealings up there, so there's no point in us getting involved. It's out of our jurisdiction anyway. We have no real power up there, and frankly, we don't know who is dodgy and who isn't. So—'

'I do,' Fowler interrupted. 'There are mostly good cops up there, but it's a question of treading very softly.' He looked at me. 'I'll make some discreet enquiries to see if I can pick up any intelligence on the whereabouts of these two geezers.'

'Aye,' Wilson said. 'Well, do it very quietly, for Christ's sake.' He glanced at me. 'You've used up about half of your nine lives, Carlson, in the last few weeks alone.'

I didn't answer, but shot him a look that he would know meant I wasn't backing away.

I left Pitt Street, where Fowler was going to be spending the next while with Wilson and the drug team discussing the next move. I knew I wasn't wanted or needed there and was glad to get out of the place. Fowler gave me a nod as I left and I got the feeling that he would find a way to keep me in the loop. We were on the same page in terms of not throwing all our trust in with the cops. But for now, I was on my own, having refused a lift from the HQ to my flat. I stepped outside into the darkness of early evening, feeling the chill of an icy wind on my cheeks as I wandered up in the direction of my flat. It was nearly seven, and as I got to Blythswood Square I could see a couple of the street girls were already out working, hanging around in the doorways on the corners or walking slowly up from Waterloo Street, tight short skirts and bare legs that must have been chilled to the marrow. I saw one of the girls approach a kerb-crawling car, and after a few seconds of conversation through the lowered passenger window, she opened the door and got inside. I watched as the car drove off through the lights and headed off, no doubt for somewhere dark and deserted where this young girl would put her life in the hands of a complete stranger who may be just another saddo, or a total psychopath. She would know soon enough. It was a shitty way to live your life and no matter how many times I witnessed a scene like that it never ceased to depress me. As I climbed the steps to the entrance of my flat, I could hear the angry shouts of a man on the corner, and the sobbing of a girl. I knew it would probably be some lowlife pimp making demands on one of the girls. I'd seen and heard it all before and I knew not to get involved. I put the key in my door, and again came the screams of a girl. I pulled my key back out again. The shouting and sobbing got closer and suddenly on the corner the girl emerged screaming as a man dragged her by the hair.

'You'll fucking stand there until you get enough. You got that, bitch?' The skinny man forced her backwards and roughly propped her up against the metal railing.

'Aye! Aye! Stop it! You're hurting me!' She stood, her skinny legs tottering on high heels.

He tightened his grip on her hair and she winced in pain. Before I could stop myself, before I could tell myself to leave it and that I couldn't make a difference, I was down the stairs and marching towards them. I held my mobile in the air as though I was filming.

'You've got two seconds to let her go before the cops are all over you,' I called out as I approached.

I faced down the guy who looked like he was in his mid-twenties, with razor cheekbones black with grubby stubble and filthy jeans hanging on him. He was wide-eyed and clearly desperate for the next fix this girl was going to provide for him.

'Who the fuck are you?' he spat at me, easing his grasp.

'I'll be your worst nightmare if you don't get off your mark right now,' I said.

He glanced at the girl, eyes blazing as she sniffed, then he backed off.

'Cunt!' He spat on the ground, then turned and ran down the street.

The girl looked at me, sniffing, wiping blood from her

nose. I fished out a tissue from my pocket and handed it to her.

'You okay?' I said, knowing it had been a long time since she'd been okay.

'Aye.' She dabbed her nose. 'Thanks. He's a bastard him. He's fucking desperate for a hit and says I'm no' working hard enough. I've done two punters in the last hour. Bastard.'

'Is he your boyfriend?' I asked.

'Naw. Not any more. He's getting worse. We used to be together, but now it's just for the work. Know what I mean?'

I nodded slowly. 'Yes,' I said. 'You work and he uses.'

'We both use. He shoplifts sometimes too.' She looked at me, then into the middle distance and her face crumpled as she bit back tears.

I stood for a moment looking at her, the scruffy shoes, the thin bomber jacket and short skirt, her legs like sticks. A few years ago, I might have taken her somewhere, bought her a cup of tea, maybe even given her some money. But it was pointless. You couldn't stop what was going on, and even if you made it better for one day or one night, she'd be back on the streets tomorrow. There was nothing I could do here and already I could see another girl from across the street glancing over, wondering if some soft touch had stopped in the street and was handing out money. Tomorrow it could be that girl who was the victim of a tragic, ugly scene like this.

'You should go to the drop-in centre,' I said. 'Talk to someone. Get off the streets for the night. See if you can get help.'

She nodded, swallowed. 'Aye. I will. I need to. I cannae do this any more.'

I stepped back and turned to go, because this was not my fight, my business, or my crusade. I turned away.

'Thanks,' she said, behind my shoulder.

I didn't answer and walked towards my flat. By the time I turned around she was gone.

Inside my flat I switched on the television for the news and the noise and went into the kitchen to take something out of the fridge to eat. I had no appetite. The delayed shock of the last few hours was beginning to creep up on me and I knew it would overwhelm me if I didn't keep myself busy. I was exhausted, but knew it would take some winding down before I could be in a place where sleep would come, if it came at all tonight. I wanted to talk to Scanlon and offload everything from earlier, because I knew he would understand, but I wasn't ready. I knew I had to be alone to get my head around the trauma of that flat across the river. I wandered around my home, closing the curtains to shut out the world, switching on lights, trying to lift the gloom that seemed to be greater in here on days like this when I was struggling. I went down the hall and opened the door to Lucas's room and stepped inside. I gazed around at the remnants of my life, opening drawers and doors of the wardrobe, looking at clothes, picturing the moments when he wore them – I could still remember where we were on those very days. I sat on the bed, my hand gently smoothing across the duvet, and picked up the soft bunny rabbit with the floppy ears that had been one of his favourites, and I clutched it to my chest, for a moment almost feeling the presence of him, the smell of him, even though I knew it was hopeless to let myself drift like that. But suddenly I could feel myself surrendering to it. I lay on the bed, turned onto my side and curled my knees up to my chest, clasping the soft toy to my cheek. Then the tears came.

CHAPTER TWENTY-THREE

My dreams had been full of terror, of being strangled by a raging fiend who was dragging me towards a stairwell and trying to push me over the rail. I'd woken up thrashing and gasping for breath and sat bolt upright in bed. It had taken me a few seconds to realise I was safe and in my own flat. I could see daylight through a crack in the curtains and I sat back on the pillows, giving myself a moment to gather the strength mentally and physically to get out of bed. My body felt stiff and achy from the struggle yesterday and the swelling on my cheekbone was tender. I told myself it was nothing that a long hot shower couldn't fix, and swung my legs out of bed and stood up stiffly, padding naked to my bathroom. I tried not to dwell on how last night I'd finally succumbed to the sadness that most of the time I keep inside. My shrink had told me that these things would happen from time to time and sometimes I just had to go with it, ride it out, and not be afraid of letting myself give in to the emotion. I think she was right in that because, despite everything, I actually felt better for having a good cry last night. I knew I could put it to the side and get on with my day. As I was getting dressed, I wondered why my mobile hadn't rung this morning. I picked it up to see that it was out of battery. I must have let it run out when I became overwhelmed last night and dropped off into a sleep. I pushed the charger into the wall and saw the mobile light up. It pinged like a jackpot fruit machine with message after message, as I was towel drying my hair and pulling on a pair of jeans. There were three missed calls from Wilson and one from Fowler, plus two from Scanlon. I got dressed and listened to them in the kitchen as I was eating yoghurt and drinking coffee. Wilson's had said 'call me' with irritation in his last voice message. It was far too early to listen to any of his moaning, but I felt I had to. I scrolled down to his number and pushed the key. He answered after two rings.

'Fuck me, Carlson! I was about to get some people to batter your door down.'

'What?' I asked bewildered.

'I've been trying to phone you. Last night, and then early this morning. Do you not answer your bloody phone?'

'Oh, sorry. I'd dropped off to sleep and didn't know the battery was low. Busy day yesterday, as you know.'

There was a two-beat silence and I knew Wilson would be getting the sarcasm in my voice.

'Anyway, you all right?'

He said it as an afterthought because really what he

wanted to do was give me a bollocking, even though I wasn't one of his cops.

'Yes, what's the panic?'

'We got information late last night that the two bastards who attacked you are in Glasgow. Whether it's genuine or not we don't know. Your mate Fowler got it.'

'I see.'

'They'll be looking for you, Carlson. And you're not that hard to find.'

I didn't answer, as I was trying to process that the men were lurking somewhere in the city, waiting to pounce.

'So,' Wilson said, 'this isn't good. If they are in Glasgow they are looking for you.' He paused. 'Well, maybe they're here for other reasons too, with this drug stuff, but they're the ones who lost the cocaine so they'll have been told not to come back without it.'

'I don't have it, as you know.'

'I know that. But these halfwits don't.'

'So I'll need to watch my step.'

'You will. But I'm getting some protection for you. Someone will be on your tail day and night. I was thinking about McCartney.'

I didn't answer. Wilson would have heard the locker room tittle-tattle about McCartney and me, and I wondered if he'd suggested him as some kind of dig. I didn't want to ask him or be seen pursuing it as that would be admitting there was something between us, even though as far as I was concerned whatever had been going on between McCartney and me was over.

'You okay with that?' he said after a long silence.

'I don't need a minder twenty-four seven, Harry. Why don't you guys just do your job and I'll do mine. I'm not a cop any more. You don't have any jurisdiction over me. I do things my own way.'

I didn't want to get sucked into the protection racket with the police, because I knew it would restrict my movements. And I didn't want them poking around the way I do business as a private eye.

'Carlson, I get that. But if I didn't get some protection on to you after what's happened then I wouldn't be doing my job. So can you just for Christ's sake live with it? This drug-smuggling up north is big stuff and the NCA are grateful that you and Fowler have brought it to them. But why don't you just wise up and recognise you could be in danger? Don't be stupid.'

I waited a few seconds then answered.

'Fine. Look, Harry, if there's going to be any protection on me, then I'd rather it wasn't McCartney. Okay? And I'm not having anyone staying at my house. If someone is there, then they leave in the evening.'

Long silence.

'I thought you two knew each other,' he said, then quickly added, 'You know, through work and stuff. I thought you were friends.'

'Yeah, well. I'd just rather it wasn't McCartney. That's all.'

I hoped I didn't have to draw a picture for him.

'Okay. Leave it with me. What are your movements today?'

'I'm going to the office shortly. I'll probably be there most of the day. I've got a bit of catching up to do.'

'Right, I'll be in touch.'

'By the way, when will I get the DNA on the samples of Astrid's clothing?'

'Later today,' he said, and hung up.

Millie looked up from her screen when I walked into the office.

'Jeez, Billie. What the hell happened to you?'

I took off my coat and hung it on the stand, then went to the coffee machine as I talked.

'You know that client who wanted me to meet him in his home?'

She rolled her eyes in despair. 'Oh shit!' she said. 'He did this?'

'Worse than that.' I turned to her, pulling the neck of my sweater down to reveal the bruising on my neck.

'Christ! Did you get the police?'

I lifted up a mug and gestured towards her and she nodded. I switched on the coffee machine.

'Eventually,' I said, 'but not before this psycho did a swan dive from the fourth-floor landing.'

'What!?'

'I'll tell you over coffee.'

She shook her head in disbelief. I knew Millie would never say I told you so, but she had always warned me against seeing clients in their homes, because you never know what kind of nutters are behind the door, she'd say. And she was right. The coffee machine pinged and I filled two mugs and handed one to her. Then I told her the story from start to finish, her jaw dropping when I described how Fowler burst in the door like some kind of superhero and rescued me.

'So, it was a trap,' she said, her mouth tightening. 'You know what, I should just have told him that you don't meet clients outside of the office.' She paused. 'I feel responsible.'

'Don't be daft, Millie. It was my decision. I should have been smarter, especially after what happened in Thurso.' I sipped some coffee and sat back. 'Harry Wilson, you know the big DCI who used to be my boss?'

She nodded. 'Yeah, I've heard you talking about him.'

'Well, he says he's got me some protection detail until this drug investigation is over. He phoned me this morning to tell me that the guys from Thurso who attacked me are now in Glasgow.' I raised my eyebrows. 'Looking for me, apparently.'

'Christ!'

Just then, the office door opened a little. To our surprise, Scanlon stood in the doorway, a broad smile across his face.

'Scanlon!' I said. 'It's you.'

He grinned. 'Were you expecting Jack the Ripper?' Then he turned to me. 'Shit, what happened to your face?'

'What're you doing here?' I asked, bewildered, my finger touching the swollen cheekbone.

He walked in and stood, arms folded.

'I'm your security, Ms Carlson.'

Millie smiled at him. 'You are a sight for sore eyes, that's for sure.'

'But what happened to you, Billie?'

'Long story,' I said. 'How come you've been assigned, Scanlon?' Then I added quickly, 'I'm glad it's you though – even though I don't need babysitting.'

'Wilson,' he said. 'He called me up to his office this morning and told me I would be part of the protection for you. There's uniform on it too. They're downstairs in a car at your door. They'll be there all day. And around the square through the night, keeping an eye on your flat.'

The stubborn streak in me was irritated that Wilson was making decisions on my life, that I'd proved time and again that I could look after myself. But deep down I had to admit that it made sense. But more than anything I was surprised by the jab of elation that it was Scanlon who'd been assigned to protect me. I felt my face smiling as I stood up.

'I hope you don't think you're going to be bossing me around,' I joked.

He put his hands up in surrender. 'I wouldn't dream of it.'

'So, what happens now?' I asked. 'You going to be sitting here all day while I work? You'll be bored out your skull.'

'No,' he said. 'I'll be downstairs with the boys. But if you're going out, then I go with you. Wilson said that the thugs who are supposed to be down here from the Highlands looking for you will know that you have an office in here. So, if they come calling we'll be ready.'

'These guys are knuckle-trailers, Danny. But I'm sure they're not so thick that they think they can harm me in my office in the middle of a big city.'

He shrugged. 'Well. We'll be ready if they do.' He glanced at Millie then at my computer. 'You expecting any clients in today?'

I looked at Millie, who squinted at the pad on her desk.

'Nope. Not so far. Everything is by appointment. So anybody coming here has to get past me first.' She gave a wry smile.

'I wouldn't fancy their chances,' Scanlon chuckled, then turned to me. 'Anyway, I'll be downstairs if you need me. Give me a text if you're coming down and you want to go anywhere, Billie. Or if you need anything brought up – a sandwich or stuff.' He turned to go.

'Sure,' I said, not really knowing what else to say.

When he left, Millie looked at me with a twinkle in her eye.

'I like that boy,' she said. 'A bodyguard. It's like being in a film.'

I laughed and shook my head, then went back to my screen to check through my emails, hoping, as I did every day, to see one from Harris, with news of Lucas.

CHAPTER TWENTY-FOUR

As I drove into my parking space outside my flat, I could see the police car sitting at the other side of the square. It pulled out and drove across, the uniformed officers giving Scanlon a mock salute as they drove past us.

'The girls will not be happy to have the cops cruising around here all night. Punters will steer clear.'

I switched the engine off and opened my door, and Scanlon got out of the passenger seat.

'They'll just go further down the road a bit,' he said. He opened the rear door and picked up a small rucksack, glancing at me as he did. 'It's just a couple of things I need for the next day or so.'

'You're not staying,' I said. 'I told Wilson any security had to be out by evening.'

I could have bitten my tongue when I saw the look on Scanlon's face.

'I know I'm not staying,' he said, 'I just want to change my clothes later.'

'Oh,' I said, feeling very stupid.

As we climbed the stairs to the front door, Scanlon's mobile rang and he answered it and listened for a few seconds as I opened the door and we stepped inside.

'So it's been quiet all day then?' Scanlon said into the phone. 'Nobody hanging around anywhere in the square?'

As he listened, I went into the living room and switched on the television then the lights, feeling a little self-conscious that Scanlon was in my flat and would be on and off for the coming days. Just relax and enjoy the company, I told myself. Your best mate has your back and that's all that matters. Scanlon strolled into the living room, hands in his jeans pockets, and looked around.

'I'll go check the rest of flat if that's okay, make sure everything is fine,' he said.

'I'll come with you.'

We walked along the hall, switching on lights as we went, into the bathroom, then my bedroom and the spare bedroom, but not Lucas's room. He turned to me as we came into the hall.

'I was thinking, it might not be a good idea to go out to eat. Wilson would kick my ass if he thought I was taking you out on the town. How about we order some food in?'

'Sure. We can watch a movie.'

'Great. And you can tell me all about your trip to Sweden. I've hardly seen you since you got back.'

'I know. It's been a bit frantic,' I said. 'The stuff yesterday in the flat with that psycho – Jesus! If it hadn't been for Fowler, I wouldn't be here.'

'He's no slouch, that guy, according to Wilson. I hope I get to meet him.'

I went to the fridge and handed him a beer and took one for myself. We clinked bottles.

'He's a good man,' I said. 'He's giving Wilson and the troops a lot of intelligence on what goes on up there. I hope they get properly on top of it and bust the lot of them when this rally brings in the drugs that are expected.' I paused. 'But that's up to them. I just want to make sure the beasts who put Astrid through that misery get their comeuppance. If they're down here, I'm going to get them.'

Scanlon nearly spluttered out his beer.

'Hold on, Carlson! It's them who are looking for you. It's not supposed to be the other way about.'

I took a swig from the bottle.

'How are we going to get DNA samples from them if we don't find them?'

Scanlon sipped from the bottle and shook his head frustrated.

'Don't start all that shit, Carlson. I'm supposed to be protecting you. We're not on the hunt.'

I smiled, but he knew I was serious.

'Is it okay if I go for a shower?' he said. 'Get changed?'

'Course,' I said. 'You want to eat Indian or Italian?'

'Indian would be good. You?'

'Yep. Let's do it. What do you want?'

'Anything, surprise me,' he said. He placed the bottle on the worktop and headed out of the kitchen.

I called the local Indian takeaway and ordered food then had a quick shower in my bedroom en suite bathroom, and quickly changed into a T-shirt and tracksuit bottoms. Then I set the table in the living room dining area, and stood back for a moment, thinking how pleasant it was to have Scanlon around like this. If it wasn't for the fact I was on some mobster's hit list, it could have been a lovely night in with some good company who cared about me. An image flashed back to me of the early days with my husband when everything seemed possible and full of promise, before he started drinking too much and staying out all night. The truth is, the relationship was dying and I should have seen it, long before my life and career hit the skids. But I'd been so wrapped up in my work. I shouldn't have allowed him to have the total control and free hand he had with Lucas.

Scanlon's footsteps on the wooden floor jerked me back and I turned to see him walking into the room, barefoot, his hair tousled and wet from the shower. I tried not to look at his buffed torso through the navy blue shirt he hadn't buttoned. There was a sudden, loud knock at the door, and we looked at each other, startled. Then the door rattled again.

'Don't open it,' Scanlon whispered. 'I'll go.'

He quickly went out to the hall and I was behind him. I picked up a heavy paperweight from the hall table and

Scanlon shot me a look. Again there was a heavy door knock.

'Who's there?' I said.

'It's me! Wilson!'

I looked at Scanlon and we both mouthed 'Wilson?' Scanlon fumbled, trying to button up his shirt as I slid open the bolts. I could see Wilson and McCartney on my doorstep and I glanced over my shoulder to Scanlon who was still struggling with some buttons.

I opened the door wide and Wilson stood looking at me, then at Scanlon. McCartney looked like he'd swallowed something deeply unpleasant. Wilson stepped into the hallway. He glanced at Scanlon, his face incredulous.

'What the fuck are you doing, Scanlon? You're not on your honeymoon, son.'

Scanlon looked flustered. 'I was just getting changed. You know. After finishing the day shift.'

'Aye, right, ' Wilson snorted. 'Your shift isn't finished yet. Keep fucking focused at all times.'

'Of course.'

'Come in,' I said, gesturing them to the living room. Then immediately regretted it when I remembered I'd just set the table.

They followed me inside, and I saw both of them clocking the table set for dinner, but Wilson said nothing.

'So has something happened?' I asked, curious as to why they were even here. 'I wasn't expecting a visit.'

'Aye,' Wilson said, glancing at the table, 'so I gather.'

I pushed out an exaggerated sigh that said 'enough of your crap, Wilson.'

'What's going on?' I asked. 'Has there been some development?'

'That's what we hear,' Wilson said. 'Your man Fowler has been on the blower up to sheep-shagging land, and apparently the two arseholes who did you over are working with the Murrell mob in the East End. Fat man Murrell has his dibs on a share of the coke that's coming in from the rally, and he's offered to make sure these two wankers deliver the stuff you took, or failing that, to deliver at least four of your fingers.'

I snorted. 'Just the four? That's all right then. I'll still have six left to eat my pakora.'

'It's fucking serious, Carlson.'

'Murrell is a total dick, Harry. You know that. He's an old man.'

'He is. But he's got some vicious bastards working with him and they will do anything for money. So, you need to understand that it's not just these two half-wits who are out looking for you. It's anybody's guess who Murrell has pulled in to get to you and get the cocaine back.'

'What about O'Shea?' I asked. 'I know he's dead, but who sent him to get me?'

'We don't know for sure, but I think you have to assume that it might be the Irishman. They'll have gathered from the newspapers that he's dead by now, but that doesn't mean they're not looking for you.'

I thought about it for a moment.

'So what am I supposed to do? Hide below the bed?'

'Well, you might need to be moved from here.'

I put my hands up. 'I'm not moving from here, Harry. No way. I've got a job to do, clients to see, and I'm not going to run away.' I turned to Scanlon. 'Scanlon's here, so I'm not on my own, and the uniform boys are outside. I'm well covered.'

'I'm not so sure.' He frowned frustrated. 'Look, it's your call. But you know how reckless you can be with stuff and you take too many risks. I want to move you, but if you don't want to go then I can't force you. But you need to be doubling down.'

'I'm fine.'

'And by the way,' Wilson said. 'Forensics came back to say there was semen on the girl's underwear from two different sources. That only shows that sex had taken place. We need a lot more than that to prove any kind of assault.'

'There's the video,' I said. 'When the time is right they'll get it.'

He let out a sigh. 'It's up to the northern boys, Billie, to find these guys. We can't get involved in that.'

I said nothing. He couldn't get involved. But I could.

Wilson turned to McCartney, who was eyeing Scanlon, his face like fizz, and glaring at me as though I was betraying him. The doorbell rang. Everyone froze.

'That'll be the takeaway,' I said, going towards the hall.

I looked through the spyhole and saw my local delivery

man carrying two bags of food. I opened the door, handed him some notes, and brought the food in. I stood in the hallway feeling a little stupid with my Indian takeaway, and three cops in my living room full of worry and protection.

'You want to stay for dinner?' I asked, holding the bags up. 'There's loads.'

Wilson gave me a sarcastic look.

'No, we're still working.' He turned to Scanlon. 'And so are you.'

'Of course.'

'So, the least sign of any problems, get on the blower and get some help. You got that? I mean, any problems at all.'

'Yes. I will.'

Wilson took a long look at him, then at me, and turned down the hallway.

'Watch yourselves.'

Once the door was closed, Scanlon looked at me and blew out his cheeks.

'Christ! Of all the people, of all the times, it had to be fucking Wilson!'

After we'd eaten, we sat at the table and I told Scanlon about my trip to Sweden and how poignant it had been after all these years. He listened, as he always did. Then I told him in more detail about the Ohio run and how it seemed Lucas had been taken to New York. I knew he sympathised whole-heartedly over Lucas, but I wondered if there would come a time when he would think that I had to stop this from defining my life, because the dark reality was never lost on me that maybe I would never see my son again. He would never say that, and if he thought it then he hid it well, because he had been with me all the way. But he was on the outside looking in, and he could never feel my pain as the months went by and Lucas was still missing.

I saw Scanlon look at his watch, then at me.

'I should get moving.' He got up from the table and crossed to the window where a police car was cruising past. 'The squad car will be going up and down all night. How do you feel?' He came back to the table and sat down.

'I'm fine,' I said. 'Tired, if I'm honest. The last couple of days took it out of me. I'll be glad to get to my bed.'

'Are you sure you're okay to be here on your own?' He fiddled with the label on the beer bottle. 'I mean, I know I'm not supposed to, but I could stay over if you want.'

I looked at him, remembering the last time we went out when he was tipsy and kissed me, and our recent encounter was more than a kiss between friends. We had never spoken about it, and with New York and Sweden we had seen little of each other. But whatever may be lying beneath this friendship, this wasn't the time to pursue it, even though I couldn't deny the desire that ran through me as I held his gaze. I knew he would also know this wasn't the time, and the last thing he would want to risk was the wrath of Wilson if he suddenly arrived unannounced tomorrow morning as he had earlier.

'I'll be fine, Danny. Honest. I'm only going to bed, the police are around outside, so I'm totally fine. I'm safe in here.'

He stood up again and I got to my feet. There was an awkward moment when it felt like both of us weren't sure what to do. Scanlon was on duty, and his work here was done for now. It was different from the night out we had when we were both easy and having fun as friends. Him being here tonight was work, and he was too committed to that for it to be anything else.

'Okay,' he said finally. 'I'll get moving, then. I've got to be in court tomorrow morning for a trial. Should be finished mid-morning. Is Wilson going to put somebody else on tomorrow to be around you?'

'I don't know,' I said. 'I hope not.' Then I added quickly, 'If it's not you, I'd rather not have anyone. It's easy being here with you for a few hours, but I don't want some cop I don't even know sitting in my house all evening.'

He pulled on his jacket and I followed him to the hall.

'I'll take that as a compliment then.' He smiled.

'Your rucksack,' I said.

'Forgot about that.'

He quickly walked down the hall and after a few seconds came back, stuffing a shirt into the rucksack.

'Hope you're not stealing my towels,' I joked.

'No, they're on the floor,' he chuckled.

Then he took me by surprise by stepping close to me. He dropped his bag and suddenly pulled me in and kissed me.

It was a hard and long kiss and I was taken aback but didn't stop him. I felt my body tense at first then I leant in, feeling the firmness of him and his arms around my back, holding me close. When he drew back, we were both breathless. I could feel his lips on my cheek.

'Jesus, Billie,' he whispered.

His mouth moved to my neck as he pulled me closer again and every fibre of me wanted him there and then as much as he wanted me. But this was all sorts of wrong. If we gave in to this, where did we go afterwards? I didn't want a relationship, and if Scanlon did he knew I was the wrong person.

I stopped and stepped back, catching my breath.

'Don't, Danny,' I said, my voice quivering a little. 'This isn't the time. You know that.'

'I know,' he said softly, looking at me, then away. 'But Billie, when this is over, we should talk. I mean really talk.'

I nodded, but didn't reply. When this was over. He meant this, this danger, this situation, but really what had happened to me in recent days was nothing compared to the real issue in my life. What moved me every morning and night might never be over. And while I could lose myself in the passion with Scanlon and try to have what would pass for a relationship, it was destined to fail, because the reality was it would never be over until my son was here in my home by my side.

CHAPTER TWENTY-FIVE

I ate breakfast in my kitchen while I listened to the news and scrolled through my emails. Two shots of coffee would give me the jag I needed to start the day. Last night's moment with Scanlon had been unsettling, and although I tried to put it out of my mind when I went to bed, I kept going back to that kiss, that feeling of being with him, that desire that I knew could ruin the friendship we had built up over the years. I considered a what-the-hell attitude and that life was too short, and that my track record and choice of men had been far from perfect so far. But Scanlon meant more to me than just embarking on something that I could see would have no future. As friends we had a future, but in a relationship I knew it could be over in six months, and then we would have nothing. I hoped Wilson wouldn't be in touch to tell me I would be getting more protection. I decided that the best thing to do was patch any calls from Wilson, and just get on with my work. In my email box were a couple of messages from Millie from yesterday afternoon with details of clients who wanted to make appointments. So I would throw myself into that until this was resolved. But I couldn't hide from the fact that the two thugs from Thurso were out there looking for me, and being helped by some other lowlifes from Glasgow. I drank my coffee. I could either spend all day looking over my shoulder, or I could just get on with it. I went into the living room and glanced out of the window where a police squad car was parked outside my flat. My mobile rang in the kitchen and I went through and picked it up, seeing Fowler's name on the screen.

'You all right, Billie?' he said.

'Safe and sound,' I said.

'That's good. Listen. I just got the whisper that those thugs – McKay and Mason – are holed up in the Marriott Hotel, you know, the one on Argyle Street under the Kingston Bridge? That's where they've been the past two nights, so someone must be footing that bill.'

'That's interesting,' I said. 'I'm tempted go down there and rattle their cage.'

'That wouldn't be a good idea. Not on your own, anyway.'

'What do you mean?' I asked. 'Have you got a plan?'

'The way I see it it's early enough in the morning, so these bastards will not be keeping office hours. In fact, I know they don't.'

'How do you know that?'

He left a couple of beats.

'I paid a visit to the hotel last night for a drink. It was

busy enough in the foyer with some function going on, so I just had a drink at the bar and sat in a corner. I saw them. The pair of them. Pissed as farts.'

'You what? You actually saw them in the bar?'

'Yep. It was busy, so they wouldn't have noticed me. And they were talking to a couple of girls – hookers I'd say, but they're so stupid they wouldn't know. They probably thought they were being chatted up.'

'Did they pull?' I asked.

'No. They were wasted, the pair of them.' He paused. 'But . . . I have an idea.'

'I'm all ears.'

'I got talking to one of the girls once she went outside for a smoke and I told her I was a private eye. I mean, she doesn't know me from anyone, but she listened to me. I asked her about the two blokes and she said they were choochters and had no money for her and her friend, so she left them. But I reckoned she'd be up for setting them up. You know, so we could get a bit of DNA from them.'

'Seriously?'

'Yeah. It's not going to be rocket science. The very least they would have to do is take the glass they were drinking out of, or get some fag end or something. There's all sorts that can be done.'

'Did you ask her if she would help?'

'I did. She said she would. Her and her mate. If the money was right. I told her the guys were bad people and they had abused a woman, and she said she'd be up for it.'

'What kind of money?'

'She said five hundred. Between her and her mate. She said they can earn that in a couple of nights in a hotel like that.'

'I like the sound of that. What do you think?'

'I've got her mobile, so I said I would ring her this morning and maybe we could meet her later. I told her we were working together.'

'That would be great, Dave. If it works, it might nail these bastards to the floor.'

'It may or may not work, but I think it's a chance worth taking.' He was silent for a moment, then said, 'We both know that evidence obtained like this is not admissable in court though.'

'Yes, of course,' I replied. 'But those two half-wits won't know that. And having their DNA by whatever means can get them brought in for questioning and might push them into a confession. Can you call her and arrange a meet this morning sometime?'

'Sure. But she said she would want a hundred up front – whether it works or not.'

'Not surprised. I'll sort that.'

'Okay. It has to be before midday because I'm going with the troops later to look at some stuff.'

'How's that going?'

'They don't tell me much. They're mostly relying on me to feed them info, which is fine by me.'

'Okay. Once you've organised the meet with the girl, let me know a place and a time. I'll be there.'

He hung up. I was more than impressed by the way Fowler worked, and not really surprised because from the first time I met him, he seemed more invested than any of the cops I'd encountered on my short trip to Caithness. All I had to do now was to lose any security that was following me around. I scrolled down and pulled up Wilson's number. He answered after two rings.

'You all right, Carlson?'

'Yep. I'm good. Nobody's even shot at me yet.'

'Aye, well, it's only ten o clock. There's time yet. Are the boys still outside your house? I told them to keep cruising.'

'Yeah, they're around.' I paused. 'But look, I need to lose the security for the next day or so. I have a job on that I need to be alone with. It's not around here. I can't be having cops on my tail or anywhere near me. It's delicate.'

Silence followed and I could see the wheels of his brain turning.

'Carlson, are you planning to go rogue on me?'

'I'm not a cop, Harry. I can go rogue any day of the week. I'm my own boss, remember?'

I heard him sigh.

'As I said to you before, this is your call. I can't force security on you. But if you're instructing me that you need it called off for a day or so then I respect that. But seriously, those fuckers are out there and they'll still be after you.'

'Yeah,' I said. 'But maybe they'll have other things on their mind. Especially if the big haul is coming down the road in the next couple of days. They're not going to chase me forever.'

'We don't know that. But it's up to you.'

'Good. Can you lose the squad car at my house? It's putting the hookers off their work.'

'Aye right. Just be careful.'

He hung up.

I saw Fowler with his dog on the lead standing outside the café in Queen Street train station concourse. He smiled when he spotted me, and the dog wagged her tail and jumped up on me excitedly.

'I love this dog,' I said, ruffling her head. 'She's got a real personality.'

'Aye, she's a great pal.'

The station was bustling and noisy with the announcer hailing the arrival or departure of various trains and I saw Fowler's eyes strain at the noise. He looked red and I wondered if he'd stayed in the bar for a while last night. He may look like he's on holiday, I thought, but I could see a big part of him was relishing his sojourn in the city and dipping into being a cop again. He jerked his head in the direction of the café window.

'The girls are inside. I saw them go in from the other side of the platform here.'

'Good, let's go then.' I looked up at him. 'And thanks for

your help here. Honestly. All going well, this is a great thing you're doing.'

'We're not there yet, Billie. But let's hope. I haven't met the other girl, so we'll see how it goes.'

I walked behind him as we went through the entrance past the takeaway and a few tables with commuters or travellers sitting eating a late breakfast. I saw two girls at the back of the café. I wasn't surprised to see that they looked fresh and clean and nothing like the pathetic waifs up around my flat on the square. The girls who worked the hotels were smart and well-dressed of an evening. They had to be to get in the door in the first place, and they had to look like classy women out for a good time. Some of them worked for escort agencies, but some just for themselves. There was serious money to be made in passing trade in any big city's finest hotels, from Glasgow to Moscow and all places in between. They both glanced up when we approached.

'Hi, ladies,' Fowler said, gesturing to me, 'this is my colleague I told you about.'

'Howsit going?' I said as both girls eyed me up.

The younger one looked a bit suspicious. The other girl looked at the dog.

'Aw, man, look at your wee dug! It's beautiful!' She stretched out a hand and the dog gladly jumped up on her hind legs for a caress.

'Can I get you a coffee, folks? Tea? Anything to eat?' I asked.

'Coffee is fine, please.'

'I'll have one too,' Fowler said.

I went up to the counter and ordered then returned and slid into the Formica-topped booth. The younger girl looked no more than early twenties, good-looking, with big trusting eyes and nothing hard about her.

'So,' I said, 'Dave has told you what we are looking for here?'

'Aye,' the older one said. 'Who are these guys, by the way?'

'Bad people,' I said. 'They raped a young girl. They're just beasts.' I didn't want to get drawn into the story of Astrid. 'What did you think of them last night when you had a brief chat?'

'Just the usual wankers,' the young one said. 'Same old shite you hear every night. You could see they weren't businessmen though, like a lot of the men we meet. As soon as they started talking, I could tell they were thick and pig ignorant.'

'They asked us whether we could come to their room for the night and how much would it be. When we told them they nearly fell off their chairs. One of them said how about a hand job round the back of the hotel. Fuck's sake! Cheap bastard! We laughed it off, but they were just arseholes.'

'Do you think you'll be able to get onside with them enough tonight?' I asked.

'Enough to get the DNA that you're asking for. I mean,

that could just be a glass they've been drinking out of or something, couldn't it?'

'Yes,' I said. 'Anything like that. It's amazing how little it takes to link someone to a crime.'

'I know,' the younger girl said. 'I used to watch all them crime TV shows. I was even at college to get enough qualifications to go to university. I was thinking of going into that area.'

We both looked at her, a little surprised, and she saw it.

'Don't look so surprised. I wouldn't be the only student who does this kind of shit. When I was at college that's how I got started for more money, with the escort agencies. Ended up making more money than I could in a job, so I chucked the uni and did this. Not just here. London sometimes too. Edinburgh. I even stayed in Marbella for a month doing it. Made a fortune.'

The other girl looked a little lost.

'I've got a wean. He's eleven. My man's got MS so he can't work, and I just do it at night to make more money than I could in any other job knocking my pan in. It's all right really.'

I nodded, not knowing what to say. The story of these two women was so different from the people I saw every day or had met as a cop. They were very clear about what they did, and confident and easy about who they were. It was a means to an end, to earn money. I wondered if, at the end of each night, they felt the grubby humiliation or any of the other emotions, but I got the impression that these girls had long since left any of that introspection behind.

I wanted to say I was glad they were doing well, and hoped they could be safe. But it would have sounded trite, condescending, and these girls were looking back at me knowing that no matter what I said, I had never walked in their shoes or spent a night the way they had. And at the end of the day I was conscious that I was using them as much as the men in the bars. It didn't make me proud at that moment, but I figured they would like to see the two bastards they were setting up behind bars.

'Okay,' Fowler said. 'So, ladies, have you any kind of plan that you think might work?'

The girls looked at each other and half smiled.

'If we could plan things every time we went to work, we would be sitting in Downing Street or somewhere running the country. No. No plans. We'll just go with the flow.'

'Fine,' I said. 'You know, any kind of DNA. Whatever you pick up should be good enough. Just don't place yourself in any danger.'

I looked from one to the other and for a moment we sat in silence.

'So,' I said. 'A hundred up front, and four when you finish, agreed?'

'Yeah, that'll do.'

'It'll be worth it if these two bastards get done. It wouldn't be the first time we've had a slap from a punter in a pinstripe suit, so, in my book, anything that can get a bad one in jail makes it worthwhile.'

'Couldn't agree more,' I said. 'So we will leave you to it and you can call Dave, or me, when you've got what you need.'

'How do you know these guys will be in the hotel tonight?'

'As far as I know they're there for a few days. If they are, then they'll be hanging around the bar as usual.'

'Don't worry. We'll get them sorted.'

I took a card out of my pocket and slid it across the table.

'That's my number if you need me any time. I mean, in the future.'

The younger girl turned the card around in her hand and gave it to the other girl who looked at it.

'Aye, that's good. You never know when you need a private eye in this game.'

They both smiled – bright attractive women, the younger one a looker, the older one somewhat distant, with so much going on in her life. Yet here they both were, keen as mustard, with a task to do.

CHAPTER TWENTY-SIX

As I left Dave to go back to my office, I made a decision that I was going to go for a backup to the attempts to get the DNA. I knew I only had one shot at this. It wasn't that I didn't trust the two women – in their line of business, rape was always a threat – but any prostitutes I ever spoke to as a cop always told me it wasn't something you ran to the police about. The ordeal of a criminal trial where a defence lawyer painted a lurid picture of a prostitute's life was one of the main reasons they seldom reported sexual assault. I was in no doubt that these girls would do their utmost to get the DNA. But I needed more. If they failed, it was over. There would be little chance of ever getting the DNA I needed. These guys were still looking for me, and it was unlikely I'd ever get close enough to them. I scrolled through my mobile and found the number for a good contact – Kevin, who worked on the concierge desk at the Marriott. I'd paid him over the years for information, and I'd once bailed his mother out after she got caught up in a money scam that emptied her bank account. Kevin had never let me down. I called his mobile and he answered after several rings.

'Kevin. How you doing? Billie Carlson here.'

'Billie!' he said. 'I'm good. Just getting organised for work. I start at two. What's happening?'

Kevin had been with the hotel since it opened in the nineties. It wasn't all tourist information at the concierge desk. He was discreet, and could procure whatever a guest requested, whether it was ideas for the best restaurant or bar, or an escort for a businessman on an overnight stay. The last time he'd helped me was on a case where a company director was having afternoon sessions with a young footballer. I had a camera set up in the bedroom and captured some graphic images. I'm not proud of it, but the wife had three kids and was being duped by her husband who was planning to ditch her. She cleaned him out financially on the strength of the hot pictures, and nobody was any the wiser about how he was trapped.

'Kevin, I need a big favour from you.'

'Sure, Billie. As long as it doesn't get me fired.'

'It won't.'

'Okay. I'm heading into work now, so why don't you meet me in Buchanan Street bus station in twenty minutes, tell me what you need and we'll see what I can do.'

'Perfect.'

*

I stood outside the bus station watching the flurry of students coming and going from Caledonian University, the travellers, and old people on day trips out of the city to Oban and the coast. Homeless punters sat at the entrance with signs saying they were hungry, some of them Romanians on the make, others shivering in the cold, just punters with their lives stuffed into plastic shopping bags. I saw Kevin walking along smoking a cigarette. He tossed it away as he came up to me.

'It's all going on here in the mean streets, Billie.'

'Sure is. What time you working until tonight, Kevin?'

'Finish at ten. I've a few things to do before I start work. What do you need?'

I told him about the guys in the hotel.

'These men are the lowest of the low. They raped a young girl a few weeks ago. I'm trying to get DNA from them. I need it to link them to the case.'

There were several questions Kevin could have asked if he'd wanted to, but he wasn't that kind of guy. He trusted me, and I knew he would do the right thing.

'You mean you need to get into their rooms?' He gave me a knowing look.

'Yes,' I conceded. 'They might be sharing a room. Not sure, but you could check.'

He took a breath and looked over my shoulder for a long moment.

'It's dodgy. If they are out of the room I could get you in, depending on where it is and where the CCTV is. Do you know where they'll be, like when they'll be out and stuff?'

'So far they've been in the hotel bar at night, talking to the girls, but not wanting to pay the asking price,' I said. 'I'd expect them to be there again tonight.'

I didn't want to tell him about the women who were also working for me. No point in complicating matters. But I gave him the names I'd been given.

He took a long time to answer, then he spoke.

'Okay. Once I get in, I'll check what room they're in. I'll deal with the CCTV. If you let me know when you arrive, if you know they're not in, then I'll get you up there.' He paused. 'Buzz me when you get to the hotel and I'll come out for a fag and give you a keycard. But after that it's up to you.' He looked at me. 'You sure you want to do this on your own? I mean, if they're rapists then they'll have no qualms about beating the shit out of you if they walk in and find you rummaging around their room.'

I looked him in the eye. 'They've already done that, Kevin.'

His eyebrows went up. 'Seriously, they hit you?'

I nodded. 'Long story. But I hit them harder.' I half smiled. 'So, believe me, I really don't want to run into them.'

He gave a wry smile. 'Okay, Billie, I'll do my best. If something happens and if for any reason I'm not able to do it, I'll let you know.'

'Thanks, Kevin. And I'll make sure you're well sorted when it's done.'

He didn't reply, he just nodded and turned to go.

'Call me.'

He walked briskly towards the lights and crossed the road then disappeared down West Nile Street.

It was nearly nine thirty by the time I got the call from one of the girls to say they were in the bar and that the Highlanders were there. I called Kevin's mobile and relayed the information. He said he'd already made sure he clocked the guys earlier and confirmed that they were in the bar, just came in about half an hour ago. I'd been sitting in my car close on Montrose Street and headed up, parking it across where Kevin told me. He came out of the hotel and lit up a cigarette and I walked towards him. Tipsy couples came out of the hotel and I could see through the glass doors there were a few people milling round the bar off the main foyer. I didn't look in the direction of the bar, just in case anyone saw me. I stood for a second, then Kevin went into his trouser pocket and held out his hand, pressing a keycard onto my palm.

'They're sharing a room,' he said, not making eye contact with me. 'Three one eight. Here's the deal. I've switched off the CCTV for the third-floor corridor where their room is. But I can't leave it that way for long. So, you've got about fifteen minutes max. Will that do you?'

'Should be quicker than that.'

'Okay. I'll go back in and I'll keep an eye on the bar. If any of them leave and look like they're heading your way, I'll call you.'

I nodded, and he backed away through the automatic doors. I stood for a moment, then went inside, Kevin winking at me as I passed the concierge desk. I walked quickly to the lift just before it closed and pushed the button for the third floor, my heart beating faster for every floor that pinged. Then the doors opened and I stepped outside, checking the numbers on the wall and heading right to number 318. I walked quickly along the carpeted corridor – I find these long hotel corridors creepy at the best of times. I glanced over my shoulder when I got to the door and slipped the key into the lock. Nothing. A red light flashed. Shit. Take your time, I told myself, and tried it again. Bingo, there was a green light and the door clicked open. I slipped inside and inserted my key in the wall holder. Lights popped on, blinding me in the glare. The room was a mess, clothes, T-shirts and underwear strewn across the floor and between the two single beds. I pulled on rubber gloves and took out a couple of evidence bags. I picked up underwear that lay on the floor at each side of the beds and put them in separate bags. I glanced around looking for anything else I could use. There was a cigarette butt in an ashtray, and I picked it up and put it in another bag. I went into the bathroom, working meticulously, like a cat burglar. There were two toothbrushes. I took both of them and bagged them separately. They would notice them missing when they came back, but they were so thick the last thing they'd think of was that I was creeping around their bedroom gathering evidence that could put them behind bars. Suddenly my mobile rang and I nearly jumped out of my skin. It was Kevin.

'Billie. You need to get out of there quick. I was with a customer at the desk and didn't see until it was too late that one of the guys got into the lift. You need to move now.'

'Shit. I'm done. But I can't come into the corridor because they know what I look like.'

'Okay. But you need to do something.' He hung up.

I glanced around, my heart thumping, looking for some place to hide. The bathroom was small. The wardrobe was big enough for me to get in, but if he opened it I was in trouble as there were only a couple of jackets hanging up. I slipped into the wardrobe and closed the door. But as I did I remembered that I should have taken the key out of the wall holder as the lights were on. Shit. Too late, I heard a key being slid into the lock. Then the door opened. Someone was standing in the hall, probably bemused that the lights were on, hopefully too drunk to think anything of it. I held my breath. Then I heard a drawer being opened and a short silence, then the sound of tapping on the glass table, scraping, then an inhaled snort. He was sniffing a line of coke, which he obviously couldn't do in the bar. I could hear him sniff again and a couple of times as he whispered, 'Magic. That's better.' Then silence again. I could see through the venetian slats that he was standing looking around the room. He came across to the wardrobe door and opened one side of it, then closed it again. I held my breath, terrified. If it came to it, I might have got the better of him because I had the element of surprise, but it would be so messy. He stood with his back to me, then he stepped towards the room door. Relief flooded through me. He looked at the key, mumbled something like, 'Daft bastard must have left it,' and pulled it out, plunging the place into darkness. I waited until I heard the door close and breathed out a sigh. I gave it a couple of minutes, then put my phone torch on, feeling my way to the door. I ran along the corridor, down the stairwell and kept going until I was on the ground floor, then out of the hotel. I jumped into my car and drove off. Job done. I was elated, thrilled and in disbelief.

When I got to my house I could see some guy – the one I'd seen before – standing talking to two guys in a blacked-out four-by-four just yards from my house. I drove past the square and headed down towards Charing Cross and quickly up to the West End, finding myself in One Devonshire Gardens, a discreet luxury boutique hotel. I'd stay there for the night. I booked a room and when I got in, I took the evidence bags out of my pocket and lay them on the bedside table, jubilant. It had been a long time since I'd felt that something had really worked and I knew that this could make all the difference. By itself, it didn't mean they raped her, but it had to be enough for them to be questioned, and I would hand over the video, which would show Mason's scorpion tattoo. Game over. I was pumped on adrenalin and almost without giving it any consideration,

I ordered a bottle of red wine and found myself phoning Scanlon.

'Can you come to One Devonshire Gardens? I'm staying here for the night.'

'What? Why?'

I told him there were a couple of guys outside my house and I felt it best not to go in. 'I'll tell you the rest when you get here.'

'Okay, I'm on my way.'

It only took fifteen minutes for him to arrive, by that time the wine was uncorked. He knocked gently on my door, and I opened it.

'What's going on, Carlson?'

'Sshh,' I said as he walked in.

We stood looking at each other for a long moment, then Scanlon's eyes took in the room, the huge bed adorned with puffed up pillows, and the wine on the mahogany table. We didn't speak. He smiled and I could see him swallowing. I took a step towards him, put my arms around him and kissed him hard on the lips. He kissed me back and then he pulled me close, his hands finding my breasts and stroking my thighs. He pulled his shirt out of his trousers as I unbuttoned my blouse. We kissed, breathless, and in seconds my blouse was off and on the bed and Scanlon was pulling his jeans off.

'What the hell, Carlson? If you've gone mad, I really like it.'

I didn't answer but felt my hands reach all over his body

as we lost ourselves in the fire of unexpected and unplanned passion that had been waiting to explode for far too long. Afterwards we lay spent, and I could feel my heart beginning to slow down.

'What was that all about?'

'Just . . . just what it was, Danny. No catches or hidden agenda. It was something we both wanted.'

'You're right about that. But . . . I'm confused.'

'So am I. But let's not pick this apart. Let's be . . . well . . . let's just be this.'

We kissed again and I lay on the bed in his arms, and I told him what had happened, about the girls and me in the hotel. We fell asleep.

I was wakened an hour later by a phone call from one of the girls.

'Got some things for you. I think we did well . . .'

I drifted off to sleep again.

CHAPTER TWENTY-SEVEN

I awoke with the noise of traffic, my arm resting against the warmth of Scanlon's and there was a sudden flash of reality that we had crossed a line last night. Twice, actually. Jesus! This wasn't supposed to happen. I was perfectly still, glancing sideways to his naked chest rising and falling as he slept peacefully. Why was it that men never woke up after a night of sex and raked over the rights and the wrongs of it? I took a slow, quiet breath and let it out, glancing again at Scanlon, images in my mind of the two of us last night lost in the throes of something I couldn't even really explain to myself. I'd never seriously considered this with Scanlon in all the time I'd known him, until recently, until the little frisson we had after dinner that night. Last night's reckless caution-to-the-wind escapade had been a bad idea. Despite my thoughts I felt my face smiling, and refused to regret what had happened. I wouldn't. I would have to live with it, but it wasn't something to get hung up about. I hoped he wouldn't either, and the last thing I wanted was for him to wake up and start asking where we went from here. I closed my eyes when I heard him stir, and he leaned over and gently kissed me on the lips. Then he got out of bed and I was conscious that he was standing looking down at me, and I was desperate to look back but kept my eyes shut.

'I know you're awake, Carlson. I can see your eyes flickering.'

I opened one eye and smiled. Then I heard him in the shower. I hoped this wasn't going to be awkward. When he came out with a towel around his waist, I opened my eyes.

'Goodness,' I said, 'how the hell did you get in here? What's your name?'

He chuckled, throwing himself onto the bed beside me, a whiff of the freshness of his body still damp.

'Don't give me all that nonsense, Carlson. It's your fault. I'm going to have to do the walk of shame through the lobby of this very posh hotel and get out of here pronto. I start work in half an hour.'

He leaned up on one elbow, and I smiled to him.

'You okay?' he asked, his fingers tracing down my face to my chest.

I took a breath and pushed it out.

'Yeah,' I said, 'you?'

'Sure.'

It was awkward, but he didn't want to get into this any

more than I did, so we'd leave it for another day. I watched as he slipped into his jeans and trainers and pulled on a T-shirt. Then he looked down at me.

'What do you want to do with the bags? The DNA stuff?'

'I'm going to call Wilson shortly and arrange to take it to forensics. I have to see these women who were in their company last night.'

'Okay.' He stood around for a moment. 'So, you want to have coffee or something later?' Then he grinned. 'You can tell me how you didn't mean last night to happen, but that you were overwhelmed by euphoria about your success in the DNA, and suddenly—'

I pulled the pillow from underneath me and slung it at him.

'Get to work, Scanlon. Call me later.'

He smiled and left, and much as part of me felt I should say more, I was glad he'd gone. I would wait until I sorted my head around last night before I even embarked on a discussion about it. I hoped I wouldn't regret it later.

Once I'd had a quick shower, I left the hotel and drove back to my flat, feeling somewhere between embarrassed and pleased that I had stayed out all night in a hotel with a man. It was a very long time since I had done something as rash as that, and if I didn't think about the potential problems it may have created, it felt good. The few nights I'd spent with McCartney had mostly been at his flat or mine, but this felt much more reckless because I might've been risking a friendship.

When I got to Blythswood, I cruised the square twice to make sure there were no suspicious-looking cars parked up or people hanging around. It was quiet. I put my key in the front door and went quickly inside. The house was deathly quiet. I quickly checked the place to make sure nobody had broken in, then went into the bedroom and changed my clothes and headed back out of the front door. In my car I called Dave and told him about the DNA I had stolen. He chuckled, saying he wasn't surprised, but telling me it was a bit reckless. He said he would meet the girls this morning to see what they had and let me know. On my way out of the office, I called Wilson.

'Harry, it's me. Don't ask me any trick questions, but I have some DNA samples from the two hoodlums from Thurso. Can I drop them somewhere?'

There was a stony silence, and I knew Wilson would be wondering if he'd heard correctly.

'You have what?' he said, his voice going up an octave.

'DNA. Samples. Not exactly swabs, but enough for forensics to work on and compare with what they have.'

There was another silence.

'Carlson, where the fuck did you get that?'

'Don't ask, Harry, it's better you don't know.'

'Christ all-fucking-mighty! I don't want to know. But you really are a fuckin' headcase.'

I didn't know how to answer that, so I said nothing and waited.

'What have you got?' he asked.

'Fag end. Toothbrushes . . .' I paused. 'Oh, and two pairs of underwear.'

'Fuck me! You were in their hotel room?'

'I couldn't possibly comment,' I replied, picturing his face, crimson with frustration.

I heard him take a long breath and blow it out slowly.

'You know what, Carlson, I give up on you. I mean, I offered you protection, but you go traipsing around hotel rooms stealing the property of the very guys who tried to kill you.'

'That's never provable, as you well know. It doesn't matter who got the stuff, or if they handed it over voluntarily, the important thing is we have it. And anyway, when did you ever start worrying how anyone managed to get DNA from a criminal? So, can I bring it down?

After a few seconds of silence he replied, 'Is it bagged?'

'Yep, all separately.'

'All right, bring it to reception and I'll have someone meet you there.' He hung up.

CHAPTER TWENTY-EIGHT

I headed down to my office once I'd dropped the bags off to the young officer at the reception area in Pitt Street. He didn't ask questions, I just told him it was for forensics on the instruction of DCI Wilson. It was almost mid-morning, the streets were busying up, and I knew Millie would be wondering if I was coming in. I hadn't heard from her, which surprised me a little. The rain had stopped and there was promise in the patches of blue sky. It made me glad that the city was beginning to emerge from the winter. At my building, I got into the lift and stood as it grunted and clunked its way to the third floor. I stepped out and went across to my office and turned the handle on the door, but it didn't move. How could it be locked? It was never locked unless we'd both left for the night. Perhaps Millie was ill or had overslept, but that never happened either. I pushed my key in and shoved open the door. Then I froze. Millie sat at her desk, her face flushed with fear and her eyes full of terror. There was a strip of duct tape across her mouth. I stood, unable to move, my heart thumping. I was so struck by the image in front of me that I didn't even notice the guy behind the door who stepped forward and was now pointing a handgun at me.

'Wh-what . . .' I tried to squeeze words out.

'Shut the fuck up and get in here,' said the man with the gun, a thuggish, thickset bruiser. 'Get your hands behind your back.'

My eyes flicked around the room, looking desperately for something I could do, anything I could fight back with, even though I knew you couldn't fight anyone who had a gun at your head.

'Tie her hands.'

He jerked his head to the man who stood over Millie.

A skinhead guy with a face criss-crossed with knife slash scars came across with gaffer tape. He grabbed my hands tight, yanked them painfully behind my back, and wrapped the tape around. I automatically flexed my wrists out a little as he was doing it so there would be a space between my hands, thinking that at a push I might be able to slip out of it if there was the slightest opportunity.

'Get her mobile. Put it on the desk.'

The scarface frisked my jacket pockets, taking my phone out and placing it on Millie's desk.

'What is this?' I finally said. 'Are we getting robbed?' I knew exactly what it was, but I wanted to test who they were and how much they knew.

The squat guy looked at me and snorted.

'Where's the coke?'

I shrugged and made a face.

'Don't know what you're talking about.'

He came across to me and leant in close to my face so that I could smell his stale sweat.

'The fucking cocaine. You took it. Some dickhead choochters managed to let you get away with it, and we're here to pick up the pieces. So where is it? Just hand it over and we'll be out of here.'

'I don't know what you're talking about.' I glanced at Millie who looked strained. 'Listen, this is my work. I'm a private investigator. I'm in an office in the middle of the city centre, in case you hadn't noticed. So sooner or later, someone is going to knock on that door or come looking for me . . . Maybe even the cops.'

He sniffed again and ran the back of his hand across his nose, red around the nostrils. He was a coke user.

'If you don't tell us where the coke is, you won't be here much longer.' He took his mobile out. 'I've to phone them and they'll come and get you.'

'Who?'

'My boss. Once you leave here, you'll not be coming back. So, don't be a tit. Just tell me where it is, and then we'll go.' He glanced around the office. 'Is it in here?'

He jerked his head in the direction of his mate, who began opening drawers and emptying them onto the floor, then pushing over filing cabinets. Millie was white with horror that he was trashing the room where she had everything meticulously filed, neat and controlled. The guy smashed a few cups against the wall and overturned some chairs. The landline phone on Millie's desk rang and she glanced at it, then at me. She knew to leave it, as it rang out a dozen times. Then silence. Then my mobile went off and everyone looked at it. I couldn't see who it was, and eventually it stopped.

'Can I sit down?' I asked, feeling suddenly weak as the tension grew. 'I don't feel well.'

He looked at me, then kicked a chair across and I sat down, my back to the window, my arms aching. I could see Millie was struggling behind the tape.

'Can you please take that tape off her mouth? She has asthma and can't breathe properly. She's not going to do anything. She's my secretary, for God's sake. Please. She'll pass out if you don't take that off.' I was lying, but it seemed to convince him.

He looked at his mate then nodded. Scarface went across and ripped the tape off viciously and Millie winced as the pain brought tears to her eyes. The area around her mouth was an angry red.

'Can I have a drink of water, please?' Millie asked, her voice thin and croaky. She looked so vulnerable.

Scarface brought her a glass from the small kitchen and tried to give her some, but her hands were tied and the water dribbled down her face and chest.

'Let her hands out, for Christ's sake. What do you think she's going to do? You've got a bloody gun on us.'

He said nothing and didn't react for a long moment, but

there was something about his expression that told me that whoever he was, he wasn't comfortable doing this. Maybe he was fine with slapping men around but it didn't feel right with women.

'Come on,' I ventured. 'Look at her. She's old enough to be your mother. Can you imagine someone doing that to your mother? You're torturing her. I don't care what you do to me, but at least let her get a drink.'

'My ma's dead, right? Don't talk about my ma.'

Silence for a beat.

'I'm sorry to hear that. I wasn't talking about her. I'm just saying, have some thought for an older woman. She could get really sick. Come on. I'm sure your ma wouldn't have wanted you to harm women.'

He turned to me, snapped, 'I never hit a woman in my life. Never.'

I could see something here, cracks in the armour. Who was this nutter, and why had someone picked him for a job like this? Was this the best Murrell could come up with to get the cocaine back? I looked at him.

'I . . . I believe that. I'm sure you wouldn't hurt a woman. But . . . But do you know anything about the people who sent you here? Because these guys have no qualms about hurting women. And see these two dickheads you talk about from the Highlands – the choochters? They have no problem hurting women.' I turned my face to the side to show them my bruising, cut healing. 'They did this to me. What do you think of that? Of guys like that?'

'I don't know fuck all about them. I was just told to get here and get this cocaine.'

'I don't have any cocaine. You can rip the office apart and you won't find any cocaine.'

He shifted around on his feet, uncomfortably, and we were silent for a bit. Then he turned to me.

'Who are these dickheads anyway?'

'Just two bad guys who raped a young girl, that's all.'

He looked at me for a long moment, said nothing, glanced at his mate.

'What you talking about?'

'They raped a girl.'

'Fuck has that got to do with me?'

'Nothing. I'm just telling you because that's the kind of people you're helping here. Those two guys are bad news.'

'I'm only here to get the coke.'

I really wasn't getting through to him, and he sniffed and twitched. We sat, nobody speaking. I glanced out of the window where, from the side of my eye, I could see a couple of police cars pulling up outside my office. I looked back at him.

'Do you work for Murrell?' I asked.

'None of your business.'

'You got kids?'

He looked at me for a long moment.

'Aye. Boy and a girl. My lassie is eighteen.'

'She working?' I glanced out of the window again and

saw several officers jumping out of cars. I had to keep him talking.

'She's a student. She's got brains. She's going places.'

'Good for her. That girl they raped, she was a student too. She's dead now. Took her own life, they say, after the rape.'

I held his gaze as I spoke and could see something was getting to him. Then he shook himself, squared his shoulders and paced the room.

'Nothing to do with me. Listen, just shut up about that girl. I'm going to phone the boss. They need to come and get you.'

I glanced at Millie. I could hear footsteps on the stairwell, and I knew she could as well. Then it happened quickly. The door burst open and three big uniformed cops came piling in, guns out.

'Don't move! Drop the fucking weapon!'

Two cops placed themselves in front of Millie's desk, guns trained on the men. In the background were two more officers and two detectives, all armed. One of them came across to me and pulled off the tape.

'You okay? Did they hurt you?'

Then he crossed to Millie, and ripped off the tape around her wrists.

It was over in seconds. They cuffed the two men and I felt a surge of relief as they marched them across the room and ushered them out the door. When they'd gone, Millie turned to me.

'What's with this old enough to be his mother crap?

You'd think I was decrepit, to hear you.' She gave me her best angry-Millie look but I knew she was as relieved as me.

'I was trying to save your bacon, Millie.' I managed a smile. 'I was playing on the scrap of decency I saw in that guy's face.'

'You did not bad there. But it's lucky they didn't just shoot us as the door opened. How in the hell did the cops come?'

I told her I had seen them arriving and kept quiet, hoping I had shown nothing.

'Somebody must have phoned in the building. They must have heard the noise with them wrecking the place.'

Suddenly the face of Joey the debt collector appeared at the door behind the police guard.

'You ladies all right? I called the police. I just knew from experience there was something well dodgy going on here with all the racket.'

'Joey! Thanks. You just might have saved our lives.'

CHAPTER TWENTY-NINE

It didn't take long for Millie and me to get the office back into normal shape, spurred on by adrenalin still surging through us. Apart from a couple of breakages there was no real damage, but Millie's real bugbear was that the filing drawers had been emptied and she had to carefully piece back everything just the way it was. Once the police had left after we'd given our statements, Millie was trying to put the coffee machine together again. I watched her, noticing her hands were trembling.

'Millie,' I said. 'Let's just leave that and shut up shop for the day. Come on, we both need to get out of here.'

She looked over her shoulder at me, and stood for a second.

'You know what, you're right,' she said, trying her best to smile.

I really wanted to take her for a stiff drink because I could have used one myself, but it was too early in the day. So, we opted for the café downstairs. I was glad it wasn't busy and we headed to the back of the room where there were a couple of comfortable sofas. Millie shook her head as she gingerly touched the area where the tape had been that was now puffy and looked painful.

'Jesus!' she said. 'That was the worst waxing job I've ever had.'

We both burst out laughing, Millie a little more hysterical than me, then suddenly she looked up and her face crumpled as though she was going to cry.

'Oh Billie,' she sniffed, 'I really thought we were both going to get shot. I was scared. I'm never scared like that.' She wiped her nose with a tissue. 'Look at me, laughing that much I'm greetin'.'

I looked at her sympathetically.

'It's just the shock, Millie. It's natural, don't worry. I was scared too.'

'Were you?' she asked. 'You didn't look it.'

'I was. Not really from that halfwit with the gun, because there was something about him that made me feel I could get inside his head. I got the impression this wasn't his thing, maybe he'd been forced to do it, who knows. Whatever, it was crap organisation by whoever sent him. He was an amateur. But I was genuinely scared in case he was going to phone someone to come and take over. We would have been in trouble then.'

Coffee arrived.

'You take some chances, Billie – you really do. One of these days . . .'

'I know, but it's not always like this.'

'I'll be glad when you're back spying on some fraudsters or bent lawyers, like a proper private eye.

I smiled. 'Yeah, me too. But you know what, we need to start locking that door and making sure that people can't come in without an appointment.'

My mobile rang and I could see it was Dan Harris. My stomach turned over. I stood up automatically, like I had to be standing to attention to be focused, and gestured to Millie that I had to take this call.

'Billie, how you doing?'

'I'm fine, Dan,' I replied, which was far from true. 'What's happening, any news?'

If he was phoning me instead of emailing, it meant something was up. As ever I lived for every phone call but dreaded it at the same time in case it was the kind of bad news that would change things forever.

'Couple of things I wanted to run past you, Billie. About New York. Lena went off the radar for a couple of days and I couldn't get a hold of her. That's why I haven't been in touch.'

'What happened to her, did she just disappear?'

'You know what these people are like, how chaotic their lives are. But she's the only lead we've got, so we're at her mercy.'

'So, did you track her down?'

'Actually, she got in touch. Called me late last night. I'm still in Cleveland and was heading back to Baltimore today.' He paused. 'She said she can't get Williams on the phone any more. Either he's just not answering or it's a burner and he's trashed it.'

'What about the people he was supposed to be taking Lucas to?'

'They told Lena they only heard from him once, that he said he was coming by with the kid but he never showed up.'

'Shit! What do we do now?'

'Well that's what I wanted to talk to you about, Billie. This kid, Lena, I know she's got problems but I get the impression it matters to her where Lucas is and she said she would help in any way she can. She said she knows New York like the back of her hand from living there and the kind of haunts where Williams used to go and she says she would be able to track him down if she went there. But obviously she has no money to do that.' He paused.

'I'm the same as you, Dan. I felt there was something about Lena – maybe I'm just being taken in, but I had a bit of trust in her. I don't know. What do you think?'

'I was thinking that if we were going to get her to New York then I would want to be with her. You know, in the background. If she gets to him?'

'Me too,' I said quickly. 'If there is a chance Lucas is in New York somewhere, I want to pull out all the stops to find him.'

'It's a big city, Billie. There are lots of places some lowlife like Williams could have taken him, and lots of outlying places too: Jersey, Long Island – that's if he's even still there.'

'I don't care. If he's there and there's a chance to track him down, I'm in.' I paused. 'Can we trust Lena to really work for us?'

'We'll never know until we give it a chance. It's at best a long shot, but it's all we've got right now.'

'New York isn't that big. If some guy is going around with a kid in tow, it depends on how many contacts and places he knows up there. But he won't have the same freedom to move around if he's got a kid, so he could end up leaving him with someone else. Every day we don't track him down, Lucas is in more danger.'

'So, do you want me to ask her if she'll work with us?'

'Yeah, I do,' I said without even thinking it through. 'And I'm coming over. I can be on a plane tonight.'

'Billie, I need you to really know that this is going to be tough and it might not work. I mean, we went through this a couple of weeks ago.'

'But it might work. That's all I think about, Dan.'

'Okay. If she agrees, I'm going to drive up there with her today, or get a flight. We can be there some time tonight, get a hotel, and wait for you.'

I was already scrolling down my phone looking for flights to New York – there was an Icelandair flying direct tonight at eleven from Glasgow.

'Okay. I'm having a look now. I'll be there. If I can't get on the flight tonight, I'll get the one first thing tomorrow.' As

I said it I felt emotion welling up in my chest, and hung up. Millie looked at me.

'Lucas?'

I nodded, but for a moment choked.

'I'm going to New York. It's a long shot, but we have to try.'

'Are you sure about this, Billie?' she asked. 'It's going to be hard.'

'It's hard every day, Millie. But it's harder doing nothing and feeling helpless.'

'I know.' She sighed, took her mobile from her bag, and also started scrolling. 'You want me to get you on the first flight I can?'

'Yes, I do. I absolutely do.'

By eight in the evening I was in the departure lounge at Glasgow Airport, shell-shocked, exhausted, jet-lagged, and I hadn't even got on the plane. Millie had booked me on a flight and I'd gone home, hurriedly thrown some things in a bag and grabbed a heavy coat and jacket as New York would be freezing. I was in a taxi to the airport before I even had a chance to think about it. My mobile had been buzzing with texts and calls but I'd switched it off. It was as though I'd walked out on that life and all that mattered was the next few days. It could have been anyone on the phone, info on forensics, anything, but right now only one thing mattered: getting to New York. I couldn't deal with any calls from Scanlon asking questions, or anyone else who might have an opinion. I would never have told

Wilson anyway. When I got there I would maybe tell Scanlon where I was. I knew he would be annoyed and that's why it could never work between us. I cannot compromise – not when it comes to Lucas, and no matter how unfair it is to anyone, that is how it is. But right now, sitting drinking tea out of a paper cup in the quietness of the departure gate, I felt like the loneliest person in the world. I had so many people to talk to and support me but I didn't want to talk to anyone. This was what I had to do. They called the flight and I went through the gate and onto the plane, sat in my seat and buckled up. Who knew what tomorrow would bring? Who knew what kind of person I would be when I returned? But there was no going back. I switched my phone off and looked out of the window at the rain on the runway. I felt the familiar heaviness in my chest whenever I sensed that Lucas was so far away from me, but just going to the same country as him made me feel I was doing something to help. And one day we would sit down and I would tell him of days like this and nights of waiting and agonising.

I must have fallen into a deep, exhausted sleep on the plane because when I woke we were already on our descent into New York, the night sky over Manhattan lit up with a blaze of colour and lights sending shafts of greens and blues across the Hudson River. It was a spectacular sight that stirred me every time I'd visited the city over the years, but tonight gazing out at the darkness beyond gave me a desolate feeling in the pit of my stomach. I knew it was tiredness and everything that had happened, but I had to nip the emotion right there because this was a visit where there was no room for that. The plane hit the tarmac and I switched on my mobile as I came through immigration and saw calls from everyone, but the only one that interested me for the moment was Harris. I called him back.

'Billie, you here?'

'Yes, I just landed at JFK. I'm going to get a taxi to the hotel. You okay? Is Lena with you?'

'Yeah, all okay here.' He told me the name of the hotel. 'We checked in. I booked you a room next door. Lena said she'd rather go stay with some friends than waste money on a hotel, but I've emphasised to her how important it is that we're in touch at all times. We'll see what you think when you get here. See you shortly.'

The taxi drove me out of the airport on the forty-minute journey into midtown Manhattan, where the streets were heaving with traffic the closer we got to Times Square in the theatre district where tourists from all over the world flocked to catch a Broadway show. In the hotel, the foyer was bustling, mostly with tourists, I reckoned, who come to this city for a short trip to take in the sights that they only ever saw in the movies, and yet have always felt were part of their lives. I checked in and went to my bedroom on the twenty-eighth floor, slinging my bag onto the ridiculously large queen-sized bed. A text pinged from Harris to say to meet him in the bar in ten. I went over to the window and looked out across the city and my insides knotted, wondering where someone would be with a little guy at this time of night, and would he be getting lugged around from bar, to apartment, to God knows where? Or would he be somewhere settled, and by this time so used to being moved around it was natural to him? Would he be missing his father who he'd been with for so long now? It didn't bear thinking of the confusion and how much damage this would be doing to his little head and heart. I went to the bathroom and splashed some cold water over my face, dabbed it dry and applied some moisturiser and a touch of lipstick. But my eyes were tired, and I could see the dark smudges in the corners that told of a life where sleep was never long or restful enough. The shadows had become part of my life in the last two years, and I tried not to look too much at them because they depressed me and reminded me why they were there. I pulled my handbag over my shoulder and made my way down to the bar.

I spotted Lena first, sitting on a bar stool, a long drink in front of her as she swirled the ice around with the straw. I stood for a moment, flicking a glance around the busy bar, and saw people out for the night, some twenty-somethings in a group knocking back shots, loud and happy and carefree. Lena looked smart and well dressed, her hair clean and washed. She turned as I approached and I could see she was wearing make-up and she looked like any other girl in her early twenties on a night out. Harris sat opposite her with what looked like a whisky or bourbon on the rocks, and eased off the stool when I approached.

'Good to see you, Billie,' he said, his reddish face breaking into a smile. 'You must be shattered.' He gave me a strong, friendly hug.

Lena smiled thinly, a look of empathy on her lean face.

'Hi, Billie,' she said.

I touched her arm.

'Thanks for coming, Lena. I really appreciate everything you're doing.'

She shrugged, her hand clasped around the tumbler.

'I just wanna help.' She looked at me, then shifted her glance around the room as though she was a little awkward and didn't quite know what to say in this company.

We stood that way for a moment, then Harris said, 'Let me get you a drink, Billie. I'm sure you could do with one right now. Then after, I thought we could grab a bite to eat in the Italian around the corner if you're okay with that?'

'Sure,' I said, taking a breath and puffing out a sigh. 'You know what, Dan – I'll have a gin and tonic. I don't want to drink much as I'm a bit spaced out from the journey, but I could really do with a couple of drinks right now.'

'Good idea,' Dan said, gesturing to the barman who stepped up.

He ordered a drink and the barman slapped down a beer mat on the marble bar top. I watched as he poured a generous measure of gin into the glass, the ice cracking as it fizzed to life with the tonic. For a moment I thought how great it would have been to have shifted several of these of an evening in a place like this. I took a long drink, enjoyed the punch as it hit my stomach, and I knew I would enjoy the feeling by the end of it, the relaxed way alcohol made me feel for a couple of hours. Lena said she was drinking a long vodka with soda and lime, that she never got a chance or could afford to go to bars like 'normal people' she said, and this was rare for her. I knew I was only having a couple, but inside I was hoping Lena, who had already told us she was an addict, wasn't about to go on a bender.

CHAPTER THIRTY

The Italian restaurant was just a short walk along the street into Times Square, where we were nearly blinded by neon lights from billboards advertising Broadway shows. The fluorescent tickertape of continuous news from all over the world was the backdrop to the throng of traffic snaking its way towards the triangle of Forty-Second Street and Seventh Avenue. As we walked, Lena was slightly ahead of us. She had two phones in her hands that were pinging with messages, and when they rang she would answer briefly. I glanced at Harris who shrugged when she took a third phone out of the pocket of her leather jacket. Then she stopped and turned to us.

'Just checking out a few people,' she said, as though sensing our curiosity. 'You know, just letting some good people know I'm in town.'

'You got a lot of phones there, Lena,' Harris said.

'Yeah. A couple of them are burners though. I find them useful sometimes.'

We didn't answer and walked into the restaurant. The waiter sat us at a table by the window where the lighting was low and the walls were adorned with images of Tuscany, of black and white pictures of old villages in the region with names underneath. Lena ordered pizza and I had some house linguine cartoccio and Harris had lasagne which he said was a special here. He ordered a bottle of house red and we sipped it, and I felt relaxed as we started talking.

'I was thinking, Dan,' I began. 'Do you reckon it would be worth going to the cops here to have a talk with them? Tell them we are here and why?'

Lena tore off a piece of garlic bread and glanced at Harris. He swallowed a mouthful of wine and pulled his lips back in a kind of grimace.

'Tell you what, Billie,' he put down his drink, 'I know from experience that they're just going to send us all the way back to the missing persons unit. I mean that's a total nightmare. I went there in the beginning, in Baltimore, and the word is being put out across the country about Lucas. They tell me the same story, that lots of kids are missing in every state in the USA and some of them never turn up. They just don't know. And I'll be honest, I don't know if they even get anywhere in their searches. All they can do is put posters up and circulate it on police websites and social media. It feels hopeless. Maybe that's just the way it looks, but that's what it feels like.'

'What about talking to the television stations again?

Like we did in Cleveland? Though, if I'm honest, I'm wary that it might attract the wrong kind of reaction.'

He nodded. 'Absolutely. I'm not sure we want to go down that road yet. Maybe in the end if we are getting nowhere, but for now, best to see what Lena can come up with. What do you think, Lena? Will you be able to get any line on this guy now that you're here?'

'I think so,' she said. 'I know people who know him, and who he talks to. And he will be looking for some deals around here.'

'But what is the point of him dragging my son around with him? That's the problem I have. Surely he's better off on his own?'

Lena took a breath and sighed, looking dejected.

'You know, I've known Williams a long time and he's always slipping in and out of deals. He'll do anything for money. That's why he took your kid with him. It's not easy to haul a little kid around everywhere, like you say. But he's thinking of making money.'

My gut dropped a bit and I swallowed.

'Like how though? I'm almost scared to ask. He's not going to sell him, is he?'

'I don't think so. I'm not sure. There are people here who would do that, you know, would buy a kid like that to sell on. It's disgusting, but it happens. There was a house out in New Jersey and kids were found there from all over the place – from down in Colombia, and Mexican kids who'd come over the border and were trafficked up here. Slaves, really. There are people who do that. I'm not sure Williams would know where to start, but maybe he thinks he'll get lucky.'

The very idea sent shivers through me.

Lena fiddled with her straw. 'I remember when I was living here, there was a guy who said he'd sold a child. I mean, maybe he'd done it before, but I remember we met him and he was bragging about it to a couple of people we were with.'

'When was this?' I asked.

She shrugged and screwed up her eyes as though trying to remember.

'I guess it was two years ago, maybe a bit less?'

I glanced at Harris and could tell he was thinking the same as I was – that she would only have dim recollections of something that happened a couple of years ago, because she'd either been high or drunk.

What she was saying was beginning to freak me out.

'What did you think when you heard that guy bragging, Lena?' I asked.

She looked at me, surprised.

'What did I think? I thought it was disgusting. How could anyone do that with someone's kid?' She shook her head and looked straight at me, then at Harris. 'I mean I lost my kid and I know I'll never see him again, and maybe it's for the best because I need to get myself straightened out. That's on me. But to go and try to dangle someone's kid in front of them for money? No way.' She paused. 'I couldn't say that to him at the time as it was nothing to do with me. But Williams? He liked the story. I could tell. But the way we were living then, these things got said, then we drifted on to another house, another squat. Some of it was just shit, man. I knew it then and I know it now.'

'But can you still make contact with these people or with that guy?'

'I'm trying all kinda things. Mostly I'm trying to track Williams, but I have to be careful because I don't want him to know what I'm doing.'

'Of course,' Harris said.

We ate in silence for a while, and I could feel my spirits begin to sink a little. I'd known this was a long shot before I even boarded the plane, but something about flying over here, being busy, doing this, meeting people, made me feel that it was better than doing nothing. It was slowly dawning that this could all be for nothing again. What were the chances that Lena could crack this wide open and lead me to my son? I knew the answer was virtually zero, but I was trying to push that thought away. Maybe we should look at going to the British Embassy in New York and I could pour my heart out and hope I'd be listened to. But I knew how difficult that would be because all I had with me were Lucas's birth certificate and old photographs of him. I had nothing of his life here except this latest picture, and what did that prove? There was the trace that he had flown here some eighteen months ago, but Harris had already established that my ex hadn't left behind any form of paper trail – he had emptied my account and gone with cash. He could have been in several states over recent months and there was no trace. All I had was what was in front of me, across this table in this city where thirteen thousand people went missing in one year and in a country where more than two thousand children go missing every single day. I needed something bigger than this to help me.

After we'd finished eating and the waiter was clearing the table, Harris checked his watch, then asked, 'You want some coffee? Or are you tired and needing to get some sleep?' He paused. 'It's just that I wanted you to meet someone who might be useful to us.'

I looked at my own watch. Coffee would just about guarantee I would get no sleep, but I was already caught in that weird time lapse where I'd travelled in a time zone, only to find that the place I'd arrived at was five hours behind my body clock.

'Sure,' I said, 'I'll have coffee, but make it decaff. Who do you want me to meet?'

'My buddy. My ex-brother-in-law, actually. Rocco. He's a detective with the NYPD. I called him on the way up and told him I was going to be here and what we were doing. He said he'll help if he can – unofficially.'

I felt myself brighten at the idea that someone other than just us could pitch in.

'That sounds useful,' I said. 'We'll see him tonight?'

'Yeah. He's been at some retirement drink for one of his NYPD buddies in a bar downtown, but he said he would join us in a bit.' He glanced at his watch again. 'Any time now, probably.'

I could see Lena shifting a little in her seat, her eyes focused on her mobile, which had been pinging throughout the meal with text messages. She looked up.

'Guys, I think I'm gonna get out of here for a bit.' She glanced from Harris, to me and to her mobile, scrolling down the screen. 'I've had a couple messages now that some people know I'm in town, and I think I should kinda touch base with them tonight – you know what I mean? Just see the lay of the land.'

Harris shot me a look that said he didn't quite believe her, but before he could answer there was a loud rap on the window that startled us. Harris's face broke into a broad grin, as he beckoned the guy in.

'Hey, bro!' he said as a big man with dark close-cropped hair came in the door and strode up to our table. 'We was just talkin' about you.'

Harris stood up and they embraced in a tight man-hug, slapping each other on the back. I could see the outline of the cop's gun under his jacket.

'How you doin'?' the big man said, a smile on his face, handsome, even with a couple of days' growth. He was big, on the chunky side of fit, but hard and solid-looking.

'I'm good, Rocco. I'm good,' Harris said, motioning the big man to the empty chair beside me. 'This is Billie Carlson, the woman I was telling you about.' Then gesturing to Lena, he said, 'And this is Lena, who's helping us.'

He shook hands with us and sat down, taking a lingering look at Lena. She looked uncomfortable, self-conscious, and then she pushed back her chair.

'Guys, like I said, I'm going to bounce. I have to move and see what's what.' She turned to Rocco. 'Good to meet you, man.' Then to us, 'I'll call you in the morning.' And she was gone.

There was a moment when we all just looked at each other, a little thrown by her sudden departure. Rocco shrugged, his hands spread.

'I have that effect on women sometimes,' he chuckled.

Harris smiled. 'I think maybe Lena might feel a bit uneasy around cops.'

'Yep,' Rocco said, 'I saw that straight away.'

'Maybe she had a few run-ins when she lived here,' Harris said.

'I'd say that's about right. Kid like that, the way she looks? How old is she? I'd say twenties, early?' Rocco said.

'Yes,' I said. 'She told us she was twenty-two, just a kid.'

'Yeah. But a kid living in the raw in New York city on her own? That says something. You met her in Cleveland, right? I wouldn't be surprised if she left New York in a hurry one time.'

'You might be right,' Harris said.

'What's she into, meth? Seems too clean for that to me. You can usually tell someone's a meth head from their spots, ravaged complexion, and rotting teeth. She doesn't look like that.'

Harris glanced at me.

'What did she tell us, Billie? Was it coke she was hooked on, or what?'

'Speed probably, and alcohol. But she seems to have been mostly sober when we've met her. I mean, she didn't look wasted any of the times, and she was sharp enough. She says she's trying to straighten herself out.' I paused and looked to Rocco. 'She did me a real turn by getting a picture of my son, Lucas. That's why we're here. That's the only real evidence we've had since he was taken from me.'

Rocco nodded slowly, and I was aware of his eyes searching my face.

'Jeez. That must have been helluva rough on you, Billie. How you doing with it?'

I sighed. It might have seemed like an insensitive question to hit someone with straight after meeting them. But I felt he meant well.

'I'm here,' I said, 'trying to hunt down someone who has taken Lucas, someone I may never find. It's rough all right. But I'm living with it. I've no other option.'

He nodded slowly, his eyes still on me.

Harris broke in, 'I think you're right, Rocco. Lena's probably just not comfortable being around cops. But right now she's the only link we have. This guy who took Lucas is somewhere in New York, so she's our best chance to find him.'

'Yeah,' Rocco said, 'I guess. When you talk to the kid, just tell her that I'm not here to start looking into her past, okay? I got more to do with my time.'

Harris nodded. 'I will.'

The waiter came and we ordered coffee, and Harris ordered a brandy and Rocco a beer.

'So how much do we know about this guy? If you give me his name, I'll run a check to see if he's got a rap sheet and who he has a history with around here.' He looked at me. 'Of course, everything I do will be off the radar, as I can't make any official investigation. For that you have to go through the proper channels, and I'm sure Harris has told you how that is.'

'He has,' I said. 'I'll just be grateful for any help you can give at all.'

Harris filled him in on the story so far. Hearing it laid out like this made me acutely aware of how desperate this all must seem to someone out of the loop. But Rocco seemed to care what happened and I was glad he was on board, however unofficial.

'So you are brothers-in-law?' I asked, once the story was over. 'How come?'

'I was married to Dan's sister. But we split up five years ago. We never had any kids, probably just as well. This job – you know, it just about kills everything outside of it.'

I nodded, blinking in agreement.

'Ain't that the truth,' I said, and meant it.

Rocco glanced at Harris then at me.

'Dan tells me you were a cop yourself.'

'Yeah,' I said, 'so I know what you mean about the job taking over.'

'The kind of work we do, the way we live, it's hard sometimes to make a marriage work,' Harris, who was also divorced, chipped in.

'For sure,' Rocco said. 'But to be honest, and I think Harris agrees with me, I don't think my marriage would have stayed the course anyway, whether I was a cop or not. We were too young, really, to make the decision to hitch for life. It happens, so I'm okay about it.' He took a swig of his beer from the bottle. 'So, what made you become a private eye?' he asked.

I wasn't sure how to answer this, but I got the feeling Rocco was just trying to get the measure of me, and at least Harris had left it to me if I wanted to spill any details about my past life.

'I shot a guy,' I said.

I felt suddenly a bit overwhelmed, and had to stop as I was feeling emotional, but I managed to compose myself after a few moments. 'Then when it all happened, when Lucas was taken by his father, I fell apart. That's the only way I can put it.' I swallowed, my eyes downcast.

'Sorry,' Rocco said. 'I didn't mean to drag you back to a bad place.'

I shrugged. 'I've never really left the bad place, if I'm honest. But it feels better if I'm doing something about it, so thanks for coming along.'

He nodded but didn't reply, and for a while we sat in silence – three people who knew a thing or two about being messed up and wading their way through it.

CHAPTER THIRTY-ONE

Harris, Rocco and I moved to the bar across from the hotel where they'd insisted we get one more drink before we called it a day. The alcohol count was notching up. They were having a good time and were glad to see each other and catch up on their stories, so I agreed to join them briefly. But I was anxious that this might turn into a night out that would leave me hungover and in a worse place in the morning. So, I drank soda and lime while they ordered beers, and we sat at a table in a corner of the bar, busy with a mixed clientele of all ages. Some of them were three sheets to the wind on the dance floor as lurid green disco lights shifted around the walls of the room, making me blink to focus. I watched as some young dude in a Stetson and denims stood on the raised stage, strumming his guitar and singing 'Friends in Low Places', and it felt like I'd tripped into some kind of parallel universe. I made my excuses and left, arranging to meet Harris whenever we got ourselves moving in the morning. There was no deadline to this mission, no place to be at a certain time, no rules to follow. But I need structure wherever I am, so it was important that I took myself out of there and went back to the hotel where I could chase some sleep before it was too late.

Once I got back to the room I couldn't resist switching on my mobile. Much as I thought I could leave everything behind and focus on Lucas, deep down I knew I couldn't. It was two a.m. on my watch so it would be seven in the morning back home. My phone jangled with text messages and missed calls. The first message I read was from Fowler. It read simply, 'Forensic match'. I was suddenly wide awake. I pressed the call key.

'Billie!' He sounded bright and I could almost see him smile. 'I was calling you earlier. Great news! Wilson called me – he couldn't get you – to say the forensics from McKay and Mason are a match for the DNA found on Astrid's jeans and pants.'

'Brilliant!' I said. 'So, what happens now?'

'Well, Wilson said he was going to contact the big shots in the Highlands and Islands and tell them in no uncertain terms that these bastards have to be picked up. Obviously it's going to look very bad back in Thurso that they fucked up by not looking hard enough at Astrid's death.'

'For sure,' I said. 'Once the press gets a hold of this they will run with it. The thing is, will there be more DNA semen samples in the police lab up north from the post-mortem or will that have been destroyed by now? As far as they were concerned the case is closed.'

'I'm not sure what they'll do, but it's not as if they can ignore this evidence now. Plus, you have the video, but I don't think Wilson has told them about that yet. There's also the DNA you collected with the help of those girls. At least they have to pick these two up and start asking questions.'

'Do you know if Wilson told the Highland cops about the cocaine in Astrid's flat? Because it's not just rape – they might be facing a string of charges from blackmail to drugs-trafficking. What do you think?'

'Yeah. He told them the full story. They have to get these guys in and nail their feet to the floor.'

We were quiet for a long moment and I knew Fowler wouldn't want to pry into what was going on in New York.

'So, what's happening with the cocaine run and the big operation with the NCA back there?'

'So far it's all systems standing by. I'm told some of the rally cars have already started arriving by ferry, but so far none of them have gone to the Irishman's place. The NCA have got all spots covered and they're ready to roll as soon as it happens. Could be any time, really.'

'Great,' I said. 'I hope it works. Keep me posted.'

'Of course.' He paused. 'Are you okay over there?'

'Yeah, just got here. I was with my private investigator tonight. Long way to go. I'm just hoping and staying positive, Dave.'

'Okay. Watch yourself.'

'I will,' I said as he hung up.

After we spoke I fell into bed, but tossed and turned most of the night in a bed big enough for six, and when I finally passed out from exhaustion, my dreams were of a crowded night-time city of flashing neon lights and ticker-tape high up on a tall building with twenty-four-hour news banging out Lucas . . . Missing . . . Mummy. And when I woke I'd been chasing a yellow cab down a street with a little boy's face pressed to the back window, forlorn, crying, his tiny hands reaching out for me.

In the morning I showered and went downstairs past the foyer which was busy with people checking out or checking in, their bags and luggage strewn around, and I was glad to step out of there into the crisp New York morning. It was just turned seven, and already the streets were teeming with traffic and early risers, wrapped up against the cold, clutching barista-prepared coffees, striding purposefully to whatever they did every day. I went into the nearest café and sat, mesmerised by the buzz outside and wondered what kind of stuff these people carried around with them in their heads and hearts each day; were they happy, driven, high achievers, or were they like most of us, just surviving and no more?

I ordered toast and poached eggs, orange juice and coffee, hoping it didn't arrive US-style with a side order of French fries and six slices of bread. I took out my mobile and placed it on the table, switched it on and began scrolling down the half dozen or so missed calls, and the unread text messages. The first one was from Wilson in his usual eloquent manner: 'Fuck's sake, Carlson. I called you six times and even sent someone to your house. Are you all right?' I felt like texting back 'I didn't know you cared.' There was another text from him saying he'd finally tracked down Millie who told him I was in New York. He didn't ask why, but he would probably guess it was to do with Lucas. His next text was brief: 'Postive DNA matches to those two bastards from the north. H&I have been informed. Over to them now. Call me.' I returned his text and told him thanks for the good news on the DNA, that I'd be in touch. Scanlon's text was brief but I could sense the hurt in it: 'I hear you're in New York. Didn't know. But good luck.' Was there a goodbye hidden in there somewhere? I knew he'd be upset that I hadn't even called or thought to tell him I was going, but it had all happened so fast and there had been no time. The truth was that Scanlon wasn't on my agenda at that time, and I knew he would take it personally if I said that to him, but he was smart enough to work it out for himself, that despite our night of passion in the hotel, I could walk out just like that. It was how I was. I wasn't proud of how I felt, but it was why I knew that it would never work between us, and probably he did too. But I wasn't going to play it over again and again in my mind. For now, I just parked the whole thing, as I didn't feel like having a conversation right now. I would deal with it later.

When I finished breakfast, I could see the waiter hovering around my table making it obvious that he didn't want me to linger here all day. This was New York. There was no need to be courteous to customers because no matter how much money you spent, someone else was waiting outside to take your place – every hour of every day of the year. People visiting the city thought it was rude of New Yorkers, but I liked them all the same. New York, with all its impatience and fast, straight talking has always reminded me of Glasgow but with more attitude and a bit bigger. It's the Irishness of both places. I paid my bill – including the already added surcharge, which always irritated me – pulled on my jacket and left. I found my bearings and set off to do what everyone else does when they have time to spare, and went for a walk in this city. There were places I could have gone further – Chinatown, the Bronx, Brooklyn – but I stayed to the main places and headed to Central Park. As I walked, I looked up at the dizzying heights of the buildings and remembered the tragedy of 9/11 when this city stood horrified amid clouds of dust and death as planes flew into the twin towers, changing the world and the way we lived forever.

All human life is here on the streets of New York, from beggars who take credit cards to weirdos wandering around who should probably be incarcerated but have slipped through the net. They contrast with the rich who come here to shop, stepping from their limos, armed with carrier bags from designer shops, and heading for the Plaza Hotel up at the top of Fifth Avenue. At Central Park, I sat on a bench watching Irish boys who'd come to America because everyone in Ireland did to make their fortune the way their forefathers had. Some made it and never looked back, others ended up driving sightseers in horse-drawn carriages around the park, until their luck changed. And I wondered if these boys dreamed of the hills and villages back home, or whether they had truly left all that behind.

It was good to get out and try to clear my head. Eventually I headed back down to the hotel, feeling the walk had done me some good. I didn't want to go back and sit in my room, so I wandered around outside, people-watching. Then I saw Lena walking up the street towards our hotel. She was with a guy who embraced her then walked away, and she stood for a moment watching his back. I approached her.

'Lena?' I said.

She turned, startled, and from the look of her, she had slept as well as I had last night.

'Oh, hi, Billie.'

'You just getting in from last night? Or are you going out?' I asked, keeping the fact that I'd seen her to myself.

She looked at me through tired eyes and flushed a little.

'I stayed with a friend. Joey. I used to know him when I lived here, so we hooked up.'

I nodded, because I couldn't think of an answer.

'But I made some calls and talked to a few people last night.' She looked at me then around. 'You want to go for a coffee or something?'

'Yeah,' I said. 'You want breakfast?'

'Yeah. Sure.'

I didn't want to go back to the same café, so we walked in the opposite direction and found a little sandwich place that had a couple of tables, and we went in and sat down. My mobile rang and it was Harris.

'Hey, Billie. You okay, did you sleep?'

'Not much,' I replied. 'I've been up since a ridiculous time. You up and about?'

'Yeah, Rocco and I turned it in not long after you left. You want breakfast?'

'I've already eaten. But I went for a walk and bumped into Lena. So come and join us in this café.' I explained to him where it was.

'Okay, I'll be there in five.'

I was glad he had called so he would be here when Lena told us whatever she had found last night – if anything. I watched her for any sign that she was on anything, but if she was it wasn't obvious. But she did look rough, like she hadn't had much sleep, and seemed weary. I thought perhaps she was hungry.

'You okay?' I asked. 'You can just order something now if you want, before Harris comes.'

'It's okay,' she replied. 'I'll wait.'

I wanted to ask her about leaving the restaurant in a hurry last night, but decided to leave it up to Harris, and was glad when he appeared at the door, because Lena looked a little awkward.

'Hey,' he said, plonking himself down on a chair beside us, his dark hair still damp from the shower. 'I'm starving.

It's always like that after a few drinks.' He turned to Lena. 'You okay, kid?'

'Yeah.' She nodded.

His gaze lingered on her as though he was reading her face. The waiter came and Lena ordered a toasted ciabatta roll and bacon, while Harris went for the full fried breakfast, shrugging as I half smiled at his appetite. The waiter came and poured us coffees.

'Lena,' Harris said, 'you left in a bit of a rush last night. We all noticed. Tell me, kid, did you feel a bit uncomfortable because Rocco is a cop?'

She flushed and swallowed, looking at both of us then away, and shifted in her seat a little as though she was looking for an escape route.

'I . . . Well, I thought we weren't having cops – you know? I was just surprised.'

'Yeah, but Rocco isn't on duty. But he noticed you were uneasy.' He shrugged. 'I mean, he's a cop. He sees things like that. But listen, kid, he's no threat to you. So, if there is anything you might be uncomfortable about from your past living here, then he's not even interested. You get my drift? So relax.'

She didn't reply, just lifted her chin in acknowledgement.

'Are you okay with that?'

'Yeah.'

Harris looked at me and took a breath.

'But listen, Lena, I want you to level with us. I don't want to be in a situation in this city where you are in some kind of trouble because of your past here and something you might have been involved in. So, is there anything you want to share with us right now? And don't worry, nobody is going to judge you. Trust me on that.'

She didn't answer, her eyes dropped to the table, then she fidgeted, pinching the skin on the back of her hands. It was awkward with nobody talking and I was tempted to say something, but I caught Harris throwing me a look that said to be quiet. Then eventually she drew her hand across her nose and looked up at us with tears in her eyes.

'I . . .' She swallowed again. 'I . . . This is where they took my kid away from me. So, I was asking one of the people I know if they had any idea where he was. It's stupid, because I can't ever get in touch with my son and that's part of the rules because he's adopted now.'

Tears spilled out of her eyes onto her cheeks and she wiped them away with her sleeve. Harris and I glanced at each other and he grimaced.

'I'm sorry, Lena,' I said, breaking the silence. I reached across and touched her wrist. 'It must be awful for you.'

She nodded, biting her lip. 'It always will be.' Then she seemed to shake herself a little. 'But it's how it is. Sometimes you just have to live with what you got. And that's all I can do.'

Her words stung me and echoed in my head. It struck me that there may come a time when I have to live with what I have, without Lucas. I pushed the thought as far away as I could, but I knew it would come back to haunt me. Lena said nothing for while. Eventually, she swallowed hard and sat up, as the waiter came and put the food down. She eyed it for a moment, and I couldn't make up my mind if she was hungry or had suddenly lost her appetite. Then her dark eyes met mine.

'But, the thing is . . .' she said, 'look . . . I'm sorry about this, but I'm okay, honest I am. Just maybe being here hit me a little hard. I'm tired too, because I was out most of the night talking to some other people about Williams and trying to find if anyone has seen him.' She stopped. 'So that's what I'm gonna do now. I'm gonna help you, because . . . because I can't help myself.'

Her mouth tightened and we sat for a while saying nothing, then Harris broke the silence.

'So, did you have any luck at all last night with anyone?'

I felt Harris was being a little insensitive. I would have given her more time and teased the information out of her, but he was clearly a man who didn't mess around, and he wanted this girl to know, even if he sympathised with her own problems, that the deal was, she was here for us. It felt uncaring on the face of it, but I know he was trying to do the best for me, so I said nothing. She took a bite of her sandwich and chewed it, then drank some tea, and for a moment we sat with Harris wiring into the food, stabbing the yolk of the eggs with a link sausage and mopping up the beans.

'Looks like you've lost your appetite there, Dan,' I said, more to lighten things a little.

He chortled, and Lena did too, and I was glad that we

were out of that dark moment when this girl just didn't know where to turn in her life. They both ate for a while and then she took a gulp of the coffee, and began.

'I talked to one of my old buddies here. Joey, his name is. He used to work with Williams when he lived here, and they made money from different scams and, well, stealing mostly. They robbed a bit as well, small stores on the outskirts, stuff like that. So, I met Joey in a bar last night and he told me he was on a programme now and that he goes to AA three, four times a week and hasn't used for months. He works in a warehouse, got a job and stuff, but he still hasn't much money. So, he told me Williams got in touch with him out of the blue a couple of days ago, and he saw him.' She looked at me. 'But he was on his own.'

'No kid with him?' Harris said.

'No. Just Williams. He told him he would only be here for a couple weeks tops and that he had some business.'

'Did he say what?'

She shook her head. 'Joey said he asked him, but he didn't say at first. Then he said that he was doing something that could make him a lot of money, and he asked whether Joey wanted to come in on it with him. He said he was trying to look for this guy – you know the one I was telling you about who ransomed a kid back to his parents and who sold someone? He said he was trying to track him.'

I felt my gut twist.

'Did your pal Joey ask him why he wanted to track this guy?'

'Yeah, but he said he wouldn't tell him just now. He wanted to know if Joey would come in with him first. Joey has a works van now he drives and drops things off, like orders and deliveries for his company, so he moves around NY and New Jersey a bit.'

'So how did they leave it?'

'Joey says he told him he would think about it. I told him to make sure he doesn't say I'm in New York, and he promised me he wouldn't.'

CHAPTER THIRTY-TWO

It was late afternoon when I got a call from Harris to say he'd been out most of the day talking to a few old cop friends – pressing the flesh, as he called it, because you never knew when you might need them. He said he'd also had a brief chat with a New York politician who he knew from some years ago – a woman – who had now risen to the heights of deputy speaker of New York City Council. He said they'd become friends while he was up in the city from Baltimore on an investigation that led to the arrest of a mid-level drugs gang, and they'd hit it off as buddies. I wondered why he was telling me this, then he said it might be useful, depending on how things went in the coming days. If she was onside in the hunt for Lucas, she might be able to open some doors for us in the police department, or any other official sources who needed a word in their ear. Harris said she stressed that she could only do so much, but that she was sympathetic and would help if she could. I caught up with him in an Irish bar, Mulligan's, on Madison Avenue, which looked like any other Irish bar outside of Ireland, with Celtic decor and trinkets to make it feel like home. Lena had disappeared after she had breakfast, saying she would get showered and organised then go out and try to meet up with some more old connections. We didn't ask her where or who, so there was a huge level of trust we had to place in her, but all the time there was this niggle that she had agreed to come up here with us because it was a free ride to the city where she could try to trace her own kid. Harris had said that to me after she left, and I had only half agreed, but I told him if that was the case then we had to just live with it, and I could see where she was coming from.

Inside Mulligan's there were a few customers at the bar, some tourists and others who could be cops finishing their shift sitting at the bar, having a few beers on the way home. I spotted Harris at a table in the far corner, and saw Rocco was with him. I was glad to see they were both drinking Coke, as I got the impression last night that these two knew how to do a night on the tiles. Rocco smiled as I approached and stood up, offering me a drink. I asked for a flat white coffee. When he came back from the bar he sat down and said he was starting work in the next couple of hours but thought it was best to meet up to tell us what he had found so far. I watched and waited.

'So, this Williams asswipe,' Rocco said, sniffing and running his hand across the days old stubble on his chin. 'He's bad news all round, Billie. I was just telling Dan. I had a look at his rap sheet – the length of both my arms. I talked to one of my buddies who busted him a couple of times over the years. Mostly it was turning guys over for money – you know, getting drunk with some guy he'd befriended in a bar, or so it seemed. Then he'd go out to help the guy into a taxi, when suddenly the dude gets rolled by Williams and his mates, beaten up, left in some shithole back alley. One time he set up a sales guy with a girl who was in on his scam. The girl robbed the shit out of him and Williams left him unconscious. That's what he did. He's a grifter, small time, but that's how he lives.'

That my little son was in the clutches of this lowlife thug made me sick to my stomach.

'Look, Billie,' Harris shot Rocco a look, 'I know this is hard.'

I put my hand up to interrupt. 'It's all right, Dan.' I turned to Rocco. 'I'm not naive. If a guy is ruthless enough to drag someone's kid hundreds of miles, he has to be a real piece of shit.' I bit my lip and looked away. 'I'd rather know everything that's going on, so don't spare my feelings.' Rocco blinked slowly, as though he wished he could have found a better way to tell me what he just did.

We sat for a moment in silence, and I looked from one to the other, waiting for more information.

'Okay,' Rocco said. 'It's not all bad news though. We have a handle on the people he knows in this city and who he deals with. He's been gone for the past eighteen months because he didn't pay up on a debt, so he had to get out of town. Ten grand or something, probably more. So, whoever he stiffed will be looking for him once they know he's here. I'd say Williams will be looking to make any kind of fast buck and get the hell out.'

'Is there any word on who he might be talking to, or anything that says he's here and he has a child with him?'

'Not yet,' Rocco said. 'But the feelers are out there, so when I get to work later tonight, I'm going to rattle a couple of cages, see what I can pick up.'

I nodded in acknowledgement, then turned to Harris. 'You hear anything from Lena?'

He shook his head. 'Not yet. But I think the kid is sound enough. I hope she's being careful not to dig up any lowlife junkies from her past who will sell her out for money.'

'I think she will be,' I said. 'This guy Joey she was talking about. He's clean at the moment and has a job, and he has talked to Williams so getting him onside with her is good.'

'Yeah,' Harris said, 'I'm pinning a lot of hope on that guy. Hopefully not too much. But we'll see how the day goes.'

We sat for a while talking about how we would get Lucas out of the country if we were able to get to him at all, and how it was fraught with all sorts of problems. My stomach was churning like an engine at the prospect of finding ourselves in a situation where the worst of anything could happen. Even the things I had been involved with in recent weeks back home were small potatoes compared to this. I told them this, and a couple of stories about my problems while I was helping Jackie find her own kid stolen by gangsters, and then about my investigation into Astrid's death which was still hanging there, and how the two men who were sent to kill me would hopefully be behind bars soon.

'You've had a rough few weeks,' Rocco said. Harris nodded, eyebrows raised.

From what I'd seen of Rocco so far I got the impression that he was a fearless, kick-doors-in kind of guy who punched first and asked questions later. I liked his staccato way of talking in his New York drawl, and his sharp attitude – a guy who took crap from nobody.

'Yeah,' I said, 'for sure. But nothing compared to this. And I don't mind admitting that I'm scared in this country about what might happen. I mean everyone has guns – everyone – so I'm a bit like, how are we going to deal with that without cops to back us up?'

Rocco nodded. 'I know. But I have a couple of people in mind who could help if it comes to us having to wade in to get the kid.' He glanced at Harris. 'But we don't want to get ahead of ourselves here. We have to wait and see what we can dig up over the next night or so.'

We'd finished our drinks and Harris looked at his watch and said he had to go. As we were about to stand up, his mobile rang, and he turned the screen to us. It was Lena.

'Lena, you okay?'

I didn't hear what was said, but Harris was quiet, brows knitted with concentration. It seemed like a long, one-way conversation, and I exchanged glances with Rocco who gave a shrug. Eventually, the call ended and Harris gestured towards the door, saying we should talk outside.

Williams had made contact again with Joey, Harris told us, and he'd asked him again whether he would come in with him on this money-making plan. He'd specifically mentioned some guy he knew of a couple of years ago, who'd sold a kid.

'He said that?' Rocco asked. 'Asshole.'

'He didn't say he had a kid, but only that he knew someone who could potentially make money in the same way. He said to Joey there was no risk, that it only involved using his van.'

'For what?' I asked.

'Joey asked that too,' Harris said, 'but Williams said he would only tell him more if he agreed to come in with him. He said there would be a big payoff. Joey had told him he'd think about it, but that he was clean now and had a good job, and didn't want to mess things up and get into trouble.'

'Did Joey get any kind of handle on where Williams is, where he's shacked up at the moment? Is he staying with some old buddies?' Rocco asked.

Harris shook his head.

'So, what happens now?' I asked.

Harris turned to me. 'Lena says she knows there is no way in the world Joey would get involved with Williams for a stunt like this, but that he's willing to help us. But he's scared because he doesn't know if Williams is involved with other people. He thinks he must be working on his own or he wouldn't have asked him for help. Plus, when Williams left New York in a hurry a couple of years ago it was because he stiffed some guy on a whole lot of money, something like ten or fifteen grand. And if this mob find out he's in the city they'll be looking for him.'

'So, it looks like he's on his own,' Rocco said.

'Yep,' Harris said.

'We need to find out where this bastard is, but it's doing it without getting the force involved.'

Harris put his phone on speaker so we could all hear, then called Lena again and asked if they could meet later with Joey as they wanted to have a look at his mobile in the hope they could trace where Williams was calling from.

'I understand,' she said. 'But he might have used a burner. I'll ask Joey if he'll meet you, though. I think he will. I mean, he's scared and stuff, and I don't know how involved he would want to be, but I can ask him. Okay?'

'Sure, Lena,' he said. 'That would be great. Call me once you talk to him.'

We all looked at each other. Harris shrugged.

'It's something,' he said, as though trying to pull a result out of not very much. 'If we can get Joey working with us, it takes us a step forward. That's all. Just one step.'

I nodded.

'Okay, guys, I have to go,' Rocco said. 'Let me see what I can dig up tonight and I'll talk to you later, or tomorrow.'

'Thanks, Rocco,' I said.

He patted my arm. 'Hang in there, Billie,' he said. 'We might be getting somewhere.' Then he turned and walked briskly up the avenue.

CHAPTER THIRTY-THREE

In the couple of hours after Lena's call I sat in my hotel bedroom and used the time to sort out some emails that were piling up in my inbox. A couple of them were from Millie, with details of calls that had come in with clients looking for me to take their cases. I called her – she was supposed to be having a few days off after our ordeal in my office before I hotfooted it out of the country.

'I thought you were having a rest, Millie,' I said brightly when she answered.

'I am, well, kind of,' she said. 'But there's only so much daytime television you can watch and all the adverts are offering special deals on funeral arrangements. So I'm better off working. How are you?'

'I'm okay. But you're not going into the office, are you?' I asked, concerned that she was going in alone.

'No, I thought I'd leave that till you get back, depending on when you get back. Though Tom Brodie called me yesterday and said we could pitch in together in the office, so I might do that.'

'Yeah, maybe do that. Tom's good company and you will work well with him. He's a good lawyer and he's chasing some company data for me on hotels in the Highlands. You know, so we can find out more of what's going on up there with the drugs and the money-laundering.'

'But you were supposed to be just up there to find out what happened to Astrid, were you not?'

'Yeah,' I agreed. 'But once you start peeling back the layers, Millie, there's a lot of murky stuff underneath.'

'No change there,' she said. 'So, is it going okay over there? I'm almost scared to ask.'

I pushed out a sigh as I tried to think of how to put it.

'We are making some contacts. The guy who took Lucas is in New York. We're trying to find him, but I have no way of knowing right now if he still has Lucas. But the guy's making moves with people from his past, so we're hoping to track him down.'

'Just be careful. How long are you going to be there?'

'I don't know, it's hard to say. Could be a few days. Could be longer. Who knows? I have to follow this lead and see where it goes.'

'I wish you were back,' she said.

I could hear a bit of a catch in her voice, and I wondered if it was the delayed stress and emotion of what had happened back in Glasgow catching up with her, or if it was just that she cared about me and knew that I'd invested so much of myself into finding Lucas that being this close would tear me apart if it didn't work out. Also, Millie lived alone after she and her husband divorced a few years after their children had been killed by the hit and run driver. I always imagined that having the structure of being in work most of the day was how she managed her life, given the tragedy that could have destroyed her.

'Me too,' I said. 'But I'll be back as soon as I can. And meanwhile you take care of yourself. Have a couple of weeks off if you want.'

'No chance,' she said, sounding more like her old self. 'I'll call Brodie tomorrow and suggest we get into the office and get some proper work done. He can buy the lunches.'

'Okay. Be careful, Millie.'

'You too, Billie. Be safe.'

The line went dead, and I felt a little homesick twinge, longing to be back in Glasgow where at least there was some level of normality and I could manage my life. Here it was a knife-edge of tension, of hope, and always teetering on the brink of fear – and probably the reality – that it could all collapse at any second. I sat back and scrolled through my mobile to bring up Scanlon's number. My thumb hovered over it as I considered what I was doing. I wanted to hear his voice. I knew I could rely on his support, but perhaps things had changed after we'd spent the night together. I wasn't sure if I was doing the right thing, but I found myself pulling up his name and pushing the key. There was a little twist in my gut when he answered.

'Billie,' he said, his voice bright. 'I was just thinking about you. How you doing over there? I called you yesterday.'

'I know. It's been pretty constant since I got here.'

'Are you okay? Are you making any progress?'

I filled him in on what had been happening.

'But it's all very much chasing and hoping for the best.'

'Are you bearing up though?'

'You know me, Danny. Getting on with it. I'm staying positive.' Then I changed the subject. 'Did you hear about the forensic match?'

'Yeah. That's what I was phoning you about yesterday. Well, and also to see how you were doing. Wilson told me. Also, he said to me he wants to nail them for attacking you. What do you think?'

'Dunno about that yet. If we can get them on the rape and whatever else with Astrid, then they'll go to jail anyway.'

'Yes, but they could have killed you.'

'I know. But hey, I could have killed them too.' I tried to sound light, but I knew Scanlon would see through it.

'We'll see when you get back. When do you think that will be?'

'Can't say really. I feel we are getting closer, Danny. We're pretty sure Lucas is here with this guy who brought him up from Cleveland, and if there's a chance we can get him then it will be as long as it takes.'

'Okay, I hear you.'

A silence.

'I miss you, Billie.' He paused. 'Listen, about the other

night. Don't worry about it. I mean, don't stress about it. It was, well, I'm not sure what it was. But listen. I . . . I just want you to be okay. That's more important to me than anything. I'm here for you. Always. No matter what.'

Hearing him say that choked me up and I knew I couldn't trust myself to speak. Eventually I managed to say, 'Thanks, Danny. You're too good for me.'

After an awkward pause he said, 'Wilson has pulled me into the NCA stuff, by the way, so I'm right up for that.'

'Really? That's great. You going to be frontline?'

'Probably backup. But there's a big team on it. Could happen any time.'

'Great. Keep me posted once it happens, will you? Fowler is in the loop too, which is great after all the information he's given.'

'Yeah. He's a good guy. I met him yesterday. Old-school. I liked him.'

'I have to go now, Danny. We're seeing some people.'

'Take care, Billie.'

'I will.'

I hung up, but I knew he was holding on to the call, wondering if I'd say any more. I lay back on the bed, feeling tired, but it was still early and I had to wait to see what the night brought. My mobile rang almost on cue and it was Harris.

'You okay, Billie?'

'Yeah.'

'Lena called. She talked to Joey and they want to meet us

and have a chat. I told Rocco and he said he may join us at some stage later but he's doing some stuff for the next hour or so.' He reeled off the name of a place down off Washington Square. 'You okay with that?'

'You bet,' I said. 'I'll see you downstairs in ten.'

The bar was a Cuban tapas place and we could see Lena raising a hand to us from a booth as we walked in. As we approached, I flicked a glance at the boy she was with. He looked early twenties, stick-thin, with a baggy grey T-shirt, tight skinny jeans and scuffed trainers. His complexion and dark eyes and lush black hair gave him a Latino look. He flicked a glance up at me from the bowl of meatballs they were sharing, and smiled a little anxiously as Harris and I slid into the booth opposite them.

'This is Joey,' Lena said, gesturing with the beer in her hand. 'Joey, this is Billie. And Harris, the guy I was telling you about.'

Joey wiped his hand on his jeans and stretched across the table.

'Thanks for coming, Joey.' I shook his hand. 'I really appreciate it.'

He nodded but didn't answer.

'Hey, Joey,' Harris said, shaking his hand. 'Good to see you, man.' Then he looked over his shoulder towards the bar. 'You guys want some more beers? Billie? Let's get some tapas to share. I'm starving.'

I agreed and asked for a beer, the same as Lena and Joey,

and when the young waitress came up, Harris asked her for a few of the best house tapas – enough for us all to share. It was good to see the way he was able to put everyone at ease with a simple gesture like that. And if you didn't know what was about to be discussed in this booth over the next while, you would assume we were a couple treating their young friends to dinner.

The beers arrived along with a couple of bowls of tapas and we all dug in with chunks of garlic bread.

'So, Joey,' Harris said, 'Lena says you got a job as a delivery man? You enjoying it?

'It's good, so far,' Joey enthused. 'It's different places every day, sometimes in the city, sometimes further out, delivering stuff. Mostly it's mail order packages. It's not a big company like TNT or anything, but good though. And it pays.'

'Sounds good. I see you're on the no-alcohol beer? How's that for you?'

He smiled. 'It's okay, I guess. Tastes much the same, and the upside is you don't end up crashed out in a shop doorway two days after you left some shitty bar.'

Harris gave him an understanding nod. 'That bad, huh?'

'Yeah, it was. Drugs too.' He glanced at Lena. 'I know Lena told you about my past. But I'm clean now and I hope to stay that way.'

'Good for you, Joey,' I said. 'We all have to be a bit careful with alcohol and stuff, I think. It creeps up on you.' I paused, noticing that Harris and Lena were looking at me. 'I used to drink a lot more but I've cut back.'

My admission kind of hung there for a moment then Harris lightened a little.

'Well, all the more for me, guys,' he joked and we all chuckled.

More tapas arrived and we ate with gusto and drank a couple more beers. We started talking about Lena and Joey's lives in New York when they had both been into drugs. They told us about Williams and how he was then, how he'd owed money everywhere and had been forced to get out of New York fast.

'So, what is it you would want me to do?' Joey glanced at Harris, then at me. 'I told Lena I'll try and help, but I'm kind of scared that I'm getting sucked into something I have no control over, and that's the truth.' He looked at me, his dark liquid eyes fixing on mine. 'But if I can do anything that will help get your kid back, then I will. I think it's crap if he's actually doing something like that.'

We talked some more, and I found myself opening up further about my life than I usually did to people I'd barely met. Somehow, I felt at ease with Lena and Joey, because there seemed to be a basic honesty about them that somewhere along the line had got tangled up in a complicated mix of all the crap that life throws at us. Most people find a way through, but many, without the tools and the innate skills to manage, end up in the kind of chaos that these kids' lives had become.

We were wrapping it up for the evening when Joey's mobile rang and he mouthed to us that it was Williams as he quickly got up from the table and went outside to take the call. We all waited, watching him pace up and down the pavement as he talked, his lean figure lit up by the vivid neon lights of the restaurant sign strung across the window. Eventually he put his mobile back in his jeans pocket and came in through the door.

'Williams,' he said, as he slid in beside Lena. 'He wants to meet me tonight. To talk.'

His eyes wandered from us to the table as he pushed a hand across his hair in a nervous gesture.

'What did he say?' Harris asked.

'He said again that if I wanted to make some good money, all I had to do was have the van and drive. He said he didn't know when it would happen as he had some calls to make with the people he was hoping to do the deal with. But he wants to talk to me to see if I'm in. He said he would tell me more details later. He doesn't know yet if the job will come off.'

Harris pursed his lips and nodded slowly.

'Sounds promising. Did you agree to meet him?'

'Yeah.' He glanced up at the clock on the restaurant wall. 'Around eleven. I said I was working and didn't finish till then.'

'Where are you meeting him?' I asked.

I couldn't help picturing a scenario where I could storm in when Williams appeared and grab him by the throat and throttle him until he told me where my son was.

Joey shrugged. 'Dunno yet. He'll call me at ten thirty and name a place.'

Harris looked at me as though he'd been reading my thoughts.

'We have to think about how we play this, Billie. If we move too early, everything could fall apart. I reckon we let Joey go meet Williams and see what he gets told.'

I nodded, somewhat reluctantly, but I knew he was right.

'You okay with that, Joey?'

'Yeah,' he said.

'Are you sure you'll be able to carry this off?' I asked. 'Will you be able to act the part so that he doesn't suss anything?'

He glanced at Lena who nodded to him, her eyes full of affection.

'I can do it,' he said, his lips tightening.

CHAPTER THIRTY-FOUR

I went back to the hotel bar with Harris and we sat drinking coffee because it felt like it was going to be another long night. Lena had gone with Joey to his apartment while they waited for the call from Williams, and she told us she would wait there until he returned, then call us. I wanted to be somewhere in the vicinity when Joey was meeting Williams, and I told this to Harris, but he shook his head slowly.

'Listen, Billie, I know how this must feel to you – like if you can get near Williams you are one step closer to Lucas. But the bottom line is we don't even know if he still has the boy. He might not have taken him all the way to New York. The kid could still be in Cleveland or somewhere in between. We just have to wait and see. If he tells Joey he has the kid, then we are in business.'

'We should still be somewhere close,' I insisted. 'Could we not follow him discreetly and see where he goes?'

He nodded slowly. 'I thought about that. Sure, we could be somewhere near.' He looked at his watch. 'Rocco is stopping by for a coffee. He has some things to tell us. So we can talk to him about that. But one thing I'm sure of is that Williams isn't going to tell Joey where the kid is – that's if he even tells him he's got a kid.'

'So, what do we do? If he tells Joey he has a ransom plan, do we just wait for the call?'

'Exactly. Williams doesn't know where we are. He might think we are still in Cleveland. He won't know we are in New York, though he might be suspicious that there was something between Lena and you because he hasn't answered any of her calls lately. So, one thing we can't do here is go too early. Let's see what Rocco says.'

As he said it, he looked beyond me and I turned to see Rocco striding across the room. He plonked himself heavily onto a faux leather chair and puffed.

'Been a busy night so far,' he said. 'One drugstore hold-up – the owner shot in the chest. And one domestic murder down in the Lower East Side – some crazed screwball shot his wife in the head after she told him she was leaving him. Guy has been in and out of psych wards for the last eighteen months. It was a tragedy just waiting to happen.' He rubbed his face with both hands. 'Christ!'

When the waiter came up he ordered coffee, then he leaned into us.

'Listen, guys, I dug out a couple of lowlifes who knew Williams when he lived here. And one of them told me he was back in town. So, if this asshole knows, then everyone will, including the mob Williams stiffed for the money.

His days in New York are well and truly numbered.' He looked at me. 'If he has your kid, Billie, he will want to hit you up pronto to see what he can get.'

'You think so?' I asked, taking out my mobile and making sure the sound was full on.

'Yep. I do,' Rocco said.

Harris nodded in agreement.

'So, what's been going on with you guys since I left?' Rocco asked.

Harris explained our meeting with Joey and Lena and the game plan, while I turned my mobile around in my hand, not wanting to leave it face-down in case I missed a call. When he was finished I turned to Rocco.

'So, do you think we could be anywhere in the vicinity when Joey meets Williams?'

Rocco thought about it for a long moment, then glanced at Dan.

'It depends on where it is. Maybe best to wait and see what Joey comes back with.'

I blinked my agreement but said nothing. It wasn't easy for me that I had to stand back a little and let other people decide how they moved on this, but I knew I had to put that aside because if I raged on with my gut instinct I could screw things up. Everything I had in me was invested in this, and I knew that could be more of a hindrance when sometimes situations called for a cold, calm mind. Just then my mobile rang: Lena. I pushed the answer button and put the phone to my ear.

'Lena. You okay?'

'Yeah,' she said. 'I had a call from Williams.'

'Jesus!' I said, looking at Harris and Rocco who were watching me. 'You got a call from Williams? When?'

'Five minutes ago,' she said. 'Christ, man. I nearly died when it was him. I was so surprised. I mean, I've been trying to get him since Cleveland, and nothing, then all of a sudden he calls me. I had to totally get myself calmed when I talked to him.'

'I can imagine. What did he say?'

'Not too much. He asked if I was still in Cleveland, and I said I was, but that I had been trying to get hold of him, but he hadn't been answering my calls. I said I heard he was in New York.'

'What did he say to that?'

'He said that he was, and that he left a few days ago. He said he had some business he was doing here and it would make him some money. I didn't want to ask him what kind of business, in case he twigged anything, so I said nothing.'

'What else?'

'Then he asked if I'd heard from Joey of late, and I said no, not for a long time, not since I left New York. I think he was trying to fish if Joey had talked to me. He knew we were close one time, and I think he was being sly and checking in case Joey was double-crossing him or something.'

'Yeah, sounds about right. So, what else did he say?' I put

my mobile on loudspeaker and turned the sound down a little as Harris and Rocco leaned in close.

'He asked me whether I have a phone number or any way of talking to you. He said he heard I had talked to you back in Cleveland that night. He said he had some information for you, about your son. He actually said, "about that kid". Those were his words.'

Harris and Rocco's eyes nearly popped, and we sat for a long moment in silence.

'You still there, Billie?' Lena asked.

'Yeah, I'm here. Just trying to take that in. So, what did you do?'

'I gave him your number.'

'Holy shit!'

'Should I not have done that? Jesus, I'm sorry, Billie.'

'No, no,' I said quickly, 'you did the right thing. I'm just shocked, that's all. Him calling you like that. And what he said.' I looked at Harris and Rocco, and suddenly my throat felt tight. 'He's got my son, Lena. I know it. He has Lucas.'

'I think so,' she said.

'Did you tell Joey this?'

'Yeah, Joey was in the apartment when the call came. He thinks the same as you. But he's got to just forget about that, because when he meets Williams he has to be like he knows nothing, know what I'm sayin'?'

'Of course. So, Williams hasn't called Joey yet?'

'No. But it's after ten now, so I think it will be soon.'

'Fine, Lena. I'll be in touch.' The call went dead.

'Shit, man!' Rocco shook his head. 'This fucker really thinks he can do business. Christ! I hope I get my hands on him.'

Twenty minutes later, Harris's mobile rang and it was Joey. We watched as he grabbed a beer mat and scribbled down an address and shoved it across to Rocco.

CHAPTER THIRTY-FIVE

I sat in the back seat of Rocco's car, low enough not to be seen, but I could still glimpse the entrance to the bar that was only about forty yards away. Joey had called Harris to say that the meet with Williams was up off Central Park in a bar on a side street. It was called Clancy's and we watched a few customers coming out for a smoke, standing chatting, smoke and breath and vapour swirling up to the cold night sky. Then I spotted a guy that looked like the photos Lena had shown us of Williams, as he got out of a cab and strode across the street towards the bar.

'There! I think that's Williams.' I dug Harris's shoulder from my back seat.

'Yep, sure looks like him.'

'That skinny motherfucker?' Rocco said. 'Looks like the mugshots.'

We watched as he idled outside for a moment or two before he went inside. Then we saw Joey cross the street and follow him through the swing doors.

'So, we just wait,' I said, more for something to say.

'Yep.'

Rocco had told us he had an ex-cop close friend of his who was sitting two cars back, and who would be attempting to keep tabs on Williams for the rest of the night. We were hoping Williams would eventually go back to wherever he was crashing, as at least it would give us an address and a place to look whenever the time came. We had no idea if Lucas was there, or even if he'd ever been there. I had to try to keep that thought at bay, because doing something felt better than sitting around worrying and missing him. Whatever happened, I knew I had tried, with every fibre of my being I had tried, and that would have to sustain me. I eased down the window to take in some of the cold air as I was beginning to feel a little nauseous after just sitting here. Rocco stretched over his shoulder with a packet of boiled sweets and I took one. After what seemed an age, but it was less than half an hour, Joey emerged from the bar onto the street, with Williams at his back. Williams stood for a moment, lit up a cigarette and offered one to Joey, who declined. They stood chatting for a bit, then we watched as they fist-bumped each other, before Joey backed away, crossing the street and heading back across to the top of Fifth Avenue. Williams stood for a couple of minutes, then threw his cigarette end on the street and walked off, hailing a yellow cab. As he got in, Rocco gave a wave to his mate who eased out of where he was parked and got two cars behind the cab. We watched as the cars disappeared into the line of traffic. That was as far as we could go. For now. Harris's mobile rang.

'Joey. Where are you, buddy?'

'Heading down Fifth.'

'Okay, we are coming your way. Meet you on the corner of Twenty-Second Street. How did it go?'

'Good. I think.'

Harris told him the car to watch for and we drove off.

Joey was on the corner of Twenty-Second by the time we got through the traffic, and Rocco flashed his lights. Joey got in the back seat beside me. He looked shivery and chilled, and I didn't know if it was the cold or nerves and adrenalin because of what he'd been doing.

'You okay?' I asked.

'Yeah.' He took a breath and blew it out as though glad he'd got that over. 'I was nervous though. I mean at first. But I think I did okay.'

'Do you think Williams sussed you were edgy?'

'No,' he said. 'I'm an edgy kind of guy, to be honest, and when Williams knew me in the past I'd have been a lot more edgy – you know, with the drugs and stuff.'

'So can you walk us through it, Joey?' Harris asked.

'Okay,' he said, sitting up straight and turning his body more towards me. 'So, I go in a couple of minutes after Williams and he acts like he's really glad to see me, you know, like we were the greatest buddies ever, which we weren't but you know how it was back then. Everyone was all fucked up. Anyway, he bought the drink, and I told him

I'm clean now and he laughed a bit and got himself a long vodka and me a Coke. And we sat at the bar and he talked real low about a business deal. I said to him that I'd heard him say that, but I had a job and I was okay, but that I'd come here to see what he had to offer, just for old times' sake. He was okay with that, and then said it was about selling something back to someone.'

'What?' I asked. 'Selling something back?' I had to quell my anger bubbling up.

He nodded.

'Go on.'

'I said selling what. And what do you mean selling something back, and was this something he'd bought or stuff? Was it drugs? And he said, no drugs. This was different. Then he talked about that guy Lena was telling you about, you know from a couple of years ago? The guy who kidnapped someone's kid and sold it back for ransom money and got away with it?'

'Yeah.' We all nodded.

'Well, he said it was kinda like that, only he said this wasn't anyone he had kidnapped himself. This was a kid that he just happened on back in Cleveland. He said the kid had nobody when he saw it at first, like that he was an orphan, and Williams's buddies had been looking after him, wondering what they could do with him.'

'Christ!' I said, my palms sweating. 'He actually said that? The kid was like an orphan? Jesus!'

'Yeah. He said that if he hadn't taken the kid, then they

were going to sell him anyway, because the kid has no papers, so officially it doesn't really exist, you know what I mean? He said they would have sold him to traffickers. So, he took him.'

'He's a damn liar!' I said. 'He knew exactly who the kid was. I was in the room in that shithole when I blew a gasket because I was looking for my son. Someone will have told him that. He could have helped me. But he didn't because he had other plans, the slimy, sly scumbucket bastard . . .' I could feel myself trembling with rage.

Harris turned around. 'Okay, Billie. Try to stay calm. I know this is tough to hear.'

I bit my lip.

'Sorry,' Joey said. 'I'm just telling you what he said.'

I touched his arm and composed myself.

'I know. I know you are, Joey. And really, I'm very grateful. You've done brilliant. So, what else?'

'Well he said to me that he now had a plan to offload the kid to somebody. He didn't say the mother though, because he'd told me the kid had nobody. But I was there when he called Lena and asked for your number, so I know he's lying through his ass. I'll be straight, man, truth is I was really angry, but I had to button it because I didn't want to screw things up. But I know that if he has your number then his plan is to phone you and offload your boy to you. Your own son. I mean, that's so fucked up.'

'So, what did he say? Did he have a plan he could put to you?'

'Yeah, he told me he would give me five grand cash if I could pick him up when the deal was agreed, and drive him and the kid to the meeting place and hand the kid over. That's all he told me I had to do. He said it wouldn't take long, maybe an hour tops, and I'd have five k in my pocket once he swapped the kid for the money.'

'Jesus! Did he say when?'

Joey shrugged.

'He said he didn't know. Because he hadn't finalised the deal yet, but he hoped to know in the next day or so. He was just asking me if I wanted to come in with him. And if I did, then I had to wait for the call.'

'You did good, Joey.' Harris leaned over and fist-bumped his knee. 'Real good. So how was it left? Did you agree?'

'Yeah. I did. I told him I would pick them up. But I didn't want to be anywhere near guns or any shit like that if this blew up. I wanted to tell him what a piece of shit he was, but I couldn't. I just had to go along with it and convince him I was in.'

'Brilliant,' Rocco said. 'You ever thought of being an undercover cop?' He grinned at Joey.

'Well, no. I don't think I'd pass the tests! Not with my past,' he said, smiling back. 'So that's when I left. He says he'll phone me in the next day or so once he knows if it's working out.'

We sat in silence for what seemed like a long time. So near and yet so far.

*

We dropped Joey at a street corner on the edge of Brooklyn, the downmarket side, and watched as he let himself into his apartment. He told us it was a one-bedroom place, but that it was large and comfortable, and he had the rent paid upfront for four months. The building looked shabby from the outside, but it was good to see how pleased he was with himself that he had come this far.

Rocco drove us back to the hotel and I left him and Harris in the hotel bar, because I needed some headspace to process all the stuff that had happened today and try to be ready for what might happen next. Harris said to phone him if Williams called, no matter what the time was. And he chose his words carefully, tactfully telling me to try and keep calm and agreeable if Williams did want to make some kind of deal. I lay on the bed listening to the sounds of the traffic, my mind constantly drifting to Lucas, wondering if he was asleep, or alone, was he dreaming, did he ever see me in his dreams as I did him. It was past midnight and I must have drifted off to sleep at some stage, because it took me a few seconds for it to register that the humming and buzzing was my mobile on my bedside table. I sat bolt upright, picked up the phone and saw that the screen said private number. I pressed the record button, cleared my throat and spoke.

'Hello?'

'You that Billie woman? The lady looking for her kid?' the voice rasped.

My blood ran cold.

'Who is this?'

'You don't need to know. You Billie? You were on TV in Cleveland? You said you had a little boy?'

I realised I was holding my breath and gasped a little.

'Yes.' My voice was almost a whisper. 'I'm Billie. My son . . . Lucas . . .'

'Yeah.' He paused and I tried to swallow but couldn't. 'I have the kid. You want him, you need to give me twenty grand.'

I closed my eyes and slowed down my breathing. I needed to keep calm.

'You have my son?' I asked. 'Where are you?'

'I'm in New York. Where you at?'

'I . . . I'm in New York. But I was in Cleveland looking for my son. Do you have him? Is he okay? Can you . . . can you please let me spe—'

'Listen, lady,' he cut me off. 'You don't get to ask anything. You want your kid, you pay the money. Why are you in New York?'

'My flight home to the UK is from here,' I lied. 'Please meet me.'

'No way. I'll meet you if you got twenty grand. You got that?'

I took a breath and let it out slowly.

'How do I know you have Lucas? Can you send me a picture? A video? I'll get the money. I promise. Every cent.'

He hung up. I sat staring at the screen. What had I said wrong? Maybe I was too calm. Perhaps he thought I was surrounded by cops, tracking his call? Was he smart enough to think that? I tried to work out what he was thinking and why he'd hung up so suddenly. I got out of bed, paced the room, then hit Harris's number. He answered.

'Williams just called me. He said he has Lucas. He wants twenty grand.'

'Son-of-a-fucking-bitch! What did he say?'

'He asked if I was in Cleveland. He asked was I Billie and had I been in Cleveland on TV about my missing son. I told him I was. And he said you want your son you have to pay me twenty grand.'

'Jesus! The fucking balls on him. What else?'

'He told me he was in New York and asked where I was, and I told him I was in New York because my flight home was from here. Then he said again, twenty grand. I asked him for proof, a photo or a video he could send. Then he just hung up. Jesus Christ, Dan. My blood ran cold. It was really him. He really has Lucas.'

'Okay,' Harris said. 'Look, he hung up because that's part of the shit these bastards do to make you more nervous. But don't worry, he'll call you back.'

I heard the ping of a message on my phone.

'There's a message, Dan. I have to go. It might be him. Call you back.'

The message came up from a private number and I stood watching a video download onto my phone. Then it unfolded little by little, and I had to sit down on the bed, my jaw dropping open as I saw him. A small boy, blond, unkempt, with too-long hair that framed the face that was leaner than I remembered. His blue eyes looked liquidy and full, and were even larger now in the thinner face. But it was Lucas, no doubt about it. Sitting at a kitchen table with a piece of bread in his hand and a plastic cup. He was just staring unblinking at the camera, a silent little soul. It felt like someone was wringing out my insides, and I sat unable to stop the tears and the heaving in my chest. Then my mobile rang again.

'You want the boy. You pay. You have twenty-four hours. You don't have much time.'

'Please don't hurt him. Is he okay?' I said between sniffs. 'Please, is he all right?'

'You got the money?'

'I can get it.'

'Tomorrow?'

'Yes. Just tell me when and where.'

He hung up again.

I called Dan, but couldn't get the words out at first, then finally said, 'He sent me a video, Dan. It's Lucas. It's him.'

'I'll come to your room.'

CHAPTER THIRTY-SIX

It had been two hours since the call and the video and there had been nothing since. I'd kept staring at my phone, willing it to ring, just to say anything, just to know that talking to him meant that I was closer to Lucas. If I'd had twenty grand in my bag I'd have met him anywhere right then and handed it over. But it was impossible. I couldn't get twenty grand in the next few hours any more than I could get a hundred grand, and neither could Harris or Rocco or anyone else I knew. But we had to play along with it, Rocco had told Harris. If he calls again, we make the arrangements for the pick-up. He said they will take care of it from there. I knew what that would mean. I could be walking into a blood bath with my eyes wide open but I didn't care.

I'd lain awake most of the night, afraid to go to sleep in case I missed another call from Williams.

In the morning it was Harris who called to say that Williams had called Joey and told him the job was on, and that

Joey was in. He'd told Joey that he should have the van ready by early evening, that he was trying to work out a place.

'Did Joey say anything about how he reacted?'

Harris shrugged. 'No. He said he was just agreeing that he'd have the van ready. So, we have to be ready.'

'But what are we going to do?' I asked. 'I mean, if he calls again with an arrangement? If he brings Lucas, he's going to want to see the money.'

'I know. We'll see.'

He hit a key on his mobile.

'Rocco?' he said. 'Game on, man. This son-of-a-bitch called. He wants twenty grand . . . Okay. See you, buddy.'

'Rocco is coming right over,' he said.

We met Rocco in the hotel café and I relayed the call from Williams. He asked to see my mobile, then made a call to a friend and gave him my phone number. When he hung up, he looked at both of us.

'My buddy is coming over to look at your phone,' Rocco said. 'He has all sorts of shit on his laptop and he might be able to get the location where the call was made from. He's basically a hacker, and everything he does is illegal, but we sometimes use him – even if we would never admit it. So, we'll see.'

He fixed his eyes on me and I was conscious of how tired I must look with the recent tears. He reached across and touched the back of my hand.

'You okay?' he asked.

I nodded. 'I'm okay. Just . . . It was tough seeing the video. Lucas has changed so much. He's bigger, but skinnier. He—' I swallowed the lump in my throat. 'He just looked sad.' I bit my lip and shook my head.

Rocco glanced at Harris and they both looked a little awkward.

'Don't worry,' I said quickly, 'I'm not going to go to pieces.'

'Okay,' Rocco said, 'I have some information too.'

The waiter came over and poured coffee and we ordered some scrambled eggs. I just had toast as I had no appetite. Rocco drank half the cup in one swig, then spoke.

'The guy I put on Williams last night? He kept with the cab and tracked him to an address in Hunts Point in the Bronx. Williams got out of the car and went into the block. He didn't come out again and my friend waited nearby until six this morning. Then he knocked a door on the lower floor and said he was looking for some name he made up, and said he was looking for a guy with a kid. The man told him there was a kid living in the apartment two up. He said that was the only kid living in the building, that he had come recently with some guy. But he said he hadn't thought there was anybody in that apartment, apart from one guy who had gone away recently, and that as far as he knew he was in jail.' He paused as the food arrived. 'So, it looks like that is where Williams is holed up.'

'Christ, I want to bang that door down right now,' I said.

'I know,' Harris said. 'Me too. But we've got a kid in there and we don't know what this asshole will do if he's threatened.'

I knew he was right.

'I know that too. But I can't help it.'

We sat for a while, my eyes never straying from my phone. I must have watched the video two dozen times, each time seeing something else – his hands, the fingers long like my father's, his lips, his shoes scuffed, the stains on his T-shirt. In the background the room looked grimy and there was a soiled sofa and a blanket on the floor. I wondered if he'd slept there last night. Rocco looked up as he saw a guy come through the door and approach us. He was thin, with greasy hair, round specs, and dressed in a baggy T-shirt and jeans far too big for him and slung low. He half smiled and sat down when Rocco gestured. He didn't introduce us by name.

'Can you let him have a look at your mobile?' Rocco asked me.

I handed him my phone, and he turned it around in his hands a couple of times, then opened his Macbook Air and began punching the keyboard, going into my recent calls on my mobile, then the settings on my phone. He began keying things into the laptop. Harris, Rocco and I glanced at each other and shrugged. The guy sat for a few minutes, clicking and typing, clicking and typing, and we sat quietly, just eating and drinking coffee. Then, he looked up at Rocco.

'I got a location,' he said.

He turned his laptop around so we could all see, and pulled up a Google map to show a street of tenement buildings.

'Hunts Point,' Rocco said, looking at Harris. 'Mother-fucker called you from there, Billie. That's where he was last night. That's confirmation from the phone he was using.'

A shiver ran through me, a mixture of excitement, dread, not knowing what would happen next, but knowing that Lucas was inside that building. It was only a taxi ride away.

'Thanks, buddy,' Rocco said, as his friend closed his laptop and stood up. 'I owe you, man.'

'Yeah,' he smiled, 'I'll put it on your tab, Rocco.' Then he nodded to us and strode out of the restaurant.

'So,' Harris said, 'we know for sure where the fucker is. Well, was, a little while ago.'

'What now?' I asked. 'I . . . I'm just thinking. Would there be a point in even considering getting the cops involved here?' I put my hand up. 'I mean, I'm all for getting Lucas out of there by ourselves by whatever means, but if we have an address where a crime is being committed, what are the chances of the cops acting on that? Rocco?'

He pushed out a sigh. 'I know, Billie. And part of me is thinking that too. But you know what? I'd have to take you down to the precinct right now, get you to talk to someone, then the wheels start turning and then they start to ask the bosses and it moves up the ranks and all that shit that goes on, and meanwhile time is running out. I'm just thinking we don't have that much time. Plus, I'm always worried when cops go in and bang the doors down that whoever is inside gets hurt. You know what I mean?'

'Yeah. I know. I absolutely know. I just feel a bit helpless right now.'

My mobile rang and I picked it up from the table, and turned the screen to show them the private number.

'Hello?' I said softly.

'You got the money?'

Harris and Rocco leaned in and listened hard.

'I can have it by late afternoon or early evening. I'm working on it. I have to get my bank in the UK to contact the bank here and make the draft. It takes a few hours. Is my son all right? Is he crying?'

I felt the catch in my throat and I swallowed hard.

'The kid is fine. You got till seven tonight. I'll call you.' He hung up.

'Fuck!' Harris said. 'Asshole.'

Rocco's mobile rang and he answered it.

We watched as he seemed to be listening, intent on whatever was being said.

'What, like a Russian mobster?' Rocco was saying. 'How come they're involved?'

I assumed the conversation was about a case he was working on, but then he talked some more.

'Chechen? You have a handle on him? So, this guy has taken over the turf? Howd'you hear this?'

Eventually he came off the phone and looked at both of us.

'Okay. So, here's the deal. This guy tells me that some Chechen musclehead is running the show in the turf where Williams owes the money. So, it's now this guy he owes the money to. That means Willlams will be shitting his pants because these Russians and Chechens don't play games. You don't come up with the money they will chop you up. Simple as that. Maybe that's why Williams is pushing for this to be all done by today. Maybe he's nervous and wants to be able to hand over the money to them. Because the Chechen, whoever the fuck he is, won't hang around. He'll take his money out of his balls if he has to.'

We sat for a long time, trying to work out a plan. Williams had given me only a few hours, so how was I going to get anything that looked like twenty grand in cash in this time? That was the first question I asked, and Rocco looked at me, then at Harris.

'I'm already thinking of that,' he said. 'Dan, do you remember that little Sicilian guy, Vitale? The forger?'

'Yeah,' Harris said. 'I remember you telling me about him. He got busted for making counterfeit money for some mob over in New Jersey?'

'Yeah. Him. He got out of jail two years ago, and we heard a while back he's still at it, but nobody can get any proof to make a case.' Rocco sniffed and looked at me. 'I got to know him a little bit before he got busted, and well, I always found him a good guy. I mean, he was no killer, or violent, just a little nerdy guy whose forgeries are impossible to tell from the real thing. Last I heard he was making fake passports for immigrants.'

'So, what are you saying?' I asked, raising my eyebrows at Rocco. 'We ask this guy if he could rustle up twenty grand for us by the afternoon?

Rocco chuckled.

'Nah. He'll have plenty in a stash somewhere, or even enough that would make it look like a lot of money. I'm sure Williams is dumb enough that if you hand him a bag of money, he's not going to start holding it under a microscope. Asshole will probably take the money and run.'

'You think Vitale would help us?' Dan asked.

Rocco shrugged. 'Worth a try. Right now we are running out of options. And I remember Vitale was a big family man. He has grandkids now. If we tell him what this is for, he might just help.'

I spread my hands. 'Then let's try him. Anything's possible.'

I drank some more coffee as Rocco left the café and went outside to call a cop friend who would have contact with the Sicilian. He was taking forever and I kept glancing at my watch, agonising with every minute that passed. We looked up when he finally came back in and he sat down.

'Okay. My buddy gave me a number for Vitale. I just

called him and gave him the lowdown on what's going on.' He puffed out a breath, his eyes full of surprise as though he'd found a winning lottery ticket. 'He's in. Vitale says he can get a package of notes bundled and made up that looks like it came straight from Central Bank.' He looked from Harris to me. 'What d'ya think?'

'He can really do that for us?' I said, stunned.

Rocco shrugged again. 'Well, you know, it's not real money, so it's not as though he's giving us his last cent. But I'll tell you what, right now he is just about as close to a fairy godmother as we might ever meet. I had a feeling old Vitale would come through.'

Harris smiled. 'So, what's the plan?'

'I'll go pick it up in a couple of hours. Then we wait for the son-of-a-bitch to call.'

CHAPTER THIRTY-SEVEN

I stood in my hotel bedroom gazing at the little boy's clothing I had just emptied out of the carrier bags and onto the bed. I just couldn't stop looking at them, the polo shirt, the T-shirts, jeans and tracksuits and a heavy jacket and boots. Was this really happening? Was I really now folding clothes and lovingly packing them into the small suitcase with dinosaurs on it I'd just gone out and bought for Lucas? Was I really going to be walking out of this place with my son after such a long time? The thought of it brought a surge of emotion that made my heart hurt. How would he respond when he saw me? Would he be frightened, or just have that sad lost look he had on the video Williams sent me? I folded the clothes and zipped up the suitcase, and placed it at the door beside my own case which I hadn't even emptied since I got here.

My stomach lurched when my mobile rang, dreading it might be Williams telling me he wanted the money now. I breathed a sigh of relief when I saw Dave Fowler's name.

'Billie. How you doing?'

I pushed out a sigh. 'If I told you, Dave, you wouldn't believe it. What's happening?'

'I won't keep you long, but I wanted to tell you the good news.'

'Yeah?'

'Those two bastard rapists have been picked up and are singing like a pair of canaries, sticking everyone in left, right and centre.'

'Really? They confessed?'

'Well, your mate DCI Wilson and his boys sweated them for a few hours before the boys came down from Highlands and Islands to arrest them for the rape of Astrid Eriksson. But before they did, Wilson told them they were also facing attempted murder charges for the attack on you, unless they started admitting everything and throwing in some names. And the dumb bastards did.'

'Jesus! Brilliant.'

'Yep. They gave Wilson chapter and verse that they stole the cocaine from a batch belonging to their boss to sell on the side, and they stashed it in Astrid's flat. They threatened her that she had to keep it there until they needed it, and if she did anything then they would make sure the video went viral. They're so thick they didn't seem to get that the video shows that Astrid wasn't actually capable of defending herself.'

'Have you seen the video?'

'Yes. They handed it over to Wilson. It's sick. Poor girl.'

'What else did they put their hands up to?'

'Everything. They admitted it was them who monstered you in your hotel room by sticking the warning under the door. But wait till you hear this . . .' He paused for effect. 'Astrid's mobile phone. It's somewhere at the bottom of the sea.'

'What? How?'

'Well this is how Rab Mason tells it, but of course there's no proof. He said the cops took the mobile from Astrid's flat after she was found dead. McPhail probably freaked when he saw the rape and it was becoming clear that his mate Donny Mason's son was one of the rapists. It was already round the town that Mason and McKay were the guys who left the bar with Astrid that night and that there was a video on the go. Instead of taking the case all the way, McPhail tipped Mason off, and he promptly told him he had to get rid of the phone. Apparently McPhail refused, but after a visit from Mason with the threat that he would expose him for leaving the scene of an accident all those years ago, the mobile seemed to vanish.'

'What? He gave the mobile – crucial evidence in a crime – to Mason? And Rab Mason is actually saying this? Sticking his own father in?'

'Yeah. I don't think Rab was getting invited to family gatherings before this anyway. He's a bad lot.'

'Yet his father was protecting him – trying to get him off with the rape.'

'No, Billie. Donny Mason was protecting the bigger

picture – the cocaine haul that was coming in on the ferry. He didn't want anything that might bring a load of police into Thurso investigating a rape when there were drugs due to arrive before the rally. So everything had to be covered up. That's why you weren't wanted up there.'

'God almighty! So what about McPhail?'

'Word is this morning that he's retiring – ill health.'

'That old chestnut. It's the jail he should be getting.'

'I know. Who knows. Might happen yet.'

I said nothing for a long time, trying to process everything he'd told me. Part of me was elated that the rapists were facing jail, but a bigger part of me was sad that an innocent young girl lost her life because she believed the thugs were more powerful than her. No level of justice would make up for that.

'What about the drugs and the NCA?'

'Will be tonight. The cars came off the ferry and straight to the Irishman's house. So we are all over it. All going well we will be celebrating tomorrow.'

I looked at my watch.

'Good. But look, Dave, I'll talk later. I have to keep my phone clear for a call.'

'No problem. Is it going well?'

I blew out a sigh. 'I'll know soon enough.'

'Take care of yourself.'

He hung up before I replied.

My mobile rang again and I almost jumped out of my skin,

'You got the money?' It was Williams.

'Yes. I'm getting it organised. I'll have it later in the afternoon. Is my son all right?'

'The kid is fine. Just listen. I'll meet you at the underground car park in Hunts Point. At four thirty. It's on Buckley Avenue off the main drag.' He paused. 'And you do anything stupid like bring cops, you'll never see your son again. You got that?'

'Yes,' I said. 'No cops. I'll bring the money.'

He hung up and I stood clutching the mobile for a moment, then called Harris.

'Okay, I'm downstairs with Rocco,' he said.

I picked up my cases and brought them downstairs, and Harris took them out and put them in the boot of the car. I reeled off the meeting place to Rocco, who said he knew it and the area well. Then he stepped away from me to call a friend of his. I didn't ask the specifics, but Rocco had said earlier that he would have a friend who would make sure he was in the location before we got there. He was glad it was a car park as vehicles came and went there and having some guy lying in wait was not going to arouse any suspicions.

'You okay?' Harris said, touching my arm.

'Yes.' I nodded, but I knew I was far from okay.

'Just hang in there, Billie. Let's hope this will soon be over.'

The next couple of hours dragged but finally we were on our way. We drove away from the city to South Bronx, and with every traffic light stop you could sense the worsening social deprivation; downtown Manhattan seemed like another world. Rocco was directing him to the area where the huge red brick multistorey car park stood on the corner of a busy neighbourhood that was heavy with traffic, street sellers and cafés. I checked my watch – it was five minutes to the time when we were supposed to meet Williams. I hoped he would call to tell us exactly where he would be as it was a huge car park with many levels. We waited behind the two cars in front of us, then we got our ticket from the machine and Harris drove through.

'So what do we do now? He hasn't called,' I said.

'We just hang around the ground floor. He might call in a minute.'

'You're not going to try to take him on, are you?' I asked, looking from Harris to Rocco.

They glanced at each other then Rocco spoke. 'We have to see how it pans out, Billie. But we can't go in there guns blazing with Lucas in the middle of it, that's for sure. So as long as the son-of-a-bitch keeps his word and you have Lucas in your arms, we can catch this punk later. And we will.'

I nodded, my stomach tightening.

I peered closely at every car that came in and out as if I was going to see something. But there was nothing. Just the sound of cars and engines and the fumes filling the air, the dark, desolate, creepy places that car parks can be. Then I saw a white van park in a space towards the far side. A guy got out. It was Williams.

'There he is,' I said, nudging Harris.

He glanced across at Rocco but their faces showed nothing. I saw Rocco turn his head around as he scanned the area, looking for any more cars.

My mobile rang. I put it on loudspeaker.

'You here?'

'Yes.'

'Where?'

'On the ground floor. I got a lift from a friend.'

'You're with someone?' He sounded agitated. 'It better not be cops, lady.'

'It's not. Look. I have the money. I can just get out of the car and come to where you are.'

'Okay. I'm on the ground floor. At the far side. Wherever you are on this floor you get out of the car alone now and step out where I can see you. You got that?'

'Yes.'

'Okay.' Harris turned to me, and silently handed me the zipped up holdall.

I swallowed hard and pushed open the car door. I got out and stood up on shaky legs, then stepped away from the car into the main driving area, the phone still on.

'I see you,' Williams said. 'Just keep walking towards me. I'm in the white van at the far side.'

'I see it. Where's my son?'

'You'll see him when you get here.'

'I want to see him now.'

'Shut up! You don't get to say nothin'. Just keep walking.'

My mouth was dry and every step I took I felt like I was carrying lead in my boots. As I got closer I could see him stepping from foot to foot anxiously, his eyes darting all around, looking for trouble. I strained my eyes to see if Lucas was somewhere in the front of the van, but I couldn't see. Then finally I was only a few feet away.

'You got the money?' he said, his eyes hard and dark.

'Show me my son.'

'Shut up. Put the bag on the ground and kick it over to me.'

I did as he said and watched nervously as he picked the bag up and unzipped it. When I'd seen inside it earlier it looked like stacks of fifty and one hundred dollar bills all tightly packed. He zipped up the bag and took a step back, his eyes still on me. Then he opened the van door and bent down. My heart thumped in my chest as though my whole life had been about this moment. Then, suddenly, when he turned around, he had Lucas in his arms. I almost buckled, my throat tight, biting back tears as I took a step towards my son. Lucas looked at me for a long moment, his eyes at first the blank way I'd seen them in the earlier photos, his expression resigned.

'Lucas,' I whispered as I went towards him. I reached out my hand and was glad he didn't flinch as I touched his soft blond hair. He looked at me, but I still couldn't read from his eyes what he was thinking as he looked beyond me. 'Lucas,' I whispered. 'Mummy's here. Mummy's here to take you home.'

Tears blinded me as I choked out the words. Williams leaned him towards me in a handing-over gesture. He was a scumbag, but he'd kept his word. Then, the moment I had dreamed of and yearned for every day for more than eighteen months. Lucas was in my arms and I could feel the warmth of his cheek next to mine. I placed my hand at the back of his head and gently pulled him closer so I could whisper in his ear.

'Lucas. My big baby boy. We're going home now. Home with Mummy.'

'Home,' he said after me, and I hugged him close, because I didn't know if he really knew or remembered what it was to be home.

But just as I turned to go I saw Williams's face suddenly blanch as he looked over my shoulder at a car screeching up behind me. I gasped. Then everything happened so quickly and I stood there like a rabbit caught in the headlights as two big guys jumped quickly out of the car and strode towards us, guns raised and taking aim. I glanced at Williams who had his hands up in surrender.

'What the fuck, man! I got your money,' he said.

'Fuck your money. Twenty grand? For this kid? No way, man.' The big man turned to me. 'Come back when you double it.'

I opened my mouth to speak but nothing came out, and I clutched Lucas tightly.

But then he came towards me as the other gunman kept on Williams.

'Wh-what?' I said. 'Pl-please. He's my son. Please. I'll get the money!'

Where were Harris and Rocco? Where was the guy who was supposed to be here? My mind was a blur of panic and terror. But I knew they couldn't come out shooting now, when I had my child in my arms. I looked at the big, musclebound Eastern European-looking guy, my eyes pleading.

'Gimme the kid!' he spat.

'Please! He's my son! He needs me! Please! I'll do anything you want. You can't just take—'

'Shut the fuck up.' He aimed the gun to my head. 'Gimme the fuckin kid!'

I turned away from him and tried to move, but he was on me in a second. He suddenly grabbed hold of Lucas and roughly yanked him from my arms, his little face confused, his lip trembling.

'Stop! Police!'

It was Rocco and Harris racing towards us. But they stopped when the big guy suddenly put his gun to Lucas's head. The man who'd been guarding Williams came across with the holdall and jumped into the car, revving the engine.

'Oh God, no!' I heard myself say.

Rocco and Harris stood still as the big guy backed towards the car. Then he opened the car door and flung Lucas into the back seat.

The car swiftly reversed, almost hitting me, and crashing into two parked cars as the driver turned it around.

Harris was ashen-faced, his gun raised, but I knew he couldn't shoot as Lucas was in the car. Rocco was on his mobile and I heard him say 'kidnapping, child, Bronx' and the name and colour of the car. I had to do something. I couldn't just stand here and let them take my son. I ran as fast as I could after the car as it eased its way through the tight path towards the exit. Then I jumped onto the bonnet and held onto the wipers, beating my hands on the windscreen, my primal screams echoing around the car park as he swerved and tried to knock me off. If I should die right now, who would tell my son that I searched for him every day since he vanished and that I held him tight before he was snatched from my arms? I clung on with every scrap of strength I had, but then suddenly I saw the passenger door open and the big guy lean out.

'Stop!' I said. 'Please. My son!'

There was the sound of a gunshot and a dull thud on my chest and I knew by instinct I'd been hit. I thought I heard more gunshots, but I didn't feel them. I began to lose my grip on the wipers as I struggled for breath. Then, in the second before I slipped off the car bonnet, I glimpsed Lucas in the back seat sitting up, staring at me wide-eyed, and I knew that there was a flash of recognition in his terrified eyes.

'Lucas! Oh Lucas!' I heard myself wail, barely able to see now through tears as I slipped off the car onto the ground. 'Lucas!' I whispered as I tried to suck in air but nothing would come. 'Lucas!'

Somewhere in the distance I heard a commotion, scream-ing and shouting and more gunshots, but I could feel myself slipping away. Then in the blur above me there was Harris, calling my name as I began to drift.

'Billie! Stay with us! Stay with us! Look!'

My eyes were heavy and everything seemed so distant now. Then I saw him in Harris's arms. My Lucas.

ACKNOWLEDGEMENTS

Family is everything. And the loss of my eldest brother Arthur has left me bereft, but with so many memories to treasure. He will always be my big brother and remain in my heart forever.

There are so many people who play a crucial role in my life that I cannot name them all here. But they all know who they are, and I am very blessed to have their support and friendship. Here are just a few family and friends.

My sister Sadie, as we grow older is my most steadfast rock and friend. Her children Matthew, Katrina and Christopher, and their own children are the glue that holds it all together, and how lucky I am that we are so close.

Lifelong friends, Mags, Annie, Eileen, Mary, Phil, Liz, cousins Annmarie, Anne, and Alice and Debbie in London.

My old journalist friends, Simon and Lynn, Mark, Annie, Keith and Maureen, and Thomas in Australia. And also the cherished veteran hacks, Brian, Gordon, Ian, David, Ramsay,

Jimmy, Brian, Tom and Neil. And to Tom Brown and Marie who are always a joy to talk to.

Thanks also to my cousins the Motherwell Smiths for their huge support over the years.

And back in the West of Ireland, Mary and Paud, Sioban and Martin, Sean Brendain. I'm grateful to have such good people around me.

Thanks to my agent Euan Thorneycroft for the work he does for me, and for being such a great guy.

At Quercus, my publisher Jane Wood, for her encouragement and impeccable advice over the years, and my editor Florence Hare for her terrific edit on *If I Should Die*. And all the team at Quercus who push and promote my books.

And last, but not least, the growing army of readers out there who have followed my novels and enjoyed them, and tell their friends about them. Thank you. Without you, I wouldn't be writing this.